THE MISSION

Also by Jason Myers

exit here.

THE MISSION

JASON MYERS

Simon Pulse
New York | London | Toronto | Sydney

SIMON PULSE
An imprint of Simon & Schuster Children's Publishing Division
1230 Avenue of the Americas, New York, NY 10020
First Simon Pulse paperback edition January 2010
Copyright © 2010 by Jason Myers
All rights reserved, including the right of reproduction
in whole or in part in any form.
SIMON PULSE and colophon are registered trademarks
of Simon & Schuster, Inc.
For information about special discounts for bulk purchases,
please contact Simon & Schuster Special Sales at 1-866-506-1949
or business@simonandschuster.com.
The Simon & Schuster Speakers Bureau can bring authors
to your live event. For more information or to book an event contact
the Simon & Schuster Speakers Bureau at 1-866-248-3049
or visit our website at www.simonspeakers.com.
The text of this book was set in Tyfa ITC.
Manufactured in the United States of America
10 9 8 7 6 5 4
Library of Congress Control Number 2009930942
ISBN 978-1-4169-8455-9
ISBN 978-1-4169-9867-9 (eBook)

For my two big sisters and their beautiful families.

*For the friends who were there for me
in those bad times during the summer of 2008:
Kimmy Litwin (the best person in the world)
Nick Zarkos
Adam Severson
Jorge Mata
Jared Anderson
Kim Nieto
Craigers
Ryan Hitchcock*

*For Chuck Palahniuk and his amazing work.
And thanks to Aesop Rock for letting me use the lyrics to his song
"Daylight," and to his label Definitive Jux.*

*And for Erik Kolacek,
who built my website and has worked tirelessly
to keep it updated and going strong.*

All I ever wanted was to pick apart the day,
put the pieces back together my way

—Aesop Rock, "Daylight"

Saturday, May 31st

THE CAR CREEPS TO THE END OF THE DRIVEWAY AND turns onto the gravel road, the tires kicking up a small cloud of dust that whips into a spiral in the dead air before disappearing just as quickly as it came. I roll my window down and swallow a heavy gulp of humidity and look at my mom and take a deep breath. She smiles real big, and it seems authentic, and this puts me at ease to a small degree. If she can feel good about my journey, then what is there for me to really, truly worry about?

My mom guides the car onto the boiling black asphalt in front of us, turns the radio up, and rolls her own window down halfway. Her long brown hair blows in the breeze coming in and shines in the sunlight. She looks so pretty. Way better than she ever has over the past six months. She's wearing an olive green dress and white flats, and she slides her sunglasses over her eyes and says, "I'm so excited for you. You're going to do great out there, Kaden."

"I'm sure I will. It's gonna be fun. New, ya know."

"Something that you've never come close to living," she says.

I turn my eyes out the front of the window. It's so sunny today, and the sky is blue. White puffy clouds that look like zoo animals float everywhere above us. And a tiny bit of me still can't believe that I'm doing this. That I'm going to San Francisco to see Chuck Palahniuk read and stay with my cousin James Morgan, and most important, that I'm seeing the final wish of my brother through. My best friend in the world. I'm doing what he wanted us to do before he died in Iraq. I'm taking care of the rest of the business he couldn't be around to finish.

We glide past giant spaces of green country, horses, cows, hogs, and big houses that have stood in place for generations. My flight leaves the Cedar Rapids airport in two hours, and I am due in San Francisco at three twenty this afternoon.

That Patsy Cline song, "Walkin' After Midnight," comes on, and my mom looks at me and says, "Just remember one thing while you're running around out there with James."

"Sure."

"Don't put too much stock into everything he says. He goes off about a lot of things."

"Like what, Mom?"

She runs a hand through her hair and sighs. "Just things. He runs his mouth, and not everything is always worth listening to. He can get really carried away sometimes."

I have no idea what she's talking about. Not one stinking clue. So I shrug and I say, "Got it." And we barely speak the rest of the ride. The rest of the way spent with me thinking about my brother, Kenny, and how big of a kick he'd get out of knowing I was actually going through with this.

I miss him so much.

My mom pulls up in front of the United Airlines terminal. She gets out. I'm trying to show that I'm not nervous. For her sake, not mine. I step outside and walk to the back of the car and help her pull my suitcase from the trunk. Then she hands me three hundred dollars and says, "I know we already gave you three, but here's some more plus a prepaid phone card. I want to be sure you have everything you need out there."

"I'll be fine, Mom."

"I know you will, sweetie." She pats my head and hugs me and says, "Call me when you land. Okay?"

"Got it."

"I love you."

"Love you too, Mom."

She hugs me again, and I drag my suitcases into the airport and check in for my flight. I make it through security with no hassles and sit down next to these big windows that look out over the concourse and, beyond that, the endless miles of farmland and country that surround this place.

I have no idea of what to expect. I'm on my way to see my cousin, whom I've met once, in a city I've never been to, and the deep unknown of these two things combined is putting me on edge, so I slide my billfold out and pull a letter from it. The last communication I ever had with my older brother, Kenny. The words on the paper that changed my life forever when I first read them on that brutal winter day in December:

Kaden,

What's up, man? If you're getting this letter, you already know that I'm not making it back from this desert of murder and madness. I'm sorry I wasn't strong enough to. I'm so sorry, man. Sorry that I'll never be able to see you again and throw the football around with you again and talk about girls and go creek dipping and quarry jumping with you in the summer at Leland's property. I just wasn't ready and prepared, and maybe I just wasn't cut out for this day-to-day hell. That's what Iraq is, Kaden. It's hell. The brutal scent of death is around every corner and along every single road in this godforsaken place. This isn't just a bunch of American soldiers shooting at shit, this is having to bear over hundred-degree temperatures. Frozen night commands. This is trying to look at a hostile crowd of people of all ages and trying to figure out which one is trying to kill you that day. We know nothing about the people or the place we're going up against each day. The only thing we know is that it's becoming increasingly more difficult to figure out who the enemy really is. A group of insurgents who arrived here to fight the jihad from one of the neighboring countries? Or members of a family who seek revenge on the soldiers who've turned their relatives into collateral damage, destroyed their neighborhoods, driven their people out of the area, and turned their country into a lawless melting pot of religious ideology and horrific street justice more brutal than you are ever shown on the screen of the televisions back home. I've seen decapitated bodies slung from buildings while entering certain neighborhoods. Children missing hands and eyes. It's fucking sickening. Me and some of the other guys in our unit would get physically ill at times while we rampaged through houses and buildings, only to find a group of Sunni men lying face-first on the floor, hog-tied, bullet wounds in the back of their heads. Or a baby, man . . . I saw the body of this baby girl who couldn't have been more than three years old in a trash can in this house. Her throat had been slit and intestines pulled through her stomach. The rest of her family was found stacked together in a pile in the living room with all of their throats cut too, and there was a huge warning note written in Arabic about the consequences of working with the Iraqi Police and U.S. Commanders. I mean, what the fuck, man? What is this madness we've been committed to. Our presence, my presence, has brought brutal death to over one million Iraqis, and they're not all insurgents, Kaden. Hardly any of them really are. We shoot at everything that makes a sudden movement. We hog-tie men and women in the middle of the night in front of their children before whisking them away in black hoods under the rotten cloak of Bringing Democracy to these people, which is just a code phrase for American Imperialism. It's not right, and all of our soldiers should leave. I have already left, little bro. In a flag-draped coffin that I'm not sure I'm really worthy

of being buried in. We need to leave now before
more Iraqis are slaughtered on these killing fields,
before more of our soldiers are bled to death in
these blinding whirlwinds of sand.

I know what you must be thinking, Kaden. Who is
this guy writing you this letter? Where did your older
brother go? Where is the kid who was so eager
to leave for this fight and win this war for this just
country's noble cause?

Well, here I really am. This is who I was turned into.
Telling you all of this is the responsible thing for me
to do. Telling you how ashamed I was before my
death by what I had taken part in: Blind homicide.
Vast torture. The pointless destruction of homes. The
massive roundup and incarceration of innocent Iraqis.

The list could go on, Kaden. And I'm certainly not
the only one in my unit who grew despaired by
how we all became complicit in the destroying of
a country and its citizens' lives. Nobody is into it
anymore. Most of us just want to go home. That
was when I first started reading books again. One
of the other soldiers on the base was really into this
writer Chuck Palahniuk. He's the guy who wrote
the book *Fight Club*. Anyway, this guy was always
raving about Chuck's books and how they were
really helping him cope with being in Iraq. He'd
been fighting for two years, and the only moments
of life he had enjoyed during those years were the
moments of downtime when he was able to be
swept away into another one of Chuck's stories
and was almost able to completely forget for those

few precious hours where he was and what he was facing. The true life-or-death scenarios he encountered in the neighborhoods and villages in and around Baghdad for fifteen hours a day.

The guy told me that anytime I wanted to get into one of his books, to just ask him. He had all of them there. I asked him what I should read first, and he told me to start with *Fight Club*. That I should read his books in the order they came out, because put together they reminded him of one giant text, each new novel a different chapter. So I asked him for *Fight Club*, and from the very first line of the first chapter I was hooked, Kaden. I read the entire book that same night. Those hours spent reading were some of the best I'd ever spent in my entire life. Something inside of me took a drastic turn. I felt awakened for the first time. Reading those books, it was like there was an author speaking directly to me and to the way I felt about my place in the world.

Most of the characters in his books were so easy to identify with. Characters who were lost and drifting amid a plastic culture. Characters who felt betrayed by the end results of doing what they were told would make them happy. It made me think hard about how natural the violence inside of us is. But how we should use it in ways other than killing people. The way we bottle things up and are scared of everything and scared of feeling life and living among each other. It was a revelation. A revelation that happened too late.

I mean, I always felt like that myself. How Dad always told us that you do this, you do that, you get through

school, and you get a job, then get married and have
some kids and then retire and then die. And that's
Happiness. He raised us as if that's the only way of
life there is and that anyone who strayed from that
path was somehow not worthy in his eyes, and even
though I think Mom didn't really agree with him, I
don't think she knew how to ever go against his word
and how he thought about shit.

It's strange to have all of these feelings about this
right now. And it's so strange to write a letter to your
best bud in the world in this fashion. Already dead.
With no chance of ever being able to say this to you
face-to-face, man. I can't say for certain or anything
like that, but I really think that if I'd thought about
what would've made ME truly happy in life beyond
Dad's direct approval, then I don't think I would've
joined the military.

And this is why I'm writing this letter to you, Kaden.
Because I need to know that you heard all of this
somehow. I want you to start getting into good shit
right now and do something fucking rad with your life.
I want you to be happy, man. Read Chuck Palahniuk.
See if it's for you. My goal was to come back on leave
and take you out to San Francisco this summer to
catch him do a reading for his new book and meet
him. Our cousin James, the author, he lives out there.
I asked him about it in an e-mail, and he told me it
would be rad to have us out there for that. But I'm not
gonna make this one, buddy.

If you're reading this letter, you've already said
good-bye to me. I thought about this for a couple of

months. That's how important this is to me. I had to
have the letter come from somebody in the States
without sending it from here because of some of the
vague information that's inside about operation details
my unit was involved in. I couldn't have the military
read it, so I had to pack it with Brady. It was also the
only way to get it past Dad. I don't want you showing
this letter to either him or Mom, Kaden. I'm gone. And
they shouldn't have to have their final memories and
thoughts about me rehashed and then smashed into
rubble. Just let them have their peace about what
they thought I still believed about this war and this
military. You're the one who matters now. I love you.
Be something. Be anything. Go see what the fuck is
out there, man.

Your brother,
Kenny

I fold the letter and put it away. Take a deep breath.
I miss him so much. Every time I read that letter, all I can
think of is him and me shooting the shit about girls. Well,
him telling me about girls and how to deal with them and
how to talk to them. He always had lots of real pretty girls
around. They were always calling the house and showing up
unannounced and waiting for him after football and basketball games in high school. With every last feeling in my gut I
miss my older brother, Kenny, so fucking much.

I walk to a vending machine and buy an A&W Root
Beer, and then I sit back down and take another breath.

Soothing the nerves. I've never flown by myself before. Never done much of anything by myself before. And here I am, fifteen years old, about to be in San Francisco for a week with James Morgan. A person I only know through the outrageous stories and tales from the mouths of other family members. Most of the stuff not very flattering. Most of the stuff pretty fucking ruthless. There was the big uproar he caused with some comments he made on the *Charlie Rose* show, when he apparently looked fucked on cocaine and went: "I'm pretty sure that the only thing in my life that has ever held me back is the loose association I still have with my parents and my brother and my sister. Once I cut those red chords completely, the sky's the limit, baby."

Or this one in *Rolling Stone*: "The only good thing I can say about my family is that they sucked. My mom and dad were Republicans, and I lost my virginity before my brother did, and he was four years older than me. I was banging chicks when I was thirteen behind toolsheds and concession snack stands while the rest of my family was busy affirming their future roles as people of no significance whatsoever. I mean, I gave my sister her first cigarette when I was twelve and she was fifteen. I was on a path to greatness by then."

He's not in touch much with his immediate family, but him and my mom have always had a close relationship. She's always talked glowingly of him and always talked about taking a trip to San Francisco to see him, much to the dismay of my dad. The only time I've ever met him was at a reading he did in Minneapolis for his second book. He nodded and said what's up to me, and then he spent the next hour talking with my mom over a cup of coffee at a table while I wandered aimlessly through the aisles of the bookstore, bored out of my mind. At that point I'd never read a book that hadn't been assigned to me in school. I was never a very big reader before Palahniuk. Never had the urge to read before my older brother's letter came in the mail.

a. my flights

I board my connecting flight to O'Hare. I have a window seat, and I buckle myself into it and put my head against the glass. I'm tired from the night before with Jocelyn. I already miss her so much. It was hard to walk away from her on Pheasant Road. Hard for me to let go of her hands and kiss her lips that last time. And I can still taste her on my lips. I can still smell her on my skin.

The flight is only half full, and I get the row to myself. It's a short time in the air. Forty minutes it says on my boarding pass, and I know the perfect way to pass the time. I take out James's second novel, *Dickpig: Confessions of a Heavy Metal Groupie*, the last one he wrote, and I start reading it, because I've never read a word that James Morgan has ever written, and from what I understand of the guy, he totally seems like someone who would get really agitated about something like that.

b. dickpig: confessions of a heavy metal groupie

Hailed as an instant cult classic by the *New York Times* on the front cover of the paperback edition, *Dickpig* tells the story of twenty-one-year-old Irene McClusky, a chubby girl from Providence, Rhode Island, who follows her favorite metal band of all time, Hippopotamus Death, around the United States and Canada during their summer tour.

A real summer vacation.

James dedicated the book to "all the trolls and frumpy babes stalking the back rooms of venues across North America. Stalking like vultures ready to pounce on the black carcass mass of beards and leather and wicked solos. I love you all dearly."

He has lyrics from that band Slayer and lyrics from the Melvins before page one.

I flip the page and read:

I was twelve years old the first time I ever hid a sandwich under my armpit. It was during a class trip to this prehistoric museum in down-town Providence. The museum served lunch that day to all the kids visiting. The lunch consisted of a bologna sandwich, a bag of plain potato chips, a chocolate chip cookie, and a carton of milk. While the museum volunteers brought out the food on these big trays and set them on these large tables in the front of the cafeteria, it was made clear to us at least three times that each student was only allowed one of each item. They practically pounded it into our heads.

What bullshit! I'm not gonna lie at all. I was really fucking fat

when I was twelve. I still am. And I knew that one bologna sandwich wasn't gonna cut it. I had to get more. There were at least
fifteen sandwiches left over, just sitting on a platter, not being
eaten at all. It was like they were taunting me. It was driving me
nuts. So I devised a plan to get more, as I dipped the cookie in my
milk and ate it. What I did was I waited until there was some serious traffic near the sandwich trays. I hovered closely, and when I
saw that nobody was looking, I snatched another sandwich and
shoved it up the bottom of my Limp Bizkit T-shirt and underneath
my right armpit, where it wedged all neatly between a fat roll and
the underside of my arm. After that was finished, I excused myself
to the bathroom, where I sat inside a stall and scarfed it down in
three bites.

   This whole thing would become a pattern for me as I grew up. Just
last week, while I was getting nailed in the butt by Ralph, the drummer for this band Wasted Fly, a blueberry muffin popped right out
from underneath my left tit. It was insane. I'd jammed that fucker
under there at least four days before I fucked him.

   I pull my face out of the book.
   What the fuck?
   I'm like, *Holy shit! What the hell is this?* I can't quit laugh-
ing. Seriously. I'm still laughing as I step off the plane in
Chicago.

My next flight is full. I have a middle seat, and it is hell.
There's an old lady to my left, who keeps snapping and

popping her bubble gum, and then this fat guy on my right, who whistles through his nose every time he takes a breath. I can't stand it, and I don't have an iPod. Never knew what that was all about until now.

I put my head against the seat and close my eyes and try and focus on Jocelyn. An image of her and me lying on our backs in a meadow full of yellow flowers and sunlight soothes me.

They announce the in-flight movie: *Quantum of Solace*. And after we take off, I buy a set of headphones and plug in. Not ten minutes later, barely after the opening credits and action are over, my eyelids get heavy and drop. I'm gone. Off to dreamland.

c. my dream

Me and Kenny are walking down the gravel road next to the house we grew up in. The house is in really bad shape. It's been deserted, and it's crumbling, and the roof's caved in, and there's all these vines and weeds wrapping around it. Kenny and I are moving at a pretty good pace. I'm not sure where we're going. It's cold and dark, but the moon is shining real bright, and Kenny looks really worried. His face is even sad. Every time that I start lagging, he grabs my shoulder and pulls me ahead and goes, "Kaden, we have to keep moving."

"But I'm tired."

"I know you are. But we have to keep moving. We have to."

I never ask him why. I just try and keep pace, even though it feels like something is following us. But when I look over my shoulder, there's only pure darkness. A wall of black midnight. It's like the Nothing in that movie *The Neverending Story*. It's stalking us.

Then Kenny just stops moving.

"What's wrong?" I ask him.

He looks at me, and his face is expressionless. He doesn't even look the same at all.

"What's wrong?" I ask him again.

And he shakes his head. He goes, "It's time." And then something grabs a hold of his leg, and he slams to the ground and is being dragged away from me.

I grab his arm and try to pull him back toward me, but I'm not strong enough. His arm rips out of my grasp, and I fall to the ground, and Kenny gets dragged through the black wall and disappears, and I sit there. I'm exhausted. Crying. I hear a crow cawing. I look up, and I see three of them perched on a power line, silhouetted by the moonlight. I look behind me. The black wall of midnight is slowly creeping toward me, but I'm too tired to move. I wipe my face and turn my head and see someone's hand come flashing at me out of the corner of my eye and slam into my face.

My head jerks forward. Eyes snap open. The plane is descending into the San Francisco Airport. There's drool on my chin and shirt. The blue bay water is everywhere. It looks like we're going to land in it. A little girl across the aisle asks her mom if planes can float, and her mom laughs, and then the runway appears from nowhere and we hit it, we land. The sun beams bright. My bad dream is over. And I'm here in this brand-new place for the first time ever.

d. complications

I go straight for the bathroom after I get off the plane. I splash water on my face and take a long piss, and then I wash my hands and check myself out in the mirror, making sure I look as rad as I can. And I think I do. I'm wearing a blue and gold flannel, a pair of white jeans rolled up my calves, a pair of penny loafers, and the gold chain I lifted out of my brother's room the night after his funeral.

I run my hands through my curly blond Afro. I rinse my face again. Wish for a second I didn't have so many freckles. Then I dry my hands off and find the nearest pay phone, take out the prepaid phone card my mom gave me, and call her to let her know I landed okay.

"Is James with you right now?" she asks.

"Not yet. I'm on a pay phone. I haven't even got my bag yet."

"All right. Well, have a great time, sweetie. Tell James I said hi."

"I will."

"And just remember what I told you, Kaden. About not listening to everything James says."

"Right."

"He goes off a lot."

"Okay, Mom."

"Just remember."

"I will. I promise."

"Good."

I get off the phone and ride an escalator down to the United bag claim area, and this funny thing happens to me. Nobody's there to greet me. As all the other people from my flight hug family members or friends or go about things like they know nobody is gonna be there for them, I look desperately around and see no one who resembles James. Not one single person is there to jump out of nowhere, grab me, get my attention, and ask me how my flight was and if I'm hungry and what I wanna do first.

I'm feeling uneasy about everything. I am. But I keep myself under control and make myself not panic and think that maybe James is just running late. Maybe he's in the bathroom.

That's gotta be it, I convince myself while I wait for my bag to spit out.

But by the time they come around to me, there's still no one there, and I'm starting to get pretty concerned. I don't have a cell phone or anything like that on me. Only thing I got is an address and phone number for James.

I dig the number and the phone card out of my pockets and find another pay phone and call James. Four times it rings before going to voice mail, so I leave him a message about how I'm standing at the bag claim waiting for him, anyone, to fucking pick me up.

This is destroying me. It really is. I could cry. And I could break someone's face. A dramatic surge of emotion overwhelming me. I think about calling my mom and telling her what's going on. How this whole thing is a bunch of bologna. Horseshit. I want to, but I also don't want her to freak out and do something like book a flight out here. Or call James and pick a huge fight with him over the phone. That wouldn't be good for anyone. The way I've heard it about James, you really shouldn't try and test his patience, even though, from what I hear, he's pretty fucking good at testing everyone else's patience.

I decide to just man up for the moment. I walk over to a pop machine near the exit and buy a root beer and go outside.

It's a zoo. Cars whizzing by. Horns honking. Shuttle buses stopping and going. Airport security shouting instructions at people.

To my left I see a taxi pickup stop. I decide I'm going to just take a cab to the address I have written down and go from there. Be adventurous and see what happens. But right as I start to make my way over to the taxis, a girl's voice screams my name.

Stopping right in my tracks, I look over my shoulder and see this blue Volkswagen with a girl inside of it creeping up along the curb with the passenger-side window open.

"Kaden Norris," she calls out again.

"That's me."

The girl slams the car into park. "Awesome!" she says, then steps out of the car, and I'm pretty sure I'm falling in love right there.

She's the most beautiful girl I've ever seen who's ever said a word to me. Boy, she's so pretty.

She's Latin. I've never met a Latin girl before. She has this real light brown hair, almost blond, that's pulled back into a ponytail. A Marilyn Monroe–like beauty mark above the left side of her lips. Her body is banging. Athletic and tight and real sleek. She's wearing short navy-colored running shorts with a single white stripe going up each side, a tight white V-neck shirt, a pair of white socks pulled to her knees, with three black striped rings around each of them, and a pair of black Adidas. She's so hot. She even has an Indian head tattooed on the inside of each forearm.

"Who are you?" I ask, setting my bag down.

"My name is Caralie. I'm your cousin's girlfriend."

"Where's he at?"

"He couldn't make it," she snaps, snatching my bag up.

"Is he okay?"

Caralie stops moving. She looks like she doesn't know where to begin or even how she might answer that. She says, "I guess it depends on what you mean by okay." Then she whips around and drags my luggage to the car and throws it in the trunk. "Let's go." She smiles.

Well, I mean, kind of smiles.

e. the drive

We shoot past the terminals and onto the highway, the front windows rolled down, the warm Pacific breezes whipping past me, through me. I notice, in between me and Caralie, the printed-out picture of me that I sent James in an e-mail a few months ago so he would recognize me when I got off the plane. And Caralie, she looks real agitated. She's holding her phone to her ear and shaking her head. And for the most part I really can't pull my eyes away from her awesome brown thighs. Her shorts are bunched up so far to her crotch that I can see the bottom of her lace underwear. They're pink-colored.

She looks at me while I stare at this, and she gives me this half smile and puts her phone away.

"I'm sorry," she says, reaching into her purse. She pulls out a pack of Camel Lights cigarettes. "You mind if I smoke one?" she asks.

"No. My mom smokes. She's been smoking packs a day in the house since December. So I don't mind at all. It's your car, anyway."

"I don't normally. And you shouldn't at all anymore. But I do have one or two on occasion."

"Okay."

She lights the cigarette, and my eyes fall away from her, around the car and through the windows, the two of us speeding down the road.

I see a bridge poking into the sky.

"What bridge is that?" I ask her.

"The Bay Bridge."

"Where does it go?"

"To Oakland and Berkeley. The East Bay."

"Where's the Golden Gate Bridge?"

"Way to the other side of the city. Do you wanna see it while you're here?"

"I do."

"'Cause you have to. Anyone who comes here has to see the Golden Gate Bridge."

I see huge brown hills with large houses on Caralie's side. The water, the beginning of the Pacific Ocean, is only fifty feet to my left.

And Caralie looks at me, the cigarette balancing between two fingers, strands of her hair blowing around, and she says, "First off, I wanna apologize for the way I look right now."

"What? *Really?*"

"Yeah, dude. I look like shit. Complete and total shit. I was in the middle of a soccer game when James called and asked me to pick you up."

Her saying this, about her looking like crap, I'm thinking, *Shit. If this is what looking like crap is in San Francisco, then easily I'm gonna fall in love fifty times over anytime I go anywhere. Easily.*

And she says, "I also need to apologize for picking you up so late. That must have been terrible."

"It wasn't so bad at all. Don't worry about it."

"No, Kade—"

"Kaden," I snap, correcting her.

"Kaden. Sorry. It's a huge deal to me. There was a miscommunication between James and me about your flight time, and he got all caught up with some other stuff."

"It wasn't bad, Caralie. I don't care."

"But it is bad," she says, grabbing my left arm and squeezing it. "It's a really big fucking deal that the two of us left you stranded at the airport for almost a half an hour. It's absolutely not acceptable."

She's getting really emotional about the whole thing. Like deep down what she's apologizing to me for is something that has nothing to do with me as much as it has everything to do with James Morgan.

She says, "All by yourself. Just a kid. How old are you?"

"Fifteen."

Letting go of my arm, she says, "It's not cool at all that this happened to you. I'm sorry."

"Okay, then," I tell her. "Apology accepted."

"Thank you," she says, then takes another drag and turns the stereo up.

Beats. Beats. And good fucking beats. She's listening to the new Cage album, and it's getting me pretty pumped up, putting me in an awesome mood the way only rad music can do to a person on a gorgeous, sunny day riding in a car with the windows rolled down and a pretty girl next to you.

"I love Cage," I say.

"No shit." She smiles. "You're into hip-hop."

"Way into it."

"Fuck, yeah." She looks at me again and winks. "I can see that, I guess. You got some good style with what you're wearing. You'll fit in perfectly in the city. There's been a huge hip trend going on with flannels and cut-offs and rolled jeans. You look cute in it."

"That's nice to know. My dad told me I looked like a bum. Like some homeless fuck."

"Well," she says, "that's kind of a trend out here too. Lots of trust-fund types dressing like they're the scum of the earth. Looking all homeless and grungy on purpose. Trying to make a fashion statement by looking the dirtiest."

"So you're saying I look like I'm homeless, too?"

"No. You don't. You look good. Your dad doesn't know what he's talking about."

"My dad's a real type asshole."

"You think so."

"He's a miserable prick."

"Okay, then."

"Sorry about that," I say.

She makes a face. "Don't be sorry at all." She lights another cigarette. "So who do you listen to?"

"Shit. Everyone. I mean, Jay-Z's probably my favorite ever. I know every song off of every album. Me and this girl from back home, Jocelyn, love him. I also like T.I.

Lil Wayne. Nas. RZA. Tupac and Biggie, of course. Aesop.
The Grouch. Cage, obviously. P.O.S. is sick. Public Enemy.
Kool Keith."

"Nice list."

"There's so fucking much, though. And I'll listen to anything that's good. Too Short is one of my favorites. And of
course Three 6 Mafia is right up there. What about you?"

"Everyone you just mentioned," she says. "Del the
Funky Homosapien. Shit, the whole Hiero crew, I guess.
Um, Common Market is great. Cannibal Ox. Naughty by
Nature was like my favorite growing up. And I just saw GZA
a few weeks ago."

"*Liquid Swords* is one of my favorite albums," I say.

"His new album is pretty sick too," she says, giving me
another side grin that makes my stomach wanna explode.

I mean, this girl, she's absolutely something to look at.
Stare at. One of those girls that takes the breath of a room
away. A girl you notice the moment she enters a room no
matter what you're doing and how crowded the room is. A
girl where everyone turns to the people they're with and
goes, "Who the fuck is that? I would do anything to talk to
her. The guy fucking her, that guy is the luckiest motherfucker in the world. I would fuck men to get to that."

She finishes her smoke and says, "I would've never
thought that James Morgan's little cousin from Iowa would
be all into hip-hop the way you are."

"James isn't into it?"

"Not anything past ninety-six really. What he calls the Golden Era of Rap."

"Really," I say. "That's all the hip-hop he gets into."

She sighs. "It's complicated." She turns to me, then back to the road. "He's one of those guys that hates everything even though he really loves everything too."

"Oh, I see. So what does he love the most, ya know, besides you?"

She puts a finger to her lips and goes, "2 Live Crew. Guns N' Roses. The Coachwhips. Aerosmith's first album. Replicator and Future of the Left. At least that's what he's been pounding in his pad for like the last four days. Only that stuff."

"My brother, Kenny, liked Guns N' Roses a lot too."

"*Lies* and *Appetite for Destruction*. Can't go wrong with any of that."

We take an exit and enter the city, and it's a quite a sight. Hills upon hills upon hills crammed and stacked with side-to-side buildings. Warehouses and stores and shoulder-to-shoulder traffic.

"Have you ever been here before?" Caralie asks me, turning the music down.

"First time ever."

"You're really gonna love it," she says. "James is gonna show you a great time."

"I hope so."

"He will, Kade."

"Kaden," I correct her again.

"Kaden." She grins. "Got it."

"Where's he at right now?"

"This crazy place that him and the kids he lives with call the Whip Pad."

"Why do they call it that?"

"Who the fuck knows. Those guys, really, they're all off in their own little worlds. It's like a damn madhouse most of the time over there."

"Really?"

"Yup. I mean, I'm taking you over there because that's where he's at, but honestly, I'm not that big into the idea."

"What's wrong with it?"

She scrunches her face and says, "Pretty much everything. The place itself is like this moldy, dark cave with bad plumbing and horrible air circulation."

"Huh," I go, looking on as we roll down Ninth Street past homeless people pushing carts, a crazy white woman in rags, yelling, and well-dressed younger-looking professional types sharing the same sidewalks and taking it all in perfect stride. "I would've thought someone like James might live in a nice place with how popular his books are and how one of them was supposed to get made into a movie."

"*PieGrinder*," she says. "That was the one."

"Right."

"Well, he has another place," she says, as we cross Van Ness, the golden dome of City Hall glistening a few blocks away. "It's in the Mission, and he stays there most of the time. He just has a room at the Whip Pad where he keeps shit and rages. And that just happens to be where he's at right now."

"Partying?" I ask, even though I know.

"Yeah," she gasps, rubbing her forehead and changing lanes. "Partying."

f. the whip pad

It's in the part of town that Caralie calls the Lower Haight, near the stoplight intersection of Fillmore and Haight streets. She says that it's a pretty okay neighborhood.

She says, "You're in walking distance to the Mission, which is rad. There are some pretty decent bars and shops. The food is great. And there's always something happening on the street. Plus," she continues, "it's not a bad couple of blocks. Although . . ." She points past Fillmore toward a row of same-colored houses with small green lawns and porches in the front. "That block up there can get gnarly. Two shootings a couple of weeks ago alone."

"What neighborhood is it?"

"It's the outer Western Addition and the start of the Fillmore. It's not nice at all the deeper you go."

"Huh," I say. "Don't have those problems in Dysart, Iowa."

"I bet you don't." She grins. "How big is your town?"

"Dysart is about a thousand people tough. I live on a farm, though. Outside of town. Right off a gravel road."

"So you're a farmer?"

"Not me. I hate that shit. But my dad is."

"What do you grow?"

"Corn and soybeans."

"Nice."

It takes forever to find a parking space. We seriously circle these three blocks maybe twenty times for fifteen minutes at least before we slide into a spot in front of this hair salon called Edo, with some real pretty girls styling hair inside of it, and this medical marijuana store with two door guys out front doing security.

First time I ever seen anything like that.

The sidewalks are filled with bodies. With the sun shining down, it feels like a festival is happening, but it's not a festival; it's just Saturday. There's a big circle of black kids, my age–looking, maybe a little older, shooting dice on the side of this store called Lower Haters. Up the block from them are groups of people eating sausages in front of this bar Tornado. A couple of kids in flannels and sideways baseball caps are grinding a curb on their skateboards. I smell weed. Lots of weed. And there's some kids on a stoop drinking forties, and one of them is selling his art.

We walk past this bar Molotovs, with punk rock music blasting through its open windows. We move past a barbecue joint that smells fucking rad. There's more stoops full of kids. More pockets of pot odor. Kids in hoodies and tight jeans drinking tall cans and listening to N.W.A. on a boom box.

A few guys call out to Caralie.

A few more even whistle.

She ignores this, like it's nothing, like it's not happening, like she gets the treatment every time she leaves the house, and then she smiles when some toothless black lady asks me to dance with her.

"I'm all right," I say, blushing.

"I think she likes you," Caralie giggles.

It's pretty cool. Just this one city block in San Francisco is way busier than the annual Fourth of July gathering in Dysart Park.

We stop at the top of a set of stairs going down instead of up. The only set like that on the whole block.

She turns to me, wiping a few shining strands of hair out of her eyes, and she says, "This is it. This is the Whip Pad."

At the bottom of the stairs is a closed door, smeared green, all chipped up and rotting. And I'm not lying here: I'm real nervous all of the sudden. I'm a tiny frame of a hundred different nerves, and I can barely suck up the intensity of the moment. I'm not joking one bit. If I would've been more like my older brother, Kenny, it might be different. He wouldn't be nervous at all. He never got nervous in social situations. He always projected enough confidence for other people to hide under the invisible cloak of it. He was the guy who owned every place he chose to be. The way Caralie seems to be. Thing is, I don't know her like I did my older brother, and I know I won't be able to ride her coattails of cool. Not this soon. Not in the cool capital of the country, entering some slumhole known as the Whip Pad.

She smiles. "You ready?"

"Sure."

Trying my hardest to project a strong sense of calm and toughness, I stick my chest out and square my shoulders and snap my back straight and clamp my jaw down as I follow her down the steps littered with trash and covered in graffiti.

She pulls out a set of keys and pushes the door open, and my whole world gets devoured and reshaped in the blink of an eye. In front of me is a dark, narrow hallway with two doors on each side of it. Picture frames and posters hang on the walls, which are covered in more graffiti. We start walking down the hall. This gross, thick fog of cigarette smoke sits heavily in the air. There are bikes and paint cans stacked together to my right. Superintense and loud thrash metal pounds from a room to my right. Screaming voices trying to be heard over the music are coming from the same room.

Caralie swats at the smoke and says, "Jesus Christ. This place is death."

Me, I have to cover my face with my shirt. The smoke is that potent.

Caralie pushes open the door where the music and voices are coming from, and I trail her inside of the room. It's really small and has a low ceiling and no windows. Six people are crammed in there. There are three way fine girls sitting on a futon right next to the door, holding beers. A glass coffee table covered with beer cans and ashtrays and empty whiskey bottles and a large, grimy mirror with a big pile of cocaine on it sits in front of the futon. Almost every inch of the walls is covered with album covers and posters and flyers for shows.

I spot James right away. He's slouched in a chair on the opposite side of the room, wearing a pair of tight black jeans, red cowboy boots, and this white T-shirt with a V-neck collar that looks like he cut it even farther down his chest.

He nods and I nod back.

His hair is real short, like he's just run over it with a quarter-inch clipper guard. His face is rough and covered in stubble. He's wearing a pair of aviator shades with pitch-black lenses. His arms and his chest and his knuckles and his neck are covered with tattoos. On the top of his right hand is the word "self." And on his left one the word "made."

He looks pretty much the way I recall him looking at the reading in Minneapolis, except for one thing. His face looks like it's aged faster than the rest of him. All the partying looks like it's catching up with him in a big-time way.

There's also a guy in a navy-blue cardigan with black-rimmed glasses and long brown hair that's combed real neatly from the left. He's sitting in a black rocking chair next to James. And then there's this other dude kneeling next to the coffee table, and he looks like he's just walked out of a

Mötley Crüe video. I'm being dead serious about this too. He has greasy blond hair that hangs past his shoulders. He's wearing a black Cradle of Filth T-shirt with some serious sweat pools under his armpits. There's a white bandanna tied around his neck, and he has on these skin-tight black jeans that look like they're glued to his legs.

It's crazy how tight they are.

"Oi," that guy snorts when Caralie and I walk in. "Who the hell are you?" he asks, staring at me. "You're not very old. Who are you?"

"That's my cousin, Kaden," James says. "He's from Iowa."

"Ha. That's the guy you were supposed to pick up from the airport," the Mötley Crüe extra says.

"Something like that," says James.

Mötley Crüe extra guy knocks some hair out of his eyes, licks his gross lips, which are chapped white, then looks back at James and goes, "Awesome job with that, dude."

Everyone in the room except James, Caralie, and me is laughing, and I feel horribly out of place. My cheeks are red. I have nothing to say.

Turning to me, rolling her eyes, Caralie says, "Kaden, that's Ally over there." She's pointing at this superthin girl, sitting on the far end of the futon, with long blond hair that goes down to her mid-back. She's wearing this blue dress that has a U cut down the front of it. And she's barefoot and has a solid black band tattooed around each elbow.

Caralie says, "She lives here. This is her room."

"What's up, man?" She smiles. Winks. "It's nice to meet you."

"You too," I say back nervously, waving a hand at her.

Then Caralie points at the guy in the cardigan and says, "That's Reed Charleston. He also lives here. Next door over."

Then she points at the guy kneeling and says, "This is—"

"I'm Ryan," the guy snaps, cutting her off. "I don't live in this dump, but I love Venom more than anyone else in this room loves Venom."

I don't know what he's talking about, so I just go, "Sure. Nice to meet you."

And he says, "I heard you were in town to see a Chuck Palahniuk reading."

"That's right."

"He's pretty good. He's a way better writer than your cousin is."

James shrugs and flips off Ryan. He picks up a bottle of Jim Beam on the desk behind him and takes a pull.

And Ryan goes, "The thing I don't like about Chuck is that he spends all this time, all those pages, building up these incredible stories, and then BAM"—he slaps his hands together—"he wraps everything up in like twenty pages. He's like, 'So in conclusion . . . ,' and then it's done. The book is finished. It's really anticlimactic."

"Huh." I don't have anything to say to that except, "That's an interesting point."

"Do you even know what the hell I'm saying?"

"What?"

"Exactly what I fucking thought," Ryan snaps.

"And what do you think you know about anything except slanging coke for a living?" Caralie snaps back.

I smile wide as a river when that rips out of her mouth. Sticking up for me like that and all. What a rad fucking girl.

"I know about books," Ryan says. "When's the last time you read anything, Caralie?"

"You have no idea what I get into, dude. So don't start."

Ryan flips the back of his right hand at her. "Whatever."

Then Caralie points at the other two girls sitting with Ally on the futon and says, with attitude, "I have no idea who they are."

"I'm Bridgette," says the girl in the royal-blue skirt and the white Van Halen T-shirt with the sleeves rolled over her shoulders.

"I'm Renee," the other girl says. She has short black hair that's cut all crooked across her forehead. She's also wearing a pair of really big sunglasses and a hoodie that has GIRLS AGAINST BOYS across the front of it.

"Hey," I say to them.

"Welcome to the Whip Pad." Ally smirks.

James stands up, cigarette ashes dropping from his shirt, and he steps toward the stereo and turns the volume down.

"Dude," Ryan cackles. "You just turned down 'Providence by Gaslight.' It's like my favorite fucking Daughters song."

"Would you just calm down," James snorts. "Just relax for a minute. My cousin just got here from Iowa. Quit freaking him out, man."

Ryan looks at me with his cold black eyes. He runs his tongue around his gross lips again. "You're not scared at all," he says. "You like this."

I don't say anything.

"You love it." He grins.

Again I don't say anything.

James moves for Caralie. He grabs the bottom of her shirt and pulls her toward him. He hugs her and kisses her on the side of the face and goes, "Hey, baby. It's good to see you."

She pulls away from him. "Your breath smells, James."

"So what? It's still good to see you."

"Yeah," she goes. "You too."

James looks at me and sticks a hand out. "It's good to see you as well, man. Welcome."

I shake his hand. It's all clammy and gross. His fingernails are filthy. He smells worse than the room. He smells like what happens when you dump a bunch of cigarettes into a half-full can of beer and leave it baking in the sun for a few days.

"It's good to see you, James," I say.

He lifts his shades and rests them on the top of his head.

"I was real sorry to hear about Kenny, man. Your brother was a good guy. I tried to get back for the funeral. Things just, ya know, popped up and got in the way."

It's about the most insincere thing I've ever heard. How he says it, I mean. As if he's actually known he was going to say those exact lines to me for the past week and just barely recalled them from somewhere deep in the gutter of his brain next to all the beer and the rainbows and the skeletons and the grime.

"It's all right," I tell him. "It was a good service. Kenny always liked you a lot."

"Right." James slides his glasses back over his eyes. "So, I mean, do you want anything, man? A beer. A pull of whiskey."

"James," Caralie snaps, smacking his arm. "He's fifteen."

"So what? I was doing blow for days in Chicago with models when I was fourteen. It's part of life. I turned out just fine." He looks back at me. "Anything you want this week, man. The world is yours."

My mom sure wasn't fucking around one bit when she said the things she did about James. It seems like everything I've read or heard about him is pretty much dead-on, from what I'm seeing in the room.

And I ask, "You got a bathroom I can use?"

"Sure, man. Down the hall and to the left, through the kitchen."

"Cool."

I slide past Caralie, into the hallway. The door across the hall is closed and says *Gerry Jones* on it in black spray paint. As I move down the hall toward the kitchen, I hear one of the girls, not Caralie, say something like, "He's absolutely adorable, James. And his hair. That curly blond Afro is so cute. And that flannel is too perfect."

"Just like a Methodist version of Bob Dylan," Ryan snorts.

"Just shut up," Caralie snaps.

"Fuck you," Ryan says.

"Fuck you," she says back.

"Both of you shut up," says James.

It makes me feel good to hear this about my flannel and hair, because other than that I feel so fucking out of place.

So goddamn uncomfortable.

It makes me feel pretty cool, and there's nothing wrong with that.

I make a left into the kitchen, across from another closed door, this one covered with Polaroids.

The kitchen is easily one of the most disgusting rooms I've ever set foot in. Probably twenty trash bags are piled into the far end of the room. There are three mini-fridges next to each other along the wall. The counters are covered with spilled whatever and ants. A mountain of dishes and food wrappers is packed into the sink.

Everything smells like ashtrays and mold.

The door to the bathroom is open a crack. I pull it all the way open.

"What the fuck?" is the first thing I hear.

There are two people inside. One is this tall, skinny black guy with an Afro and purple jeans even tighter than Ryan's, a white V-neck cut just like James's, and a pair of Chuck Taylors.

The girl he's with is also black. She's a fucking fox. She's wearing this black dress and sandals. Her body is slamming, too. She's fit. Short hair. Nice boobs. This insane gold necklace with a fake-diamond bulldog hanging on it.

"I'm sorry," I say, taking a step back.

"Who the fuck are you?" the guy asks.

I'm all red and timid again. "No one."

"You don't knock," he snaps. "Where's your fucking manners?"

"I didn't think anyone was inside."

"Who the fuck are you?" he snaps again.

"I'm Kaden. I'm visiting James. I'm his cousin."

"Oh . . . shit," the guy says, a smile crossing his face. "I'm sorry, man. I forgot you were coming."

Whew. I take a deep breath. "No worries, man."

"I'm Gerry Jones," he tells me. "Nice to meet you, man."

"You too."

"I'm Michelle," the girl says next.

"Hi."

"You gotta piss?" Gerry asks.

"Yeah."

"All right. We'll get out of your way, man."

The two of them start to leave, and Michelle goes, "I really like your flannel and your hair." She runs a hand through my curls. "You got good style, man."

"Yeah, those loafers are sick, man," Gerry snaps.

"Thanks."

Michelle rubs my forearm and winks. I'm already in complete awe of the city. All this beauty in one single dump pad. All this coolness. This radical debauchery. I'm enamored by the lifestyle. Getting wasted all day. Listening to records in rooms with beautiful girls.

I close the bathroom door, and it smells like sewage in there. Half the ceramic tiles are missing from the ceiling and stacked into piles next to the toilet, with magazines like *Vice* and *National Geographic* on top of them.

The toilet water is brown. There are cigarette butts floating in it and empty Pabst Blue Ribbon cans filling up the back of the seat. As I piss, I notice this pretty awesome shit written in black Sharpie on the wall above the cans.

That says:

Code of the Grifter:

1. Grift or be grifted.

2. Never grift a grifter.

3. Grift or die trying.

4. Grift now . . . ask questions later.

Awesomeness. *What the fuck is a grifter, anyway? Who the fuck penned that shit?* I'm laughing as I leave the bathroom.

The Grifters . . . is that who these dudes are? Like a modern-day *Outsiders*.

The new Greasers.

But as I'm exiting the kitchen, I notice the door across the hall is open just a tiny crack, and I can hear people arguing inside of it. James and Caralie.

I put my ear next to the door to listen.

Caralie is going off on James about how he needs to get himself together and become a positive part of my trip.

She snorts, "James, he's staying with you. You're the only person he knows in the city, so you need to start acting like a fucking adult right now."

"Fuck you, Caralie," James snaps back. "Me act like an adult? Don't forget what I do for you."

"None of that shit matters right now, James. Your fifteen-year-old cousin is here, and you are in charge of him. That's the only thing that matters."

"Will you please take him somewhere for me?" he says. "I am not in the right state of mind to play babysitter. Just take him for the next few hours, and I'll meet up with you later."

"Jesus," she snorts. "You have no regard at all for my life."

"Please, baby."

"What am I supposed to do with him?" she asks.

"I don't know. Do some bonding. Introduce him to some of your babe friends."

"He's fifteen, James."

"So what? I fucked a twenty-six-year-old grad student in the back of her car when I was sixteen."

"Would you stop it with that shit, James? I don't wanna hear it."

"Take him."

There's a pause.

"Please, Caralie. Pretty, pretty fucking please."

There's an ever bigger pause.

"Come on, baby," he says. "For me. Huh . . . what do you say, beautiful girl? Do it for me."

It's just like listening to my mom and dad argue about doing anything with me since my brother died. It feels so similar. Me listening to the argument through a door. Neither of them exactly excited about dealing with me or even wanting to talk to me.

More silence ensues until it's broken again. Not by the shitty sounds of combative voices, but instead by the sound of lips and tongues slapping into each other. I hear Caralie moaning. I hear James go, "Damn, baby. I love your lips."

And Caralie says, "I know you do."

She says, "Okay, baby. I'll take him."

"Thank you."

"I love you," she says.

"I love you too, baby."

I bail from the doorway and move down the hall back into Ally's room.

The Guns N' Roses song "Sweet Child O' Mine" is blasting, and everyone in the room is singing along with it. I watch Ryan lift the mirror of drugs off the table and hand it to Ally. He looks back at me, and he goes, "Destroy!" Then throws up the rock horns.

I'm actually feeling okay about being here now. Maybe it's the combination of the familiarity of the song, all of them singing together, and how much fun they're having. The ugliness of the physical surroundings blending together with the lovely faces of the girls in the room. That Michelle girl dancing all sexy and sweaty with a beer in her hand.

James and Caralie come back in. He grabs my shoulder, leans in to me, and goes, "You're gonna go with Caralie. I'll meet up with you two later."

I nod. Look back at Caralie, who puts on a big fake grin just for my benefit.

Stepping over the back of Ryan's legs, James whispers something to Reed, who nods, then pulls out his wallet and hands a card to James.

Flipping back to me, James hands me the card and goes, "Do not lose this shit, man."

I look down at the card. It's a fake California ID with the same picture of me that I e-mailed him, and I'm twenty-two on it.

"Be very careful about this ID, Kade."

"Kaden," I snap.

James grins. "Kaden. My bad."

Caralie taps me on the shoulder and asks me if I'm ready to go.

"Sure, I'm ready."

James grabs my hand again and goes, "It's good to have you here, man."

"It's good to be here."

"San Francisco, baby. Destroy."

"Let's go," Caralie says.

I tell everyone else good-bye and then Ryan says, "Fine, Reginald VelJohnson. Just go run off into your little world of glasses and loafers and vacuum cleaner toothbrushes."

"What?" I ask.

"Bubblegum gasoline," he hisses.

"Huh?"

"Just fucking leave," he snarls as Caralie pulls me out of the room and the apartment. But before the green door can close all the way, I hear James snort, "Dude, really. You need to chill the fuck out. You're a grimy fuckhead Xanie troll, and you're scaring people."

And Ryan says, "You wanna lick the sweat from my armpit and boil my cats in caramel mustard?"

The door shuts.

"What's that guy's damn problem?" I ask Caralie at the top of the stairs.

"He's a fuck. He hasn't pulled his head out of the coke bag

in eight years," she tells me. "That's his fucking problem."

"Jesus."

"That's Ryan Hastings for you. James says they're good homeys and stuff. But I don't think they are."

"Then why is he hanging out with him?"

Caralie smiles. "He's a drug dealer who cuts him deals and stays up with him while he parties and tells him how awesome his books are."

"Really?"

"That would be the gist of the friendship."

"Doesn't sound like a good basis for one."

"Well," she goes, "it's the basis for most of the shit going on out here, and in no way am I exaggerating about that." She pulls another cigarette from her purse. "Trust me. You'll see."

"So where are we going?" I ask.

"I'm gonna take you over to James's other place in the Mission. The one you'll actually be staying at."

"Awesome."

g. the valencia street apartment

The Mission neighborhood has a different feel and aesthetic to it than the Lower Haight. There's used clothing stores and taquerias and bars on every block. Markets with fresh fruit and vegetables. Huge, amazing, gigantic murals on the sides of buildings. Kids flying by on bikes. Girls and guys on sidewalks in hip outfits and done-up hair and big sunglasses.

Latin music stores and banks and families enjoying the sunny day.

His apartment is on Valencia Street right near the intersection of Eighteenth, above this restaurant, Luna Park.

Again it takes us some serious time to find parking, and we end up having to take a spot nearly five blocks away from his pad.

It's such an amazing feeling to step out of her car in this neighborhood. It's like nothing I've ever felt and breathed before. The culture. The used-book stores. The urban clinics. The small restaurants. The mix of ethnicity.

We start for James's and walk past this empty slab of concrete with soccer nets at each end of it, and Caralie tells me that's where she was playing before she picked me up.

"You play a lot?" I ask her.

"I try to play at least three times a week."

"You any good?"

She makes this sweet, lovely face, nudges me in the arm, and says, "Shit, man. I'm good at everything I do."

"Does James play?" I ask.

"Ha!" she blurts out, stops walking, and bends over, her hands on her knees, laughing.

She's laughing so hard that other people on the sidewalk stop walking and check her out. This table of girls and boys in front of the coffee shop we're next to starts laughing just because Caralie is laughing so hard.

It's pretty funny, actually.

For like the next minute I stand there next to her watching everyone watching us, until she leans up straight and wipes her face with her shirt. She takes a bunch of short breaths and goes, "I'm so sorry. I forgot you don't know that much about your cousin."

"It's okay," I say.

"I'm not laughing at you at all," she sighs.

"You're laughing at James."

"Exactly." She takes another breath and goes, "Whoo." Then pushes the sides of her hair back. "Damn. Whoo."

Just a few moments later and we're in James's other apartment, and it's so much better than the Whip Pad. It's a huge one-bedroom with a living room, kitchen, two bathrooms, and three walk-in closets. The hardwood floors of the living room are clean and shining. There's a coffee table in the center of the room with neat stacks of *SOMA* and *Vice* magazines on both sides of it. A futon is pushed against the wall to the left, and there's a brown leather couch across from that. On the far wall of the room, underneath two windows, is a desk and computer. Thin black sheets hang over both windows. There's another desk to the right of the computer with a record player and stereo speakers on it. The walls of the living room are colored crimson, and there's an autographed poster of James Spader from the movie *Crash* framed and hanging above the futon. Every inch of the wall to the right is covered with album covers, and there's a flat-screen television on the back wall.

The kitchen is even nicer. A complete one-eighty from the Whip Pad kitchen. There's a small, round table with two chairs, white place mats, and four yellow tulips in a vase. He has a stove and a dishwasher, and the walls are a perfect white. The counters are granite and sparkling, and he has a set of steak knives. He's even got hand towels draped on the handles of the drawers.

His bedroom is the awesomest yet. The walls are black, with large oil paintings of nude black women hanging on each one. The bed is made with red sheets and blankets, and books are piled around his nightstand with boxes of condoms on top of them.

Setting my bag next to the futon, I say, "This is so much nicer."

"I know it is."

"How long has he lived here?"

"Since before me and him started going out."

"How long ago was that?"

"It's over three years, I guess."

"Jesus," I say. "That seems like such a long time to be with someone."

She grins. "It's a very long time."

"How old are you?" I ask. "You look real young. A lot younger than James."

"I'm twenty-one."

"Wow. How old is he?"

"Thirty-three. Almost thirty-four."

"Damn," I say. "That's a pretty big difference."

"Yeah, well, he might be older in calendar years, but he doesn't always act like he is."

"Does he always act like he was?" I ask.

"Not always. I don't mean that he's always doing that type of shit. I meant, ya know, that he can be really immature at times. Not all the time, but sometimes. Like today, ya know, when he should've been at the airport on time to get you."

"At least I got picked up."

Caralie nods. "You did. And it's so good to have you here too." Pause. "Are you hungry?"

"Starving."

"So am I. What do you think about some Mexican food?"

"Sure."

"There's an awesome taqueria across the street. I'm thinking we can grab some takeout and hit Dolores Park, which is like three blocks up from here."

"Sounds good to me."

"Cool. I'm gonna change into something warmer, and then we'll bounce."

She steps into the bedroom and closes the door, and I pull out my wallet and look at the fake ID. It's cool to have it. My brother had a fake when he was in high school. He got it his sophomore year, only his didn't have his actual picture on it. His was the actual ID of this guy Mitchell Redmond, who was like seven years older than Kenny but still partied tough with the high school kids. That was when Kenny started drinking a lot, even on school nights. He would show up at home at eleven, all shitfaced, after my parents were in bed. And he would try to make these tiny Totino's Party Pizzas but pass out in the living room while they cooked, and I would smell the smoke and go downstairs and shut the stove off and help him to bed.

Caralie comes out in a pair of black tights and the same shorts and a black hoodie.

"You ready?" she asks.

"Let's go."

The sun is still bright and it's a little past six, but it's cooling down. The wind has picked up. Caralie and I walk across the street to this pretty busy taqueria.

I've never been to a legit Mexican place to eat before. In Iowa, around where I'm from, the only Mexican food comes from Taco Bell and chain restaurants like Carlos O'Kelly's. This place is completely different. It feels authentic, just like the neighborhood we're in.

In line Caralie goes, "Order whatever you want. I got it."

"I have money."

"You're not paying for your meals while you're here. Don't even think about it. And besides, it's actually on James. He gave me a hundred dollars before we split back there."

"That works."

"Yes, it does."

I order a carne asada quesadilla and a root beer, and Caralie gets two fish tacos and a mandarin Jarritos soda.

We sit at a table in the far corner near the restrooms and wait for the food to come up. Caralie is texting almost the whole time, and then she makes a call, and I listen to her going, "Yeah, I'm so sorry, but I'm not going to be able to make it. . . . I'm sorry. . . . I really am, girl. . . . Let's reschedule for next week. . . . He's a real cool kid. . . . You'd never guess he's from Iowa. . . ."

She grins at me after saying that and hangs up right as this guy walks over to us and goes, "So who the hell is this? Is this your new man or something?"

Caralie swings her eyes at him and says, "Oh, hey, man. What's up?"

And I don't like this guy at all just by the looks of him. You can smell the arrogance and taste the conceitedness dripping off of him. He looks like someone trying to be the coolest kid in the room even though there's nothing rad about him at all.

He's got this tiny moustache on the top of his lip, just like a lot of the guys I've seen so far in the city. His hair is brown and shaggy and wavy. He's got an LA Dodgers baseball cap flipped to the side of his head. And he's wearing a short blue and black striped T-shirt under a short brown leather jacket, skin-tight black jeans, and all-white high-tops.

He goes, "So who is he, girl? Who is this chucklehead you're with?"

"Huh," I say.

And Caralie goes, "Stop it, Chris. This is Kaden. He's James's cousin. He's visiting from Iowa."

Chris rolls his eyes. "Iowa, huh. Great. You guys still fucking sheep out there?"

I don't say anything.

"Still beating faggots and hanging black people from trees?"

"You shut the fuck up now, Chris," Caralie snorts. "That's not funny at all, so shut your mouth."

Chris smirks. "It was a joke."

"No, it wasn't."

"Whatever, babe." He looks at me and rolls his eyes. "So you're still with James, then?"

"Of course I am."

"Why?" Chris asks.

She makes a face. "Because I love him. Because I wanna be with him."

He smirks again. "Right. I get it." He shakes his head. "Well, I don't have time to play cute with you. I gotta go. Why don't you call me when you get bored of that shitty writer man of yours. When you wanna be with someone who's a big deal."

Caralie's mouth drops, and she lets out this quick laugh. "Sure, dude. Okay. Will do." She laughs again.

And Chris goes, "Peace out, girl."

He walks away, and I look at Caralie and say, "'Peace out'? Really? What year are we in? 'Peace out'? What is that? Is this 2001?"

She laughs for real this time and says, "No shit, dude. Good point. What year *are* we in? 'Peace out.'"

Our food is up, and we grab it and leave, and while we're waiting to cross the street, I say, "Hey. I really appreciate you hanging out with me like this and all. I know you don't wanna be doing it."

"What?" she snaps. "No. Don't say that, Kaden."

"It's cool," I tell her. "It really is. I don't care. I know you got other crap to do besides babysitting me, and I just want you to know that I appreciate this a ton. It's nice to know at least someone wants to kick it with me."

"Oh, man. Don't get down on James so easily. He's totally excited that you're here. He just got a little sidetracked is all. It'll be better. I promise you that it will."

And I'm thinking how lame it kinda is that Caralie is making all these excuses for James's asshole life. The same way my mom is always bending over backward for my dad. Deflecting any criticism of him. Stretching the truth all over the place just to stick up for him.

But I shrug it off.

Just like I do with my mom.

And I say, "I'm sure it will. Just please, though, thank you."

"You're welcome."

The light changes to green, and we cross the street.

h. dolores park

A sea of people sprawling deep on the grass. Circle after circle after circle of kids drinking beers and smoking cigarettes. There's kids playing bingo and other board games. Kids with boom boxes listening to music that even I know. Jams from the first *Chronic* album. Mötley Crüe. I hear a House of Pain song. And I even hear that song "Slam" by Onyx.

The smell of marijuana creeps out of every pocket of the park.

Caralie and I find a patch of lawn near the tennis courts. It feels great to sit down and stretch out and relax under the sun.

I really like it at Dolores Park. Memories come floating back to me of days spent kicking it at the park in Dysart. Hours spent watching Kenny play in slow-pitch softball tournaments with his friends. Eating pork burgers and bratwursts and watching the fireworks rain in the sky from the infield of the ball diamond. Slamming my first beer with Jeff Penchley from the glass I stole out of the beer tent and smoking my first cigarette in an ally a block from the park.

Sitting in this pretty park with pretty Caralie brings all these old feelings rushing back, and I ease into a comfort zone and let the pressure and the anxiety fall from my shoulders.

Dumping salsa onto the edge of my quesadilla, I say, "So what else do you do besides pick up the pieces of my cousin's life?"

Caralie smiles. "Not a ton right now. I work a few days a week at a coffee shop on Hayes Street. I was in school last year, but I'm taking some time off right now."

"Why's that?"

"Because I wasn't into it the way I should've been."

"What were you studying?"

"Poli sci. But I'm thinking about switching things up to either art history or maybe even international studies."

"Cool."

"James is pushing me hard to pick a major and go back and finish at City College so I can transfer into a four-year school."

"Why is he pushing you? He didn't go to school."

She takes a drink of her soda and wipes her mouth with the side of her hand. "Because he thinks it'll be good for me. That it'll make me into a more well-rounded person. Plus, he's been paying for it."

"Oh." Pause. "That makes sense."

"I guess so. Thing is, I wanna be sure that whatever I decide to go into is something I feel good about and love studying. That's been my biggest holdup so far. Committing to anything other than your cousin."

"How did you two even get together?"

She sighs. "Well . . ." She shakes her head with a half grin. "I actually met him at a book signing for his second book."

"So you were a fan?"

"Oh, shit yeah. Big time. I read his first book, *PieGrinder*, when I was sixteen and just loved it. It was like my bible. Me and all of my friends would go to Ocean Beach and lay out and take turns reading chapters from the book out loud to each other. I just really like the way he uses words and his style of writing. The way each line cuts glass. I love that kind of literature."

"I haven't read his first one yet," I say.

"You haven't?"

"Nope. Just parts of *Dickpig* on the plane here."

"Don't tell him that," she snorts. "He gets real anal when people close to him have never read his stuff."

"I'm not that close to him."

"You are now," she says, taking another bite. "You're part of his crew now."

"All right."

"So anyway," she continues, "it was kinda big news around the city when word got around that his second book was coming out, and he was going to be doing a reading for the release of it at this store the Booksmith, so me and a couple of my friends went, and when it was my turn to get my copy signed, I swear to God he was nervous talking to me. He ended up signing it like this: 'To the best thing I've seen in this city so far.' It was fucking killer. I was awestruck. And so on our way out of the store Ryan—"

"The guy I met today?"

"Yep. Him. He stopped me and handed me a piece of paper and said it was from James, and I looked at it and there was his phone number. I couldn't believe it. So I called him a week later, and we made plans, and three years later here we are."

"That's pretty cool. So you grew up in San Francisco, then?"

"I was born here, but my family was in Mexico before that. They lived in Santa María del Oro in the state of Durango. They moved to the States about two years before I was born, and I grew up my whole life in the Outer Mission."

"Nice."

"So what about you? You got a girlfriend back in Iowa?"

"Yeah, I do. Her name is Jocelyn."

"That's a pretty name."

"She's a pretty girl."

"I bet she is."

"Not as pretty as you," I say. "But real pretty for a Dysart girl."

"I bet she's beautiful."

"She's my first girlfriend ever."

"No way. I don't believe that for one second."

"It's true."

"A handsome kid like you."

"Nah," I say. "I'm not handsome. Not like my brother was. Now that guy, he had a lot of girlfriends. The girls fell over backward for him. It was crazy how much they all adored him."

"He must've been special."

"You wanna see a picture?"

"I'd love to."

I take out the same picture of him that's been hanging from the mirror in my room since the day after I found out he died. It's his senior year football picture. Him kneeling with his right knee on the ground, his silver and black Knights helmet perched on his left knee. The red Union High jersey. The silver, red, and black pants. A goalpost in the background. Total confidence spilling from his face and body language. Man, he was real good at football. Real good at everything. All the girls just loved him. He was tall, like six feet tall, and had blond hair and tan skin and these big, bright blue eyes that could light up any room he ever walked into. He coulda been a movie star easily. Lots of people told him that.

Me, on the other hand, nobody ever told me anything like that. I resemble Kenny, but I don't look much like my older brother. Not with my curly hair and my pale skin and the freckles on the tops of my cheeks.

Kenny was built. In shape. Me, I'm skinny as hell. A

wimp. He was a local sports star. I was just his little brother.

Caralie looks at the picture. "You're totally right. He was a stud. But so are you."

"I'll never be as good with the girls as he was," I tell her, putting the picture back in my wallet. "Maybe if he was still alive, with him teaching me about girls and how to talk to them better. He used to. He used to give me a ton of advice even though I was so young. He always had some kinda something to say about the way to approach women. He was great like that."

"You miss him a lot, huh?"

"So much."

"He died in Iraq?"

"Yup."

"How?" she asks. "I mean, if you don't mind telling me."

I bite my tongue and close my eyes.

"Kaden, if you don't want to talk about—"

But I cut her off.

Opening my eyes, I say, "It was just like my parents and the papers said it was. During a shoot-out with insurgents. He got hit in the neck with a bullet and bled to death. That's how he died."

Pause.

I swallow the lump in my throat.

"Honestly," I say. "That's how it happened."

"I remember when James heard about it. He got pretty weird. He'd actually been talking to your brother through e-mails about you two coming out here for the Palahniuk reading together when he got out for a break."

"I know he was. That's why I'm here, ya know. To see this thing through. I mean, I couldn't believe my mom talked my asshole dad into letting me do this all by myself. I had to up my grades first, but after I started reading the Palahniuk books, life changed for me. I started working out and getting really into school. I felt a purpose for the first time in my life. Reading his books set something off inside of me. I connected with them, and something woke up in me, and I haven't been the same since. And I owe it all to my brother."

"Wow," she says.

"And I miss him so damn much."

Caralie nods, and there's this long silence, and we both look away from each other, my eyes falling on this girl sitting against the cement wall of the tennis courts holding her legs, looking really sad.

The saddest girl in the world.

And Caralie grabs my arm, and she goes, "You wanna see something?"

"Yeah."

"Come with me."

We stand up and throw our trash away and walk all the way across the park to where no one is at and stop in front of this white-colored building that's empty and locked up.

"Over here," she says, and I follow her around the side

of the building and watch her climb on the blue recycling bin. She jumps up and grabs the edge of the roof and pulls herself onto it.

"Come on," she tells me.

The sun is dropping fast, and the sky is pink and blue now, and I can still hear the people and the music in the park as I follow her lead and pull myself to the roof.

"This is it," she says.

It's a tiny swimming pool.

She says, "This is the Mission pool."

"Fuck, yeah," I say.

It's so small, just a circle of water like five feet deep.

"This is rad," I say. "Just this pool all far away from everything."

"I know it. It's one of the hidden treasures in the city. Hardly anyone knows about it. Even a lot of my close friends have no idea this is here."

"How did you know about it?" I ask.

"James brought me here the first night we kicked it. He took me to this real cute Italian place, and then we snuck forties into the Lumiere Theatre and watched this special screening of *The Dreamers*. And then he asked me if I wanted to go swimming with him, and he brought me here. We were the only two people at all and swam all night and drank some more. It was one of the best nights I've ever had in my life."

The two of us sit down, our legs dangling over the edge

of the roof, and I say, "This might be one of the coolest things I've ever seen."

"It's so nice, too. I try and come here at least once a week to fuck around if the weather's nice enough. It's really fun."

"Cool." I look at Caralie and nudge her arm and say, "Thank you for bringing me here. I think that if I lived here and needed a break from something, or was having a really stupid night, this is where I'd come."

"Good."

Her phone begins to ring, and she pulls it from her hoodie pocket and goes, "It's James."

I'm bummed that my cousin is calling. Being with Caralie is so nice to me, and I was hoping that James wasn't going to call at all and I wouldn't have to see him until tomorrow.

She gets off the phone and goes, "He wants me to drive you to the Upper Haight. To Ryan's pad."

"Really?"

"Yeah. I'm gonna drop you off with him, and then I don't know what you two are gonna get into."

"All right."

We get back on our feet and climb down from the roof and leave the park, and the sun is gone.

i. ryan's pad
It's in the Upper Haight, the big mecca of counterculture in the sixties that I couldn't give a shit less about.

Caralie stops her car in front of his building and puts the hazards on.

It's nine o'clock.

I'm pretty exhausted.

"You're not coming up?" I ask her.

"I can't, dude. I have shit to do now."

"All right."

"But I had a great time with you today."

"I had a good time with you, too."

She leans over and hugs me and gives me a kiss on the cheek. She smells really good. Like a candy store and coconuts.

"Here," she says, handing me a piece of paper. "This is my cell number in case anything happens. Call me if you need anything, anytime, this whole week."

"You're gonna be around, though . . . right?"

"Of course. It's just if I'm not, and something goes wrong, then I want you to call me. Okay? And take this too," she says, handing me a key. "It's for James's place in the Mission."

"Okay." I put the paper and key in my wallet and get out of her car.

"It's apartment three thirty. Just ring the buzzer."

"Cool."

I close the door and walk to the gate and ring the bell while watching Caralie drive away. The buzzer sounds from upstairs, and I pull the gate open, and Ryan comes down to meet me.

"What's up, dude," he croaks, a lit smoke between his fingers.

"Hey."

I follow him into his place, up this set of winding stairs that smells like garbage and smoke. There's a giant W.A.S.P. poster at the top of the stairs. Empty fish tanks and trash bags in the hallway. Fruit flies everywhere.

I trail him into his bedroom, and there's a naked girl with her eyes closed under the sheets. I sit down on this yellow and brown couch next to the door and watch him walk around a pyramid of beer cans and a stack of porn magazines.

He sits down at his computer and says, "Your cousin will be back soon. He had to run an errand."

"How soon?"

Ryan shrugs. "Real soon, I hope, because I really need to fuck this girl, and I can't do it with you in here, ya know. Unless you wanna watch?"

"No, thanks."

"You sure about that? Learn a few things on your trip to the big city."

"I'm sure, man."

"Suit yourself. You want a cigarette?"

"Nah."

"Some coke?"

"Nope."

"Whatever, then." He flips around to his computer and moves the mouse. "Do you like Pantera?"

"I don't know."

"If you don't, then I don't know what to do with you," he tells me, then plays the music and turns back to me, pulling out a baggie of coke and some keys. "Your cousin and I got wasted last week and stayed up for two nights and watched all the Pantera videos." He takes a hit. "Does that even mean anything to you?"

I shrug. "No."

He leans forward and stares hard at me. "Are you even related to James Morgan?"

"I'm his cousin."

"Then start fucking acting like it. Christ!" He does another bump, and the doorbell rings. Ryan looks out the window, then back to me, and says, "That's James. You wanna buzz him in."

"Sure."

I jump off the couch and let James in, and he says, "Just wait here, man," and walks into Ryan's room.

I peek inside and see James hand Ryan a wad of money and go, "That's everything."

"Awesome."

Then Ryan hands James more coke, and James hugs him, and I duck back into the hall, and James comes out.

"Let's go, man," he says.

We leave the apartment and walk down to the corner.

"Where are we going?" I ask.

"To my place in the Mission."

"I was just there."

James looks at me, his shades still covering his eyes, and he says, "And what's your point?"

I don't say anything. A cab drives up, James hails it, and we jump in.

j. the cab ride

James sits behind the driver. I sit behind the passenger seat. He asks me what Caralie and I did, and I tell him as his phone rings. He quits listening to me and answers. "You should really come over. . . . It's cool. . . . Nah. . . . It's just me and my cousin. . . . We'll have some fun. . . . Trust me, baby. . . ."

He hangs up.

"Was that Caralie?" I ask him.

He looks out the window next to him and says, "No. Not quite." Pause. "So what do you think so far, man? You having fun?"

"It's pretty cool, I guess."

"It's gonna be a rad week, man. I think you're really gonna like it here."

"I hope so."

"How'd you like the Whip Pad?"

"It's crazy over there. Pretty disgusting."

"Right."

"Why do you guys call it that?"

James looks at me and says, "There's this amazing band called Big Business. Used to be just a two-piece with Cody from the Murder City Devils drumming and Jared from this band Karp playing bass and singing. Anyway, Jared used to have this band before Karp called the Whip, right? And it was so good. Some of the best metal I've ever heard. So when we found the place, Reed was the first one to move in, and for the first week he was there, he got fucking loaded every day, all fucking day, and the only thing he played was the Whip record. It was playing anytime that any of us walked into that dump. So we just started calling it the Whip Pad after that."

"I've never heard of the Whip," I tell him.

"Oh, you have now. You're gonna hear a lot of new shit this week, kid. We're gonna get you all caught up on what's good while you're here. That's one thing you can totally count on."

"Sweet," I say. "By the way, do you know some stupid kid named Chris?"

James lets out this heavy sigh and runs a hand over his face. "I know a few Chrises, man. What'd he look like?"

"Kinda tall and skinny. Real cocky. Had a turd-looking piece of hair above his lip."

"An arrogant piece of shit with some bullshit sense of entitlement to him?" James says.

"Yeah."

"I know him. Why?"

"He was talking some major shit about you to Caralie at this taqueria earlier."

James sighs. "It's nothing. They all fucking do that when I'm not around her."

"Why?"

James looks right at me and lowers his shades. "Why?"

"Yeah. Why?"

"Look at the girl, man. She's the most beautiful thing in this city. They all want her so bad, but she loves me." He slides his shades back up and looks back out the window. "I fell for her the first time I saw her. I really did, man. She's the best thing in my life. The best thing in this whole damn city. You ever seen *25th Hour?*"

"Nah. Why?"

"There's a part in it where Edward Norton's character is talking about his girl, Naturelle Riviera, who's played by Rosario Dawson. And he's telling his buddy at this bar, he says that Naturelle Riviera, he says, 'She's the only girl I've ever fantasized about after I've had sex with her.' And that's how it is with Caralie Chavez, man."

Pause.

"Shit," I say.

And James says, "I really love that girl."

k. the valencia street apartment II

I'm so spent by the time we get back to his place. With the time change it's only ten, but for my body it's midnight, and I hardly got any sleep the night before with Jocelyn.

"So what do you wanna do?" James asks. "You tired? You wanna pass out?"

"I think so."

"Cool."

He grabs a couple of blankets and some pillows and hands them to me. "Just pull out the futon and hit it."

"What are you gonna do?"

"Hang out for a little while."

He goes into his bedroom and closes the door, and while I make my bed, I can hear him pounding his drugs out on the nightstand. I hear him sniff a couple of times, and I shut off the living room light and lie down.

Then James comes back out and stands over me. He's smoking. I sit up and he says, "Nothing you see tonight, nothing you see this week, leaves your fucking lips. Got it?"

"Sure."

"You understand me, man?"

"Yeah."

"Do you really understand me?"

"Yes. I do. I got it. Nothing leaves my lips."

"Good."

He goes back in his room, and I close my eyes, and I'm out right away, and then I'm up right away.

Someone's knocking on the door. I poke my head over the pillows and watch James answer it and let in that girl Michelle I met at the Whip Pad. I watch them kiss, and then he slaps her butt and tells her to get into his room.

She does.

Then James takes off his shirt, whips it into his room, walks into the kitchen, and re-emerges with a six-pack of beer.

He stands over me again and looks down at me and whispers, "This isn't really happening."

Then he goes back into his bedroom and slams the door shut behind him, and probably ten minutes later I hear Michelle moaning and James calling her a bitch.

It gets louder.

Way louder.

And soon they're fucking, and I can't get back to sleep. It's too loud. I try and block out the noise. I put a pillow over my head. I put both pillows over my head. I even try humming to myself and plugging my ears, but none of it helps. I have to wait it out.

My first night in San Francisco and I can't sleep because my cousin is having loud sex in the next room over with some girl who isn't even his hot girlfriend.

Hours later Michelle leaves, and as she's bailing, James goes, "I hate you. Ya know that. I fucking hate you."

"I hate you too," she says back.

"Screw you."

The girl walks out and I'm thinking, *What a fucking head case.*

But at least he seems to be having a blast with all of it.

His awesome life.

Sunday, June 1st

I WAKE UP THE NEXT AFTERNOON TO CARALIE WALKING
into the apartment. I sit up and look down the hallway and
watch her coming toward me in a yellow sundress and flip-
flops, a big pretty smile on her face, white framed sunglasses
resting on the top of her head.

She's holding two plastic bags filled with takeout orders.
"Hey, there," she says, stopping in front of me the same way
James did last night. "Did you sleep good?"

I pause. It's not like I can come out and just say, "Um,
no. Actually I didn't. I actually slept like crap because your
dickheaded boyfriend was pounding beers and drugs and
some girl who was all friendly with you just a few hours
before she got nailed by your man." It's not a real feasible
scenario to spit those words out of my mouth, especially
with James in the next room, so I say what I have to.

I say, "Like a rock, Caralie. I hit the futon and I was out
in a minute."

"Good. I'm glad to hear that," she says. "Sometimes
James likes to keep people up with him just so he has someone to talk to until he's done getting loaded."

"Not last night," I tell her. "It wasn't like that at all last night with me here."

"Good," she says again, then moves into the kitchen.

And I still can't believe how gorgeous she is. I can't. It's not only a combination of her looks and the way her presence commands all the attention in the room. It's also in the way she looks at you when you talk to her. Like she's truly listening to what you're saying and understanding what you're telling her. It's in the way she carries herself.

With pride and confidence.

With the grace of an angel.

And how her smile makes you feel alive.

I stand up and stretch and go to the kitchen. She's pulling the window shades up. The boxes of food are on the table.

"I hope you're hungry," she says.

"I am."

She moves back into the living room and opens up both windows after pulling up the shades, then enters the kitchen again while I'm fingering over one of the boxes.

"He keeps it so dark in here all the time," she sighs.

"Isn't that what people who do a lot of hard drugs do?" I say. "At least that's how I always see it in the movies."

"It's true," she says. "But he keeps it like that even when he's sober. Or just kicking back and sipping on beers."

"Huh." Pause. "So what's to eat?"

"Well . . . I didn't know what you liked, but I remember

James telling me that you can't go wrong with bacon, sausage, eggs, and pancakes when you're dealing with anyone from the Midwest. So that's what I got."

"I don't think you can go wrong with any of that when you're dealing with anyone from anywhere," I say.

"Good point."

I sit down at the table and open one of the boxes, and Caralie sets some Tabasco sauce and ketchup out and sits down across from me.

"So what'd you two do after I dropped you off?" she asks.

"Came right back here."

"Oh. Okay. Well that was a waste of a trip to the Upper Haight. How long were you at Ryan's?"

"About twenty minutes. He had some naked girl under his sheets and asked me if I wanted to watch him fuck her."

"Jesus Christ," she snorts, shaking her head. "That guy is fucking stupid."

"Why do you guys hang around him, then?" I ask. "Because he has drugs?"

"That's a huge part of it. But him and James have known each other for a while. They have a pretty twisted love-hate thing between them, where they do and say really fucked-up shit to each other but also have each other's backs so hard. It's one of those things, ya know. That only those two truly understand."

"I guess. The dude was kinda funny. He was so fucked up and confused it was a little funny to me."

"And that's how you have to deal with him. On that level. Most of those guys, actually. A lot of people don't get how to be with them. They don't know how to handle being around all that bullshit, and they take it the wrong way. People get in those situations, like you were in yesterday, and they can't hang or be around it, because it's so much. You just gotta understand how to deal with that mindset. Those dudes are all criminals and hustlers, and you have to be able to think in those ways when it gets like that. Stick up for yourself and talk shit back to them, because it's all a big fucking joke to them . . . most of the time."

"You obviously don't have a problem with it."

"I did at first," she says. "I didn't know what the hell was going on when James and I first got together and he would drag me into that, but then I realized how to communicate with them in the ways they could understand, like talking shit right back to them when they're ripping on you, or calling out their bullshit when they're going all intellectual, or just knowing the words to most Faith No More or Guns N' Roses songs. It was like nothing after that. It can get annoying. But they don't mean any harm by any of it. They're just fucked up and trying to have a good time. And they do."

"Yes, they do."

James's door slams open. Footsteps coming down the hall. The words "I feel like a two-dollar whore who got slapped around by her speed-smoking pimp!" being yelled.

My body tenses. Just the sound of his voice gets me uptight. I'm not really all that fond of him so far, except for the fact that he's with Caralie.

Whipping around the corner in just a pair of jeans and those same sunglasses, James snaps, "You guys start eating without me now, huh?"

"I didn't know you were up, baby."

"Forget about it. I'm not sure I have the stomach to eat, anyway."

Caralie drops the forkful of food she was scooping to her mouth and says, "You did a wake-me-up line, didn't you?"

He puts his hands on her shoulders. "Maybe . . ."

"Damn it, James," she snorts. "You're already doing coke. For fuck's sake."

"Oh, stop it," he groans. "Don't get your panties in a bunch. It's my fucking life." He leans down and kisses her neck and then reaches over and smacks me in the shoulder. "Morning, dude."

I take a bite of my eggs. "Morning."

James pulls a glass from the cupboard and opens the freezer and pulls out a bottle of Ketel One and a couple handfuls of ice, and then he opens the fridge and grabs Bloody Mary mix, some celery and olives, and some horse-radish and Worcestershire sauce.

"James Morgan," she says.

"What's up? You want one too?"

She rubs the back of her neck. "Please."

"I knew it."

I look down at my food, a little bummed that the people in charge of taking me around to do anything are gonna be wasted and high on drugs the whole time.

He brings the drinks over and pulls up a stool and dumps some Tabasco into his glass. "So is there anything in particular you wanna do this week?" he asks me. "Cool places you heard about and want to check out?"

"Maybe," I tell him, then pull out the list of things to visit that my dad gave me yesterday morning before I left the house with my mom. "My dad thought I might like these places."

James rips the list from my hand and looks it up and down. "Nope," he says. "This list is shit. Total fucking crap. We're not doing any of this."

"Why not?"

"Because your dad's a fucking tourist, man."

"What's that mean?"

"There's two types of people who come to this city. You got your visitors and you got your tourists."

"What's the difference?" I grunt.

"Visitors are people who come here because they already know people here. They stay with their friends and do the rad shit that their friends are into like going to killer shows at dive bars in the shittiest parts of the city. They eat at grease-trap hole-in-the-wall diners that ain't in any

'Where to Eat While You're in San Francisco' brochures. And they stay up all night doing good drugs with strangers while arguing about the genius of Body Count and Gil Scott-Heron. Whereas tourists are people who come here usually without knowing anyone at all. And they hang out at Fisherman's Wharf and Pier Thirty-nine. Or," he says, looking back at the paper, "they go to Alcatraz and ride the cable car down Powell Street." James looks back at me. "You're a visitor, man. And your dad is a stinkin' tourist. He always has been, and he always will be." He crumples the list into a ball and throws it into the trash can. "Now, your mom, on the other hand."

I tense again and say, "What about her?"

"She's a rad lady. She's a visitor."

"Not anymore," I tell him. "Not since Kenny died."

"Bullshit," he snaps back. "She let you come out here, man. That takes one pretty cool chick. Now, she may not act like it all the time, but I know her real well, and she's a visitor. The complete opposite of your asshole dad."

"James," Caralie barks. "Calm the fuck down and quit talking so much shit."

James sneers at her and turns back to me and stares at me from under those shades while he slams another drink.

It's awkward. And I can feel myself getting red. But I'm not gonna shy away. Not from him. So I go, "Cool. Then what the hell are we gonna do today, since I'm a visitor and all?"

James smiles and grabs a slice of bacon from Caralie's

box and says, "I'm glad you asked." He takes a bite. "We're going to this block party down in SoMa. Thee Oh Sees and Master Slash Slave are playing a stage on the street, and my friend Lauren lives in the building right above it all. There's gonna be kegs on the roof and some DJs spinning between sets." He shoves the rest of the bacon into his mouth. "That's what we're gonna do."

"And that's the plan for the whole week, then," I snap. "Partying?"

James swipes his nose. "What the fuck else is there, man?" He nudges Caralie, who takes a sip from her drink. "Right, baby?" he snorts.

"Sure, babe."

Jumping to his feet, James storms into the living room with his drink, and like seconds later heavy metal music starts blasting.

"Who is this?" I ask Caralie.

"The Saviours," she answers. "They're from Oakland."

"It's pretty good," I say.

Then James pops back into the kitchen and throws up the rock horns and says, "First time I saw these guys, they played on stacks at Thee Parkside! Like holy shit! These dudes were playing on stacks at a bar about as big as my living room. How fucking ruthless is that?"

I don't say anything.

And James points at me. "It's metal for breakfast around here, Iowa boy." Then he lights a cigarette.

a. block party in soma

The three of us roll to the party in a cab, and the scene when we get there is something like I've never seen before. This three-story building with all these people spilling through the walls. All these hot girls in summer dresses and tube tops and short skirts. Tattoos and moist skin. Tight jeans and flannels and flipped-bill baseball hats. All kinds of people. Kids as far as the eye can see.

I follow James and Caralie through the packed hallways and crowded stairwells full of spilled beer and cigarette smoke as we ascend to the top floor of the building.

James is wearing a light blue polo shirt and black jeans, and I'm wearing a Chicago Bears T-shirt, a pair of cut-off jeans, and some white Vans.

Those two seem to know almost everyone here, and the ones they don't know seem to know who they are. And I'm not gonna lie; it does feel pretty cool to be rolling up like this with James Morgan and his girl, Caralie Chavez. Part of the big-time published author's posse. Part of the group with the prettiest girl in the world on their side. It's such a different feeling of relevance than the feeling of being Kenny Norris's little brother. With Kenny, there was always this implied pressure to be just as good as him, because we shared the same last name. There was pressure to be better than him, almost. To at least be in the exact mold as him. And I could never get over that or really understand it. How people wanna put those kinds of pressures on someone else, onto their own kids. Trying to hold them to ridiculous standards set by other people who are radically different from them. And this is the difference I feel rolling into this spot with James. Just being in his presence is more than good enough for everybody else. Save for a few horribly jaded girls and some insanely jealous guys.

We hit the third floor where James's friend's apartment is and go inside. More girls in loose clothing and seventies funk music bumping. There's people dancing and smoking weed and shotgunning beers. Wasted faces with big smiles and tired eyes, and it's barely four.

We go down this bright hallway with all these photos on the wall of people—friends, perhaps—posing for the lens. The complexions are washed out, and the images are grainy, and I don't really care too much for it, because I don't think it's that good or even close to original.

In the kitchen there's a keg in a bucket of ice and two metal tubs full of soda and beer. This really short guy in a blue beanie and a skateboarding shirt whistles at Caralie from the corner and yells, "What's up, bitch? Come talk to me. I wanna know your name!"

It pisses me off to hear him say that to her, and I wanna deck him in the face with his own skateboard and destroy him, but Caralie takes care of it for herself. She looks at him and says, "Say something like that to me again and I'll fuck your face up, Tiny Tim." Then she flips him off, and all of that guy's friends start laughing at him, and so do I.

Caralie looks back at me and says, "It's typical shit."

"That guy is an asshole."

"That guy was nothing," she says. "Took care of him in a fucking sentence."

"You did."

James hasn't seen any of this. He missed all of it, or if he didn't, he ignored it. I guess he did tell me last night that he's used to guys coming on to her and saying shit and trying to undermine him when he's not around. So maybe it's like that. Just some background noise. Something he knows he doesn't have to worry about because Caralie can handle herself pretty good.

He's also started busying himself with two pretty girls. One has short black hair and is covered in tattoos and has this red velvet outfit on that looks like lingerie. And the other girl has blond hair and blue eyes and is wearing this tight black and white dress.

He waves me and Caralie over and introduces me to the girls. "This my cousin," he tells them. "He's visiting me for a week."

"From where?" the girl in the red asks.

"Iowa," I say.

"Potatoes," the other girl says.

"No," I say. "Corn."

"Cool," she says back.

Lauren is the girl with black hair and tattoos, and it's her place we're in, and the other girl is Emily.

And it's obvious that Caralie knows both of them but she's only friendly with Lauren. They hug each other the way you expect good acquaintances to do, but when Emily says hi to her, Caralie says nothing and looks away. Like maybe there's some shit between them. Something to do with James Morgan, perhaps.

And I'm thinking, *Yeah. That's probably it.*

I'm thinking, *I'm pretty sure it has something to do with my cousin James.*

"So what brings you here from Idaho—"

"Iowa," I say, correcting Lauren.

"Yeah. Iowa. I know. What brings you here?"

"I'm gonna see Chuck Palahniuk read on Friday. My older brother, Kenny, wanted to bring me out here for the reading, but he couldn't because he died in the war, so I'm doing it for him."

All four of their faces change after I say this, as if somehow I'm saying something too inappropriate. As if speaking of my brother's death is in some kinda bad taste. But it's all me being honest, and that's the thing with being out here. The lines between fact and fiction seem severely blurred in this San Francisco scene.

And Lauren goes, "Well, I'm sorry to hear that about your brother."

"What?"

"About your brother," she says. "That sucks."

"It does more than that."

And James goes, "Well, Jesus Christ, I need a drink." He looks at me and Caralie. "You two want a beer?"

Caralie says yes but I say no, and James says, "Take the stick out of your ass, Kaden. Christ. Your mom and dad ain't here. It's just you, man."

"But I don't want a drink right now."

"That's pussy talk, Kade—"

"Kaden," I snap back. "It's Kaden. Always."

"I know," James snorts. "Just settle down. I was only kidding with you. What do you want to drink instead of beer?"

"I'm gonna grab a root beer from one of those tubs."

"Good for you," James says, before going to the keg.

Caralie turns to me and says, "He's just messing with you."

"Well, it's not very funny," I snap, then go and grab my root beer and cuff it in my hand.

The thrill of being in the Morgan posse has dissolved, and I'm just irritated with the guy. Irritated all over again.

I dry my hand on my shirt and open the can and go to look around the rest of the apartment. It's not like I was going to be this huge part of any conversations anyway, so I slide back down the hallway with the pictures in it and see that one of the doors is open and hear some kids freestyling inside of it. I push the door open, and a cloud of blunt smoke rolls out of it, and I walk in. There's six people total in there. Two girls. One with long black hair twisted into two humongous braids and like three piercings in her face. She's wearing black pants and a wife beater and kinda looks half Latin, although I don't think she is.

The other girl looks half Asian. She has dark brown hair, and her cheeks are blotchy and red, and she's wearing a red dress.

And the other four kids are guys with backpacks and baggy jeans and baseball caps flipped to the sides and bad jewelry all over them. It seems pretty stereotypical. Pretty much the way you'd imagine it looking like if you hadn't walked in the room yet and someone told you what was happening inside of it.

It's the two girls who are rapping. They're flowing to beats coming from computer speakers, and they're not very good, either. The one with all the piercings is going off about period blood and getting fucked in the ass, and that's it. And she's struggling with it. Like it's not making too much sense. Most of it doesn't rhyme. And she's using the same words way too much.

Then it's the other girl's turn, and she's not very good either. She raps about the exact same thing as the girl before her, and it's boring and not funny the way I think they want it to be funny. And even though I know I can't do any better than them, I figure I know enough to keep from embarrassing myself the way they are.

As that particular beat, a Murs one, begins to fade out, the door is pushed back open, and James walks in.

"Your rapping is bullshit," he snaps. "Fucking stupid, I tell ya."

Both girls stop, and everyone looks at me and James.

"Goddamn it, Ellen," he snorts. "Why are you still doing this to yourself?" He's talking to the girl with the braids. "Don't make yourself look like a clown in front of other people."

I start laughing, because it's kind of funny what he says, and then Ellen, she gets all agitated and snaps, "You're a little bitch, James."

"And your rap sucks, baby. It's bullshit. Give it up. Nobody's buying the gig anymore." James is grinning big while saying all of this. He grabs my shoulder and says, "Let's get out of here. The live music shit is about to start on the street. Time to hear some real fucking music."

We turn and leave while Ellen is saying something about James having a small cock, but he doesn't seem to care that she's even talking. He lights a cigarette and goes, "Those broads don't have a clue, man. Thinking they're gonna be all big and shit and make a real album. Bullshit."

"They're actually trying to be for real?" I ask.

James smirks. "Trying, but it ain't working. It's a fucking gimmick, dude. A ploy. Two white girls rapping about cocks and periods, and it ain't even funny. It's a shitty ploy."

"What do they call themselves?"

"Bacon."

"That's a stupid fucking name."

Sliding his shades back over his eyes, James says, "It's a fucking disgrace to hip-hop, kid. I mean, did you hear anything in their rhymes other than dudes who come too fast and how their periods suck?"

"I don't think so."

"Exactly. 'Cause that's the only thing those two know how to talk about. There's nothing else to their act. And it could actually be funny if it was done the right way."

"But it ain't."

James smacks me in the shoulder. "No, it is definitely not."

b. the roof

There are two more kegs up there with the black tar and the tiny pebbles and the Bay Bridge pointing to the sun. I can see a city of houses in rows, spread across the horizon like a chessboard, black and white, the sun drilling down on the skin. A DJ spins soul music. There's a cute girl in a blue dress laughing so hard that beer sprays through her nose: something about a fat gay guy eating the ass of a fat girl while she was passed out on a bed. Another guy makes an absurd gesture at Caralie, but she's too busy watching James to really notice it. She's watching him like a record store clerk watches a teenager with a backpack. A thousand people in the street below us.

This hot blond girl in a black and white flannel dress

and black tights runs up to James and throws her arms around him. She seems really wasted, like a lot of people. Everyone is wasted except for me.

James hugs the girl back and points to me and says, "Hey, that's my cousin."

"Hi, cousin!" the girl shouts. "I'm Bailey."

"Kaden."

"Hi," she says, her lips covered in gloss and glistening. She's so drunk. She looks really happy.

Caralie waves at Bailey and then moves away from us, over to a group of kids in flannels and mismatched blouses standing near the DJ. James doesn't pay attention. He just points at me again and says, "Kid's from fucking Iowa. Can you believe that, Bailey Brown? How awesome is that?"

"My band played in Iowa with Lamborghini Dreams last month," she says.

"Where at?" I ask.

"The Picador in Iowa City."

"Who's your band?"

"Bloody Flowers."

James takes a drag of his smoke. "It's metal as fuck," he says. "And she's the singer. She's awesome."

Bailey looks back at James, a cigarette between her fingers, and says, "Ya know we're playing with the Dreams and Ally's band on Wednesday at Bottom of the Hill."

"I know this, darling," James says. "It's gonna be one of

the best shows of the year. Fucking Lamborghini Dreams and Bloody Flowers. Ya listening to this, Kaden. And you're just in time for it, dude."

"Awesome. I can't wait," I tell him, even though I have no idea who the hell any of these bands are except for Lamborghini Dreams, who I only know in name because they're all the rage on the MySpace music scene.

I kill the rest of my root beer, and one of the bands starts tuning up on the stage right below us.

The soul music stops.

"Sweet," James says. "Showtime."

"I'm fucking pumped for this," says Bailey. "I haven't seen Thee Oh Sees in a while, and Dwyer's my boy."

"Master Slash Slave kills it too, B."

"I've heard that."

The three of us swerve around people to get to the edge of the roof, and everyone is lining up to see. Two hundred legs dangling over the side of the building.

On the stage are two guys. One of them is wearing a brown corduroy suit and bow tie and is holding a guitar, and the other guy is sitting behind his drum kit. A large synthesizer sits on the right side of the stage, and the guy with the guitar tunes it. The drummer puts on a pair of headphones, and then the other guy strolls up to the mic and goes, "How's everyone doing today?"

People scream and hold up their drinks and whistle.

"That's good," he says. "So we're Master Slash Slave

from right here in San Francisco, and this first song is called
'You Never Write.' Get into it."

They start playing, and I gotta say that I like it. It's
dancey, but really loud with heavy undertones, but pretty
poppy, too.

And they get everyone going. People start dancing and
getting really into it. Even James is dancing. Even I catch
myself shaking my stupid white hips around by the third
song.

It's pretty cool, actually. These girls in front of me keep
backing their asses into me and slamming their thighs
against me. One of them even smiles and winks at me. The
drunken euphoria of a perfect afternoon. And they have no
idea how old I am. No one does, except James and Caralie.
I look like a lot of the kids there with the way I'm dressed
and all. And I think about how rad it would be to make out
with one of them and then show them my high school ID. I
think about this scenario until the music has stopped and
the band is done.

Everyone's cheering and screaming still, and I need
another root beer and to pee, so I climb back into Lauren's.

I decide to pee first and remember seeing like five or
six kids rubbing their noses and talking real fast when they
were walking out of a bathroom earlier, and I find it and
walk in and it's total bullshit.

Christ!

Those two girls from Bacon are in there, and they're

laughing about something, and the half Asian–looking one is holding a comb.

"My bad," I tell them, and start back out, but Ellen snaps, "No. Hold on. Don't go yet. Stay in here."

"Why?"

"Just because," she says. "We wanna talk to you about some stuff."

I get this feeling that I shouldn't stay. That these two can't offer anything good at all. They seem real shady and conniving, and they're a turnoff because their rhymes are bad, but I stay.

I close the door and go, "So what is it you wanna talk to me about?"

"Who are you?" the Asian one asks.

"I'm Kaden."

"Kaden what, though?"

"Kaden whatever. Who the hell are you?"

"I'm Raquel," she answers.

"Raquel what?"

"Rosenburg."

"That's not an Asian name."

Ellen laughs, and Raquel goes, "I'm not Asian."

Pause.

They're both giggling, high as fuck, and Ellen says, "Now it's your turn, mmmmmkaaaaaayyyyy? I know your first name, but what's your last?"

"Norris," I say.

"Like Chuck Norris," she snorts.

"I guess. I don't know any other famous one."

"Cool," she goes.

"Is that it?" I ask.

Ellen glances at Raquel and says, "No."

"What else?"

"You're here with James Morgan?"

"Yeah. I'm his cousin. I'm visiting him for a week. Gonna see Chuck Palahniuk read on Friday."

"Who?" they both ask at the same time.

"Chuck Palahniuk."

Blank stares.

"He wrote *Fight Club*."

"Oh," says Ellen. "I saw the movie once."

"A lot of people did," I say. "Let me ask you something."

"Go for it," Raquel says.

"Why did you name your rap group Bacon?"

"Because bacon is the best," Ellen snaps.

I roll my eyes.

And she goes, "Did your cousin tell you a little about us? Is that how you know about our grab?"

"He told me a little."

"Did he tell you that he's fucked me before?" asks Ellen.

"Nope."

"Well, he has."

"Cool."

"But now he's with that bitch Caralie," she snorts.

"Hey," I snap back. "She's not a bitch. She's awesome. Like the raddest person I've met in my life so far, besides my older brother."

"No, she's not awesome," Raquel chimes in. "She just puts on a good show."

"No shit," Ellen goes. "She's just as bad as James is. She hooks up with other dudes all the time. I've even heard her talk shit behind his back to a room full of people."

"Well, he hooks up with other girls, so it equals out, I guess."

"He still wants me," Ellen says. "He texted me like four months ago, but I wouldn't meet him."

"Good for you," I say. "You obviously have a thing for him, though."

"Whatever," she grunts.

"Yeah. Whatever." I pull the door open. "Good luck with all your Bacon stuff."

"Loser," I hear one of them mumble as I leave.

I move back through the kitchen and grab another root beer. I don't have to pee anymore. Those two girls drained enough from me.

On my way back to the roof I run smack-dab into Gerry Jones.

"Oh, snap." He grins. "Look what we got here. What's up, man?"

"Not much." I smile.

"Where you going?"

"Back to the roof."

"No, you're not. Come with me."

"Where to?"

"Just come on." He puts an arm around my shoulder and takes me into a different bedroom than the one I was in earlier.

Like twelve kids are in there. That T.I. song "Whatever You Like" bumpin' from some stereo speakers. Ryan is there, cutting up lines of coke on a mirror, and pretty much everyone else is singing with the song. . . .

"Stacks on deck, Patrón on ice, and we can pop bottles all night. Baby, you can have whatever you like. . . ."

Gerry lets go of my shoulder and drops into a wicker chair next to the bed. He's trashed and sweating.

"Yo, Ryan," he says. "Look at this motherfucker right here."

Ryan looks up from the mirror and throws up the rock horns.

"James Morgan's cousin from Iowa. Fuck. Now that's some shit," Gerry finishes.

"It's not that big of a deal," I mention.

"What's not?"

"Me being from Iowa."

"I never said it was, kid." He wipes the sweat from his face with the back of his hand. "Why are you drinking root beer, man? What the hell's wrong with you?"

"I like root beer. It's one of the greatest drinks ever."

"Nah," he snorts. "James Morgan's cousin don't drink root beer at kegs with babes around." He reaches for a bottle of Jim Beam on the floor and unscrews the cap from it. "Have some of this," he says.

"No way. I'm good off that."

"Come on," he presses. "Just take a pull or two. It's not like your parents are hanging out. It's all you. It's your time, man." He slams a pull from it. "Your time. Take a pull. It's your time."

"Okay," Ryan cuts in. "Enough of the prodding *Goonies* fan freak."

"Shut it," Gerry snaps. "Just take a drink, man."

He holds the bottle at me, and like that everyone in the room seems to hone in to what's happening, and they start chanting: *"Do it! Do it! Do it! Do it!"*

I mean, fuck. How can I not now?

In a room full of sweaty, hot girls and the coolest dudes in town.

Right?

With the whole big fact that I'm James Morgan's cousin. *Right?*

So I put the bottle against my lips. I've never done a shot of anything before. The smell is strong. It smells like throat burn. I close my eyes and tell myself, *Fuck it.* *"Late-night sex, so wet you're so tight, I'll gas up the jet for you tonight. Baby, you can have whatever you like...."*

Like, *What would T.I. do?*

And I tip the bottle up and take this huge pull. This gigantic gulp. And my first reaction is I hold it in my mouth. Holding it for a few moments while everyone watches me with big eyes and wide smiles.

"Swallow that shit," Gerry snaps. "Put that down."

So I do. It drops straight into my gut, and my breath is on fire. My insides scorched. I gag like I might throw it back, and everyone cheers, and then I slam the bottle against my lips again and take another drink.

I do it a third time, and Ryan goes, "Holy shit, kid." He stands up, hands Gerry the mirror, and gives me a high five. "That was legit. That's what I'm talking about. Some David Lee Roth shit right there."

Gerry blows a rail and hugs me.

This girl with short platinum-colored hair and a gnarly tattoo of a shark all the way down her right arm comes up and hugs me too, and she even kisses my lips and goes, "Your cousin can't even do that anymore."

I don't believe her, but it feels good to hear it. I feel a little woozy. I open my root beer and tell them all I need some fresh air and go back to the roof.

The second band is just starting. Thee Oh Sees is their name.

And they're really fucking awesome. Dark and folksy and psychedelic. And loud. Really fucking loud and kind of experimental, too.

The guy singing and playing guitar is killing it. Flying around on stage and swallowing his mic and shredding it.

Everyone on the roof and on the street is going off. And I'm all over the place. Dancing and smiling all big and crazy, and I'm drunk, I think, and girls are grabbing me and grinding against me. Everyone just loving me. It's the first time in my whole life that it's ever happened. So many people not giving a fuck about anything else except the moment, loving me just because I'm there.

And right when the last song ends, the soul music starts back up, and Caralie and I lock eyes. It sends shivers down my spine the way she looks at me and me her. And she struts toward me, strutting with a swagger like nobody's ever seen before, and it's insane the way my heart starts speeding up. Insane how gorgeous she looks with her hair pulled back and her skin moist and dripping from the heat. Her yellow dress blowing to the side. Her perfect eyes glowing.

Grabbing my hands, she places them around her waist and digs herself into my crotch, moving slowly.

An instant boner for me as she whispers into my ear, "Boom, swagger, swagger, boom, boom, swagger, boom, boom, boom."

"What's that all about?" I say back.

"Just this great song by this great group."

"Who?"

"Murder City Devils."

"Cool."

"I know," she whispers.

She grinds my crotch and holds my hands tight against her. She even pushes them down to the tops of her thighs, and life seems really swell.

It feels like the best it's ever been.

The good time I'm having. The dark clouds of the past six months parting and blowing away to the ends of the horizon.

And then everything changes.

It gets nuts.

Of course it does.

Caralie pushes me, shoves me away from her, and before I can say a word, she snaps, "I hate your stupid fucking cousin sometimes."

"What are you talking about?"

"Goddamn it! I hate him!" she screams, then grabs that Chris guy, that asshole from the taqueria yesterday, and splits from the roof with him.

And I have no idea what's going on, but I'm really self-conscious all over. My buzz is gone, and I'm red again, and I don't know what the hell is happening until I turn around and see James on the other side of the roof with an arm around Bailey Brown's waist, whispering something into her ear.

"What the hell," I grumble under my breath, before walking over to him and tapping him on the shoulder. "Hey, man," I say.

He looks at me. "What's up, dude?"

"Your girlfriend's gone."

James drops his hand from Bailey's waist and says, "Where'd she go?"

"She bailed. She left with that asshole Chris guy I was asking you about last night."

"What Chris guy?" he snorts.

"The one who was dumping on you in the taqueria. You remember me asking you about him in the cab. It was that guy. That's who she left with."

Whipping his glass cup to the ground, James goes, "Why didn't you stop her, dude?"

I'm stunned. "What?"

He grabs my shirt. "I asked you why you didn't stop her. I asked you why!"

Bailey grabs James's arm, allowing me to pull loose from his grip, and I say, "It's not my job, James. Don't blame me for this shit. I don't know what's going on."

"Obviously." He flips a hand at me, takes his phone out, and tries to call her. There's no answer. Then he folds his arms. He puts his hands on his face, his body turned toward Oakland, and grunts really loud.

"James," I say.

He turns to me. "Let's go."

"Where?"

"It doesn't fucking matter where. We're getting the fuck outta here right now. Fuck this bullshit party anyway. It's all horseshit."

c. wandering and stopping and wandering

We get into a cab, and James tells the driver, this real nervous-seeming Arab guy, to take us to Hyde and Eddy streets. He punches numbers into his phone and says into it, "Are you home right now? . . . Cool . . . I'm already on my way." He puts his phone away and smacks me in the arm. "You better be ready to crush the world tonight."

I nod. I don't really care what he says. I'm way more focused on the changing neighborhoods. We've crossed Market Street and are in a whole different world entirely, it feels like, looking through the dirty window of the cab. It's a beast of a change, too. Sidewalks lined with some of the most broken and terrifying people I've seen in my whole life. There are women hunched over and screaming with their hands out and their pants wet from piss and sweat. Old men with no teeth and rotting faces stumbling around in a constant vowel screech. Doorways full of ghosts holding faces in their hands. Shirtless kids with chests barely moving. Garbage and shit in random piles everywhere.

"Where are we?" I ask James.

"The Tenderloin," he answers. "Looks pretty bad, huh?"

"It's gnarly."

"Don't worry about it. This isn't even that dangerous at all. The Fillmore, the West Addy, and Hunters Point, now those are your trouble spots, with guns-blazing type of shit. But down here it's your prostitutes and drug goblins, mostly, and you won't get fucked with unless you're acting the fool. Got it?"

"Yeah."

"Good." The cab begins to slow up. "Right here's cool, driver." James looks over at me. "I'll be right back. Just sit tight and hold it down."

"All right."

He jumps out, and I watch him disappear through an apartment front gate. I sit back and look at the sky. It's darker over here than it was at the party. It's more gray and more cold-feeling, and I notice that all of the store windows have bars on them.

Minutes go by, and the cab driver is getting antsier and antsier. He keeps looking at me in the rearview mirror, his fingers tapping furiously against the steering wheel, and I wonder what the kids in my grade are doing right now back in Dysart.

Swim team practice.

Baseball practice.

Walking beans.

Dancing in machine sheds.

Walking on the train tracks.

Catching fireflies.

Whatever it is, it's nothing like this.

And I ask the driver, "How's your day been so far?"

"Fine." His accent is thick and Middle Eastern.

"That's good. Busy?"

He doesn't answer me this time. He's too preoccupied with looking around and being fidgety. It's like he thinks he shouldn't be waiting in front of a building like the one James went into.

But finally he speaks again. He says, "When is your friend coming back?"

"I don't know. Soon, I hope."

"Can you call him?"

"I don't have a phone."

He rolls his eyes, and then the sound of sirens. Two cop cars zoom by us with their lights blazing, swirling, and the driver turns back to me and says, "You must get out of my cab now."

"Why?"

"Because your friend is not coming back, and I have to go. Give me the fare and get out. Now. Out of my cab!"

I look at the meter, and it's twenty dollars already. Fuck! I take my wallet out, hand the guy a twenty, and wait for him to unlock the door. When he does, I get out and watch him squeal away.

I squeeze my forehead. *Fuck!*

It's cold, and the wind is strong and wild. I feel very uneasy with all these ghosts and ghouls and fiends watching me with secret ambition as I lean against the building James is in with my arms wrapped around myself trying to stay calm and warm.

I miss Jocelyn.

And my brother.

A gate opens to the side, and James re-emerges with a smile until he sees me standing there. The smile disappears and he's like, "What the hell are you doing? Where's the cab?"

"The driver guy kicked me out."

"What'd you do?"

"Nothing, James. I didn't do anything."

"Then why are you standing out here like a scared little bitch?"

"The guy kicked me out because you took so long. What was I supposed to do?"

"Stay in the fucking car. That's all you had to do. Stay in the fucking car!"

"Sorry," I say, even though I'm not at all.

And James lights a cigarette. He shrugs. "Fuck it," he says. "Whatever. Don't worry about it now. Let's just get outta this dumphole."

He starts down the street, and I follow him like some lost puppy with big eyes, and the next cab he sees, he hails it and tells the driver, "Nineteenth and Folsom. The Homestead is where we're heading." He rubs his chin. "It's early still. Nobody I know that well should be there."

He looks out the window, agitation consuming his face, and he looks pretty hurt. Like Caralie cut a nice hole in him.

"So what was that?" I ask him.

"What?"

"Did you just buy drugs?"

He nods.

"Did you know Ryan was at the party? You could've gone to him."

He glances at me, fingers still on his chin, and he says, "Fuck that guy and fuck his shitty coke. He cuts that shit with sugar, and I'm done with it. Makes my nose slimy all damn night. Fuckin' cocksucker."

"But you bought from him last night at the end."

James sighs. "Because I was with him. It was too convenient at that point. I didn't wanna go running around the city in the state I was in, so I went with him. But that doesn't change the fact that he's a fuck and a d-bag."

Caralie hadn't been messing around at all about those two and their name-calling.

And he goes, "Anyway, just drop the fucking drug digging, all right?"

"All right, man."

d. the homestead bar

The place is like a throwback to those Western-style saloons in old films like *Tombstone*. There's low orange-tinted lighting and peanut shells covering the floor. All these gigantic paintings of pirates and madams and cowboys and Mexican bandits hang on the wall. Only three other people and the bartender are even there.

I lean against the bar with James, who orders two beers and a shot of Jameson for both of us, and the bartender doesn't even ID me, because she knows James pretty decently.

We take the drinks to a booth near the entrance. Then James goes over to the jukebox and picks out music, and by the time he sits down, Frank Sinatra is reigning heavy through the bar.

Lifting his shot glass in the air, James goes, "To this beautifully shit life." Then he clanks my glass, but this time when I dump the whiskey, it's way smoother and goes right down, and I only make a tiny wince of hurt.

"That's good shit, man," he says. "I'm glad you're indulging now. It's about time."

"I haven't drank much in my life."

"Why not?"

I shrug. "I don't know. I haven't had this great urge to. Watching my mom get all shitfaced on bottles and bottles of wine every day and totally cut herself off from everyone else and lock herself away in a room ever since she found out about Kenny ain't no joke. It doesn't look very appealing when you're watching it unfold like that."

"Give it this week," he says. "I bet you'll feel differently."

"Is that like a thing for you, like the people around you have to get messed up all the time?" I ask him.

"Not all the time, man. I mean, shit, if it ain't for you then it ain't for you, but I love this," he says. "All of it."

"The lifestyle?" I ask.

And James leans forward and motions me with his fingers to do the same. I do. And then he sets his sunglasses on the table and goes, "It quit being a lifestyle a long fucking time ago, man. Now it's just my life."

He leans back and I nod. "All right."

"Like I said, man. If it's not for you, then so be it. Have fun going to bed early and banging ugly girls."

I smirk. "All right." I take a gulp of beer. "So why did Caralie freak out like she did when she saw you talking to Bailey?"

"Here's the thing with Caralie, homey. She overreacts to a lot of shit. Pretty much everything. She flipped because Bailey and I used to fuck like forever ago, and she knows about all of it, and it might suck for her to see me around Bailey, but if she'd just quit being psycho for like two seconds, this thing called rationality would come back to her, and then she'd remember that Bailey would never fuck me again, she was over me from basically the start, and that it's just two kids talking on the playground of wastedness."

Pause.

"Caralie needs to fucking relax," he finishes, then slams like half of his beer, and I'm thinking about how maybe he should be the last person talking about a "thing called rationality," but I go with it. I don't wanna shake things up too quick with the guy. He seems fairly unstable, emotionally at least, and I totally wanna get a better feel for him.

Swallowing more beer, I go, "So you working on anything new?"

He hesitates. It's almost like I throw him off with that. And when he recovers, he's like, "Always, dude. I've quite a few new projects in the fold. This new novel that's totally cutthroat about this small-town housewife who gets all bored and seduces these teenage boys, who then form a small rebel group called the Bottlecap Gang that terrorizes the local town and does whatever she wants." He takes another pull. "I also got this series of interviews I'm doing with members of bands that I really like."

Pause.

"Shit like that," he says. "I'm also outlining a screenplay."

"Nice."

"So I'm keeping busy, ya know." He finishes his beer. "You read any of my stuff?"

A lump forms in my throat right away, and I swallow it, almost choking on it. I tell him, "Yeah, I've gotten with the books."

"Which one did you like better?" he asks.

Choking down another lump, I say, "*Dickpig*."

I say, "I couldn't control myself on the plane after reading that opening paragraph. It was nuts."

"It's the fucking shit, huh?"

"So good, man."

"Cool." He goes back to the bar, and Sinatra fades into

Patsy Cline, and then he comes back with another beer and two more shots of Jameson.

He pushes one of them to my side of the table and I tell him I wanna hold off for a second.

"I don't hold off," he says, then pounds his before grabbing mine and pounding that one, chasing them both with another big gulp of beer.

The guy's a total maniac.

And he goes, "Is your mom doing okay? Besides with the drinking and stuff, which isn't that bad of a thing."

I sigh. "She's doing better than she was right after we got the news. I mean, back in the winter, in late December and January, she was gone. There was nothing there. She was empty. You could see it in her eyes how there was no life inside."

"Fuck. Really?"

"Oh, yeah. She seriously locked herself in a room for four weeks and made a scrapbook out of Kenny's life. All twenty-one years of it. His school pictures and sports pictures and prom pictures and homecoming pictures. All the newspaper clippings about his big-time athletic achievements. All the awards he got. Everything. For a month, man, the only time she came out of that room was to throw a frozen pizza or fish sticks or whatever garbage she could into the stove for dinner. Or just to grab a new bottle of red wine. She even quit taking phone calls and shit like that. It was a house of ghosts for a while after he died. Kinda creepy," I say. "All that quiet. She even quit listening to her Connie Francis and Nancy Sinatra albums."

"Shit." James rubs his head. "It was that bad?"

"It was horrible."

He looks truly concerned. "But she's been getting better now?"

"Yeah. A lot. The color's back in her face. She's gained back most of the weight that she lost. She's getting out more. She just started teaching her jewelry and purse-making workshops at the community center in Dysart again. It's a huge turnaround, and ya know, I gotta say that it started with the idea for me to come out here for the Palahniuk reading."

"That was crazy when she called me to ask like that about you coming out here."

"Honestly, I couldn't believe she said yes to it. I was totally shocked."

"Nah. Your mom's rad. She's a good lady, and she knows what's up."

"Okay, well, I couldn't believe she talked my dad into saying yes."

"Well, your dad's a total fuck, and your mom's—don't take offense a total fox. I mean, come on, man, she could've passed as a cover model until her early thirties."

"I know. I hear it all the time from kids in school."

"She's a babe."

"She's your aunt," I snap.

James bites his bottom lip and nods. "I know. I didn't mean it like that, man."

"Right." I finish my beer. "So did you know Kenny well?"

"Hardly at all. I knew him better than I know you, but not well. The way it was is that I didn't leave home until I was nineteen, so he was around when I was still getting dragged to family reunions and bullshit like that. And he was always trying to play football or basketball with the older kids like he was the shit and all, and I even remember this one time, I had to have been about eighteen, so he was probably like six or something, and we were all playing football, and your brother intercepted this pass and started running it back, and our cousin Tom for some reason decided to just lay Kenny out. It was gnarly. Fucking brutal, dude. But Kenny shot right back to his feet, and he kicked Tom in the balls and called him his bitch and said he was gonna fuck his girlfriend."

The two of us are laughing hard, to the point where I have tears welling up in my eyes, and I go, "Goddamn, I miss him."

"I bet you do," James says. "It's fucking crazy how I got that e-mail from him about the Palahniuk books and coming for a reading. Just out of the blue, like that, he's asking me if it would be cool if when he got back from Iraq he could bring you out here with him to see Palahniuk read, and I was like, shit yeah. Of course, man. I was stoked that he was into really good shit."

"I was surprised by it too," I tell James. "He never read anything in high school or college. And then I get this letter from him telling me about this Chuck Palahniuk guy, and I got big-time into him, and seriously, his books really helped me a lot."

"How so?"

"With things like coping with Kenny's death and moving forward and, honestly, seeking out a better purpose for myself. His books make me feel alive, man. I get this total excitement inside me and can relate a lot to the characters, and it gets me going. It got me working out. It made me wanna cut myself out of stone and do some shit, and now I'm out here with you, ya know. His books are like these friends that are always there when I start to get down about something, and they bring me right back up."

James smacks his hands together. "That's cool, man. That's real fucking legit. I like that. So what's your favorite book?"

"My favorite one is *Choke*. But *Fight Club* is like my fucking bible and shit."

"Yeah, *Choke* is probably my favorite too. That and *Invisible Monsters*, I guess."

"All his books are rad."

James nods. "And so you learned about Chuck from a letter your brother sent you, huh?"

"Yup. It came after he died. My parents don't even know about it. He wrote it to me as if he was already fucking gone and gave it to an injured friend of his and told him to mail it to me if anything happened to him."

"Really?"

"Yup. And I've carried it with me everywhere since the day I got it."

"Wow. That's kinda twisted, isn't it?"

I shrug. "Twisted? You really wanna go there, dude?"

"What?" He grins.

"You were smacking some black girl and calling her a bitch while you were fucking her and then told her you hated her guts when she was leaving. That's fucking twisted."

"That's the glory life, man." Pause. "But good try, anyway." He pauses again. "And that shit doesn't leave your fucking lips again . . . got it?"

"I remember."

"You fucking better, kid."

He gets up and goes into the bathroom, and I'm feeling pretty all right again, having a little bit of fun, but still trying to figure out James. On the one hand I think he's a stupid, conceited prick, unrelenting in his disdain for anyone who dares to challenge him. Completely and totally selfish. But on the other hand he does seem to care about some things. He seems to be somewhat understanding, out to make sure that everyone's having a good time. He's confident, not cocky, and there's a difference. It seems like he has these masks he puts on, then changes them in an instant. Part of me thinks it's just maybe who he is, this sociopath who can turn on a dime. But then another part of me wonders if maybe it's all just a game, like a real-life play where he changes his part whenever he sees fit. Some big-time plan to keep people from ever getting too close, or wanting to get close. That everything in front of him is just one big fucking game.

When he comes back out, he's rubbing his nose real fast, and he buys another round of beers and brings them back to the table.

"So what's a grifter?" I ask him.

"What do you think it is?" He sniffs.

"A scumbag."

He smiles and shakes his head. "Kind of, but not really."

"Then what does it mean?"

He takes a drink and goes, "I'll tell you what, man. Why don't you give me that answer yourself at the end of the week?"

"All right."

He rubs his nose again and says something about going to another bar and finding some girls for the both of us.

"Can I ask you something, James?"

"What's up?"

"How can you fuck around on Caralie if you're into her so much like you're saying you are? I don't get it. I thought it would be the opposite."

Leaning forward, white chunks of coke residue on the end of his nose, he says, "It was at first."

He says, "But you're looking at it the wrong way." He

wipes his nose again. "The other girls I fuck don't mean shit to me at all, only she does, but the thing is, I'm so into her that I need to be able to make sure that if we ever do split up, I know that I can still have all these other women."

"That makes no sense to me at all," I tell him after swallowing a gulp of beer.

"It doesn't have to, man. This is the game that moves you as you play. There's no time to make sense of things."

"Whatever."

"Have you ever had sex?"

"No."

"How old are you again?"

"Fifteen."

"Jesus Christ, dude. What are you waiting for? I was bumping uglies with broads when I was thirteen and shit."

"I know. I've heard you say that shit more than once since I've been here."

"Good," he snaps, leaning back. "You need to hear it. You need to loosen up a little bit like your older brother and start getting fucked up and having sex. That's what I'm gonna get done for you this week, man. I'm gonna get you laid."

"I have a girlfriend already, man. I'm not like you."

He grins real wide and goes, "You might be surprised how much like me you are before you're through out here. You just really might."

I don't say anything.

And he pounds the rest of his beer and goes, "I think it's time to split."

"Where to now?"

"The fucking Whip Pad, mang."

e. the whip pad II

We sit in James's room, him on the couch and me at his computer. On the way over we picked up forties and whiskey, and now we're listening to this band Triclops! that he's super into.

"One of the best live shows I've ever seen," he says.

"Why is it so good?" I ask.

"Because it's a fucking show all around. The music is tight as fuck, and their lead singer, this short kid Johnny who used to sing for the Fleshies, too, this kid goes off. He jumps onto people from the stage and crawls around the floor and gets beer and God knows whatever else dumped all over him. He makes these retard gestures from the stage and sings with this voice modulator. I mean, the shit goes off. It's incredible. You walk out of a Triclops! show feeling like you really got your money's worth. It destroys!"

And it is real good and all. I do like it a lot. But I wanna play something I wanna hear. So when the song we're listening to ends, I grab the mouse and start scrolling through his music, and when he sees me doing this, he jumps off the chair and stops me.

"What the fuck do you think you're doing?" he snaps.

"I'm trying to play something I wanna hear."

"No way," he snorts. "This is my room, which means my music. My room, my music. I mean, honestly, what are you really trying to play anyway? The Cool Kids. Fuckin' Dirty Nasty or Mickey Avalon. Come on, kid. I ain't trying to whack this shit up right now. So get up, and go sit over there. Capeesh?"

And like that the asshole mask is back on and taking over.

I sit on the couch and take a drink, and James sits down and changes the song. "Now, this is some shit," he snaps.

Feedback and pounding drums is all I hear.

"Who's this?" I ask him.

"Lighting Bolt, dude. Get into it."

He jacks the volume way up, then takes out a gram of coke and dumps it on a mirror on his desk.

Cutting it with a razor blade, he says, "So the deal tomorrow is that I have to get some writing done. I'm feeling this surge of creativity coming on, and Caralie has to work, so I'm gonna send you with Gerry for the day."

"Where to?"

"He works at this supernice gym on the Embarcadero, right on the water. It's pretty neat."

"Neat?"

"Yeah. It's fucking neat. Now listen, okay. What I figure is that you can roll with him there at ten and shoot some hoops and go swimming. Sit in the hot tub for a while and unwind."

"Does he know?"

"Of course he does, man. I talked to him about it last night. It's cool. All the Gs wanna hang out with you."

I'm pretty bummed. "That's cool," I tell him. It's like here I am, out in San Francisco for the first time, wanting to kick it around the city with James, and here he is, telling me he's pawning me off on his friend, who's gonna take me to work with him.

Real fucking cool!

James's phone is ringing. He looks at it and tells me to hold on, that he has to take the call, and then he leaves the room.

For probably five minutes I sit there and sip on my forty before finally getting up and scrolling through the music again. He has a ton of hip-hop on his computer, and I find some Dr. Octagon and play it.

"Blue Flowers" is the song I pick.

And then I go back to the couch and wait, and this funny thing happens. James doesn't come back. He's disappeared. He's gone. A solid half hour goes by before I go look for him.

I walk down the hallway and find Ally in her room with Reed, smoking pot. Popping my head in, I ask them if they've seen James.

"He left," Ally says.

"Do you know where to?"

"I don't. But it was a while ago."

And Reed says, "A long while ago. I'm pretty sure I heard him on his phone saying something about the Hemlock."

"What's the Hemlock?" I snort.

"A bar in the Tenderloin," he answers.

"Fucking great," I snap. "Can I use one of your phones to call him?"

Ally hands me hers, and I find his name and call him, and it goes straight to his voice mail. "Jesus Christ," I say. "That asshole ditched me again."

"Welcome to life," Ally quips.

"How do you mean?"

"If you haven't been ditched by the James Morgan show, then you haven't lived yet."

"That's some real-type asshole shit," I snort.

"Well James is a real-type asshole sometimes," Reed shoots back. "Are you drunk?"

"Maybe," I say. Pause. "Yes."

"What were you two doing?" asks Ally.

I run down the whole entire day for them in excruciating detail, ending with, "Then we get back here and he lays a bunch of coke out and tells me he'll be right back, and now he's just gone."

Reed's eyebrows grow high and he says, "Is there any coke left?"

"All of it, man."

Ally and Reed shoot each other a look, and Ally goes, "Let's do that shit, then."

And the three of us go back into James's room.

Ally cuts lines, and her and Reed do three each, their demeanors changing instantly with the first dance with the powder.

It gets really chatty, too.

Since I don't know either of them for anything, I ask them what they do. . . .

Reed: "A little bit of this and a little bit of that. Speedballs and painting and writing. I write some good shit that your cousin says he likes. I'm also trying to get this band together. I got like fifty good songs ready to go. Trying not to work, either. Ever fucking again."

Ally: "I model mostly and make good money. You'll see my shit everywhere. I'm fucking everywhere, dude. I front a metal band called Jigsaw Hearts. We're playing on Wednesday, and you're coming!"

I say, "I heard about the show today. James was talking to a girl who sings for a band playing that night too."

"Bailey Brown," Ally says. "She's good and all, but she's not as good as me."

I look at Reed. "How do you get by without working?"

"I have a stipend."

"From who?"

"Don't really know anymore. Someone died in my family a ways back and left me some dough, and since I cut my folks off a long time ago, I never bothered to find out. But the money still comes every month. Lots of it."

"Huh. So that's your deal. Some rich kid trying to live like a dirtbag to piss off some people in your family."

"Damn," Ally snaps. "He fucking called you out, Reed."

Reed shrugs and gives me the finger. "Asshole."

"Hey, I'm just saying."

"I got what you're saying, man. Just don't say it again."

I shrug, and Ally lights a smoke, and Reed bums one of hers.

"You're from Iowa?" he asks me.

I take a drink. "Yes I am."

"Whereabouts?"

"Do you know Iowa?" I ask.

"I don't. Does it matter?"

"Not really?"

"So where in Iowa are you from?"

"This town called Dysart. There's like a thousand people and no stoplights and a train track. I live on a farm outside of town. Five hundred acres. Right off a gravel road."

"Sounds like hell," Ally says.

"It's not at all. Just a different way of living, I guess."

"You guys got like cows and pigs and shit like that?" Reed snorts.

"Nah, man. It's just a crop farm. Corn and soybeans is what we grow."

"What's there to do out there?" asks Ally. "I think I

would get bored as hell living on a farm outside of a town that size."

"Ya know," I start, then stop. I say, "You use your imagination. It's all you got. You create your own world in your head, and suddenly you've turned a barn into a giant robot-killing machine or the trees into huge totem poles. Shit like that is what you do. It's not the best when you're my age, but when you're a kid, growing up, there's nothing else like it."

They each do another line.

Then Reed goes, "And your brother just dies in Iraq."

"Yeah."

"If you don't mind me asking . . . what happened to him over there?"

My body tenses, and for a second I can't breathe. My stomach gets into knots, and I say, "It was like my parents and the papers said. He got hit in the neck by a bullet and bled to death."

Exhale.

Another sip.

And Reed jumps to his feet and says, "This fucking war. Goddamn these motherfuckers sending people to die over there. Your brother, dying in some third-world desert. They didn't need to be there. They shouldn't be there."

I say nothing. I'm conflicted, actually. I agree with what he's saying; it's just that it's coming from the mouth of a guy who never worked a day in his life for anything. Kenny didn't join the Marines because he had to or anything like that. I don't really know all the reasons for why he signed up. I guess it's just that criticism about anything from a guy getting a stipend from some long-dead relative leaves a bitter taste in my mouth.

Twisting his smoke out in an ashtray, Reed barks, "Bush and Cheney should be tried and hung for war crimes. Teach these assholes that they can't get away with this shit anymore."

The whole conversation is making me tired. The whole day is hitting me hard. Ally looks at me, and I think she senses the fatigue pouring out of me, so she grabs Reed and says, "The beer's gone, dude. We should go to the store and grab some more."

"Cool." He turns to me. "You coming?"

"No, I'll wait. I wanna relax for a minute. Decompress."

"Cool."

I wait until I hear the Whip Pad door shut, then I get up from my seat. Since they cut those very first lines, I've been half eyeing the pile of powder. I'm enamored with the shit. How it can change the entire dynamic of a room. It makes it funner and way more interesting. And everyone I see doing it looks like they're having a fucking blast. Much more fun than all the people smoking weed or just drinking. And I think, *Shit. Everyone is doing this but me....*

So I pick up the rolled bill they left behind and chop off two lines and lean down and take one up each nostril.

Head back.

Swallowing.

And everything goes different.

But in the best way ever.

All I can think of doing is calling everyone I know. Pacing the room. Sweat begins to seep from my pores. I want to call my mom and talk about getting some back-to-school clothes. I want to call Jocelyn and tell her how wonderful and awesome she is and how she's my diamond in this rough world. My Tupac album in a music bin full of boy-band CDs.

Nobody can fuck with me. That's how I feel. That and I want someone to talk to. But no one else is there, and it's like the walls of the room, those moldy pieces of poorly put-together drywall, are closing in fast. I want more room. I want the world. I need some fresh air, so I bail.

f. the streets of san francisco

Wild shit going on, although not as wild as it was yesterday. Kids are spilling off of a stoop next to Molotov's. More boom boxes and more early-nineties rap and more skateboard wheels grinding against the street. A tiny dance party of crackheads at the end of the block, and it's really cold here. I can see my breath. But I'm on fire. My breath is a gurgling flame of havoc, and I don't give a fuck about nothing. This world is my giant play toy, and I'm forgetting all about the bullshit with James and Reed and Ally. Only thing sticking tough in my brain is this part from the book *Fight Club*. Chapter sixteen. Page one twenty-four to be exact. When Tyler Durden fantasizes . . .

You'll hunt elk through the damp canyon forests around the ruins of Rockefeller Center, and dig clams next to the skeleton of the Space Needle leaning at a forty-five-degree angle. We'll paint the skyscrapers with huge totem faces and goblin tikis, and every evening what's left of mankind will retreat to empty zoos and lock itself in cages as protection against bears and big cats and wolves that pace and watch us from outside the cage bars at night.

I want to destroy everything pretty and shit in the eyes of the god who took my brother away. My chest pounds; my cheeks are pumping; the veins in my forearms stick out and grow. I find a pay phone and call Jocelyn, but her dad answers, and I freeze the fuck up. I say nothing, and he hangs up, so I call back, and he answers again, and this time I ask if she's around.

"Who the hell is this?" he snaps.

"Kaden Norris."

"Do you know what time it is, son?"

"Late, I'm guessing."

"It's one a.m. Jocelyn's in bed."

"I didn't know."

"Well, now you do. So you quit calling here, or I'll be having a talk with your dad tomorrow."

Click.

"Fucker!" I yell, slamming the receiver against the phone about a million times before moving on.

Past intersection after intersection I stomp. Around packs of loud, drunk people hogging the sidewalks and past this ugly girl in a bad outfit bitching into her phone about the "lame crowd at Blowout," whatever the fuck that is, and how some guy in a blue shirt told her today that she should start doing coke again because her ass is getting bigger than it used to be. And for a split second I think about stopping her and describing my cousin, because it sounds like something he's cool with saying to someone's face, and he's wearing a blue shirt today. I really do think about doing this before thinking that I don't really wanna stop and talk to her, so I shit the thought out of my head and pound on.

The blast pushes each step ahead. The white monster turns the wheels from down inside and keeps the machine running, keeps me on the go, the white monster running everything and wielding his power with epic screaming and chanting from the gutter in my brain.

I find a liquor store and pop into it.

My first time ever using a fake.

And I ain't even nervous at all.

I walk to the cooler with the cheap forties in it, grab a High Life, go to the counter, and ask the balding fat guy behind it for a pack of Parliament Lights. It's what almost everyone else has been huffing on all day.

The guy rings up the smokes and beer and then asks to see my ID. I whip it out like I've been doing this for years, and he glances at it for about five seconds, then hands it back and tells me it's seven dollars and asks me if I need matches. It's so damn easy, and I think about all those movies with those nervous wrecks for kids going into stores to buy beer with fakes. Acting like it's some sorta huge offense. It's like what are they gonna do, anyway? Take the fake and tell you to scram. That's it. The whole thing is pretty fucking simple. And I'm sure it doesn't hurt that I'm loaded with the white monster.

I leave the store and look at the street signs. Hayes and Divisadero. Up the street I see this venue called the Independent. Common is playing. It's sold out, though, and I think about sneaking in but know it's not gonna happen. Security looks supertight, plus I don't feel like being around a bunch of people anyway. All crowded and sweaty and obnoxious. Looking up the block on Hayes, I see a park. It looks perfect, and I slam over two blocks of hill and a set of stairs and then I'm there, standing at the top of Alamo Square, overlooking the entire city under a crystal clear sky and a clear white moon, just like in that Warren G song.

And it's beautiful. I'm all alone up there except for a few lurkers cutting through the park or past it on the sidewalk.

In front of me is the entire city lit up like a mini village inside one of those glass balls that you shake up and the lights flash on. I feel like a king for the first time in my life.

King Kaden.

King of the fucking park.

Sitting down on the grass, I twist my forty open, sniff real hard, take a drink, and almost puke it back up. It tastes disgusting now. I take another sip, and the same gross happens. Then I sniff again but there's no coke left to swallow. My mood is changing hard. The good feelings are disappearing with a quickness, being replaced just as quickly with bad ones, horrible ones, and these dark thoughts start creeping around my head. Thoughts like how shitty everything is and how I hate my life. I'm really cold, shivering again, and I feel so fucking alone on top of this hill overlooking San Francisco. As alone as I've ever felt in my life, even back in December when the military officers showed up at our front door during breakfast and my mom collapsed, screaming Kenny's name.

Thoughts of my brother come rushing back to me. I'm missing him so much right now, and all these memories are fighting each other for prevalence inside of my brain. But one fights the others. The memory of the good-bye party my mom threw for Kenny two nights before he was shipped to Camp Pendleton in San Diego for training.

g. kenny's good-bye party

You shoulda seen how many people showed up. Teachers that he had all throughout school, town leaders, friends of friends of friends of friends, old girlfriends and their families. It was some scene. My mom, she turned our machine shed into this small-town Times Square. There were tables of food and a DJ. There were banners and balloons and kegs of beer and an open bar. Man, it was some sight. All these people popping out of the woodwork like they were Kenny's best pal from childhood. All of them shaking his hand, taking photos with him, cracking jokes, making him out to be this goddamn celebrity of some sort. It made me wanna puke. It really did. Because I could see how uncomfortable all that attention was making him. I could see it in the fake smiles he flashed, in his halfhearted handshakes, and in his vague recollections of the stories these people were telling about him.

The way some people always wanna say they were there with you the whole time the moment you become the center of attention.

It was so fucking lame.

All of those attention whores prostituting for my brother's acknowledgment.

And as the day slid into night, all of those shitheads got even drunker, and some of them began making these long-winded speeches about Kenny and what they thought of him.

One by one these d-bags took their turns slurring and stumbling and stammering on about how much they respected him for what he was doing and how they knew he'd do the whole community proud while serving out his special duty. They proclaimed to all of them who gathered and to those who couldn't make it that he was already a hero who'd be back in a blink of an eye to share his patriotic experiences about combat and all the Iraqis who would cheer his arrival.

Or so the fairy tale went.

Seriously. It came out of this d-bag Gary Rogers's mouth. And the thing about Gary was that he'd never been out of the state, as far as anyone knew. He lived in a trailer with his fat-ass wife, had a handlebar moustache and a beer gut full of cheap beer, and worked as a lawn-mower mechanic. But apparently, despite his lack of experience and education, this fuckhead hick had his finger on the pulse of the psyche of the Iraqi people.

Man, it was so much bullshit. Half the motherfuckers who ended up making the speeches just stood there with their heads bowed, eyes to the ground, thinking about what they were gonna say when it was their turn to finally talk instead of listening to the people who spoke before them.

As if it mattered anyway.

Most of the turd burglars who stood there, thinking real hard about what to say, most of those fucking troll humpers just fucked it up anyway.

What a nightmare it all was, capped off at the very end when this one kid Kenny had gone to school with his whole life pulled him aside. The kid's name was Chester Matthews, and he'd flown all the way back from New York City just for Kenny's big send-off to the shit in the desert. He'd come all the way back to celebrate Kenny's departure to a place in backward land where he was going to fight door to door against a bunch of fanatics.

So anyway, this Chester Matthews kid, this big NYC art-school graduate with his arms covered in tattoos and his flipped-bill Oakland A's hat and his tight jeans and his white Adidas Top Tens. This dude, with his tight pink Babyshambles shirt and his burned CDs full of Arctic Monkeys and fucking Decemberists songs. This trashhole pulled my brother aside, cigarette in his fingers, fucking bubble gum in his mouth, and he told him, "Here's the deal, homey. You know how I feel about this war. You know I don't agree with it and how much I hate it. But here's the thing, man. I'm not gonna say a fuckin' word about any of that shit to you tonight. This is your night, man. It's about you. It's not about the politics of anything. So there you have it, man. My word to not say anything disheartening to you about any of that shit, because if you go over there and you don't believe in what you're doing, the bull's-eye on your back will just get that much bigger, man."

I wanted that motherfucker's blood.

Fuck that guy.

My brother, though, he just patted that asshole on the back and said, "Thank you. I appreciate that. And I understand what you're saying."

Of course he was just being nice.

It was a load of complete crap what that New York hipster art dumbass had told him.

I mean, if you don't believe in the things you're doing, the answer isn't fooling yourself into thinking you believe it. If you don't believe in what you're doing, then you just shouldn't be doing it.

And Kenny, he shouldn't have been all the way over there fighting against those Islamic freaks. Because I know he didn't really believe in any of the empty rhetoric that spewed from his lips about the war. He even came close to telling me as much.

It was way later in the night, after every single troll from his past was gone, all of them feeling so swell about themselves for giving my brother the proper send-off, a send-off fit for a star-spangled-banner coffin.

Kenny and I sat on the garage rooftop right outside of his bedroom window. I even drank a beer with him. It was an Old Milwaukee can, still wet from the melted ice in the bottom of the cooler it was pulled from.

From where the two of us sat, we could see the whole world, the only world either of us had ever known, laid out all around us. One gigantic flat spread of Earth.

Facing Kenny and me was the town of La Porte City and all of its thirty or so streetlamps shining in the dark. A one mile by one mile patch of houses and lawns and trailers and tiny roads, sprung out in between nowhere and fucking nowhere.

Behind us Dysart and its one red blinking light and its train tracks and tire swings. Imagine the quietest place on Earth, and you're almost there.

On Friday nights, before the merger of the Dysart and La Porte schools, way back when Kenny was like four, he told me that he used to be able to see the lights from the football field from up there on the roof, and that if the wind carried just enough, sometimes you could hear the crowd cheering for a touchdown and the marching band playing the fight song. He said that back then on Friday nights in Dysart or La Porte a football game was the only show in town.

Me, I told Kenny, "It still fucking is, man."

The sky that night was clear, and I could see some of the stars and the moon, and except for a gust of breeze here and there that rustled the crops in the fields surrounding us, it was dead quiet. The crickets chirping and Kenny and me talking was the only noise being made at all.

We bullshitted for most of the conversation about nothing important. Like how many people showed up. How hot so-and-so was looking. This chubby motherfucker Martin who puked on his aunt's titties while he was telling everyone how not drunk he was. When finally it just got real between us. Finally, after both of us were finished with our beers and done laughing about how this slut high-school chick was getting nailed by Chester on the weed-covered basketball court behind the paint-chipped barn, Kenny looked down and rubbed his forehead and said, "Jesus Christ, Kaden, I can't believe this is actually happening."

He turned his eyes to the vast country in front of us and

said, "This is for real, dude. They sure don't tell you about this feeling in any of those fancy recruiting brochures."

"So what are you saying?"

"It's just, I don't know. I've been doing a lot of reading about the war and stuff. I've been doing a lot of research about what we've been doing to people in some of those cities and what they've been doing to us. I mean, if you get captured by any of those goddamn monsters, they leave you wishing you'd just been killed right away. They will rape you. They will skin you alive and feed your skin back to you. They'll cut your balls off. And after all of that, they'll slit your throat and leave your fucking body on the side of the road like a piece of trash. Like a fucking piece of road-kill, man."

"Jesus, Kenny, don't tell me this shit," I said. "I don't need to know all of that, man."

"Well, fuck, Kaden. Welcome to my world. This is the thought I've been living with every day for the past two months. The thought that it's better to be killed right away instead of a week later. Do you know what that's like?"

"No. How could I, man?"

"It's like making arrangements for your own funeral or something."

"So don't go."

"I have to."

"No, you don't, Kenny. You don't have to. I'll fucking take a bat to your knee, man. Right now."

Kenny smacked my arm and went, "No. Jesus Christ. No. I have to do this. It's too late for all of that other crap. I have to go. And I wanna go. It's an honor, man. Serving is an honor."

And just like that he reverted right back into that machine of rhetoric, tossing out those vague catchphrases and bumper-sticker mottos.

It's like, if you're such a shallow person that a goddamn bumper sticker can sum up your beliefs, then Jesus Christ, are you even worth fighting for in the end?

But that was the exact moment I knew Kenny was scared shitless, scared out of his mind, caught in the web he'd thought he spun just right, and we sat together in silent agony for at least a minute, the both of us staring off into somewhere, neither of us even knowing what we were looking at.

And then Kenny turned to me and went, "Here, Kaden." He said, "I want you to have this."

What Kenny was giving me was his Chicago Cubs baseball cap. He loved that hat too. He'd had it since he was twelve, when the four of us went to visit my mother's side of the family in Chicago. My uncle Tony took Kenny and his own kid to a Cubs games at Wrigley Field. And in between innings Kenny found it lying on the ground near a concession stand and had hardly taken it off since. And that's what he was giving me. I don't know a hundred percent why. Probably because *Stand By Me* was his favorite movie, and there's that scene in the middle of the film where John Cusack gives his little brother Gordie his Yankees cap right before he dies in a car accident. I always figured he was just re-creating that scene in real life.

I took the cap and fitted it on my head; then Kenny stood up and went, "I have to get going, man."

"Where to?"

"I've got Misty Piper meeting me down the road in her car. One more piece of ass before I go to sand land, man."

"Nice."

He walked over and leaned down and bumped my fist and told me to take care of myself. "Go big, man," he told me, before turning away and crawling back through his window, on the fucking prowl for one more meat pit to shred.

And even though I knew his death was a possibility, it actually didn't occur to me at that exact moment that after he left I might not ever see my big brother again.

The memory dissolves. I'm back in the park, tears filling my eyes. I'm empty-feeling, just so fucking drained. Maybe this is what my mom was going through the whole time right after Kenny's death. The constant battle against the nostalgia of a time that can never be real again.

Never. Ever.

You can never go back.

I try another gulp of the forty and gag it down, but this time it won't stay in my stomach. It shoots right back up, and I puke beer and bacon all over myself.

And I can't remember where I am in the city. My head is thrashed. I get up and stumble away from the park, down two blocks, and find another pay phone next to this Popeyes Chicken place. I dig out Caralie's number and call her.

"Hello," she groans, her voice strained and exhausted-sounding.

"I need you to come get me. Can you, please?" I snap, trying so hard to hold back the sobs.

"Kaden?"

"It's me."

"Where are you?"

"I'm outside of a Popeyes Chicken. It's close to the Whip Pad, I think, and I'm all by myself and I'm cold. I don't know what the fuck is happening."

"Jesus Christ," she snaps. "Just stay put. I'll be there as soon as I can."

Maybe twenty minutes pass, maybe more, before Caralie shows up. I'm sitting on the dirty cement with my back against Popeyes, my arms wrapped around my knees and my head against my legs.

"Kaden," I hear the voice of an angel say. "Get in."

I stand up, dizzy and light-headed, and I stumble over to her car and fall in. After I shut the door, Caralie rips right into my cousin.

"That irresponsible piece of shit!" she screams. "How could he leave you all alone like that?"

"It's okay—"

"It's not!" she shouts. "You're wasted. Were you doing coke?"

"Yes."

"Goddamn it!" she yells. "He is the most selfish piece of shit in the world."

"And what about you?" I shoot back. "You're the one who left that party. That's why he got pissed and ditched me. Because you were gone with that stupid Chris fuck. Like what the fuck, Caralie? Did you sleep with that troll? Because if you did, you're not as cool as I thought you were, and you're not my friend. You're not any better than James if you slept with that crusty hipster."

Caralie cracks her window, lights a cigarette, and rubs her forehead. "I'm sorry I left like that," she says. "I was mad."

"Did you sleep with that guy?" I press.

"No, I didn't sleep with him, Kaden. I was going to, I really was, because I know how much James hates him, but I didn't."

I slide my hands down my face. I'm confused and feel really lost. "Why is everyone in this place so fucking ruthless to each other? Doesn't anyone care about feelings in this place?"

Pause.

"Do they?" I press.

"I don't know," she finally tells me. "I wish I did, but I don't anymore."

Three blocks of silent tongues, that P.O.S. song "De La Souls" bumping softly from the speakers. She makes a left and hums along with the chorus. . . .

"I've been living with my chips all in and I'm still in, see . . . No one will ever be like me. . . . No one will ever be like me. . . ."

"Where are you taking me?" I ask her.

"To my apartment," she whispers in the softest voice ever.

h. caralie's pad

The nicest place I've been to all day. It's real nice like that. It's on Octavia and Washington in this part of the city Caralie calls Lower Pacific Heights.

It's huge inside. The ceilings are really high, and the walls are a perfect white. She has all hardwood floors that shine. It's a one-bedroom with a large kitchen and bathroom. In the living room are two couches and two wicker chairs and a flat-screen TV on the wall. Huge bay windows wrap around the corner of the room and look out on Washington street, and even farther out into the deep horizon of the bay and beyond.

I slip my shoes off, and the first thing out of my mouth is, "How much is a place like this?"

"Fifteen hundred a month."

"And you can afford it by working at a coffee shop?"

"Nope."

"Then how do you pay for it?"

"How do you think?" she barks at me in an irritated tone.

"James Morgan," I say.

"Bingo. He pays a thousand of it and takes care of all the bills."

I move around the living room and already feel better about my life. "So how does he have enough money to pay three different rents?" I ask.

"He made awesome money from his books," she says. "They were both bestsellers. Plus *PieGrinder* was optioned for a movie—you know about that—so he gets a sixty-thousand dollar check every year, even though the project is dead in the water right now."

I move to the windows and stare into the street below me full of cars and trees and steps, and I say, "It must be nice to have James Morgan's life."

"You jealous?"

I turn to her. "Maybe a little."

"'Cause it's okay to be. Most everyone else who knows him is too."

"Really?"

"Yep," she nods, grinning. "You should try to get some sleep now."

"I know. I have to be back at the Whip Pad by ten tomorrow to meet Gerry."

"That works out perfectly," she says. "I work at ten, so I can drop you off on my way."

"Sweet."

Caralie makes a bed for me on one of the couches in the living room.

"Thank you for coming to get me," I tell her.

"Awww, dude, it was nothing. My pleasure." And she smiles and walks into her bedroom.

Monday, June 2nd

WAKING UP IS THE WORST. IT'S LIKE THERE'S SOMEONE drilling brick inside of my head. My throat hurts bad from being so dry. It's hard to swallow my spit. And it hurts to move, almost like somebody slammed me against the street and kicked me in the chest.

I sit up, groaning loud, and rub my face. Hard, piercing sunlight shines into the living room through the windows. Caralie is already up and about. I can hear her singing that En Vogue song "Giving Him Something He Can Feel," and I can see her. She's wearing a pair of dark blue jeans so tight they look painted on her, a pair of pink slip-on shoes, a black hoodie, and a navy-blue bandanna tied backward around her forehead.

Planting my feet on the floor, palming my face, I groan again, and Caralie looks at me from the kitchen, then walks to me and hands me a glass of ice water.

"You look like you could use some of this," she says.

"Thanks," I croak, the words barely audible to even me. I take a drink.

The water hurts my throat even more, half of it spilling

from the corners of my mouth before I finally choke it down.

"Thank you," I say again. "So this is what a hangover is like. Death."

"Awwww." She grins. "Was last night the first time you've even been drunk?"

"Yeah." I take the last of the water and swallow, and the term "splitting headache" takes on a whole nother meaning. "How the hell do you guys do this day after day?" I ask. "I don't think I've ever felt worse in my whole life."

"Believe it or not," she says, "you start getting used to it. What you're feeling right now, dude, it becomes almost second nature. Nothing that an energy drink or a cup of coffee or another beer for that matter can't help you get over."

"It's as easy as that, huh?"

"I'm not even kidding at all," she says.

Once more I groan and stand up. Caralie gives me a hug, my nose pressed against the skin of her neck, her skin that smells like tulip gardens and citrus orchards.

It gives me a boner, her smell does, which is the only part of my body that feels all right.

Stepping back from her, I say, "That song you were just singing."

"The En Vogue one."

"Yeah."

"What about it?"

"My brother Kenny found that song as a single on a

cassette tape in some thrift store and gave it to this girl in his class for Valentine's Day."

"Oh. That's sweet. How old was he?"

"Thirteen."

"Did she like it?"

"He told me how she laughed at him and made fun of him and how he was crushed by it. After that I only saw him treat girls like shit."

Caralie winces when she hears that, like she's insulted by it, or shocked, even though she doesn't say anything about it.

Instead she says, "We need to get moving. You need to shower?"

"That would be great."

"There's clean towels and washcloths in the bathroom."

"Thank you."

"You're welcome."

"For everything so far," I say.

"You're welcome," she says again.

"It feels good to be around you."

Caralie grins and nods, and then I walk into the bathroom and take a huge piss while the water gets warm. When it does, I step in and take the best shower of my life.

On our way to the Whip Pad we stop at this café and order two coffees and two bagels with cream cheese and tomatoes. I've never cared for coffee the few times I've tried it, and I tell Caralie this as we sit at a table next to a big window staring out onto Polk Street.

And she says, "It's because you've never had a good reason to until today."

She's so fucking right, too.

It does amazing things for me, like it's some superwonderful miracle drink, and within minutes after my first few sips I'm going from the tired, discombobulated wreck I woke up as to normalcy and fidgeting.

Things are so much better with my head almost done thrashing.

"So this girlfriend of yours is the first one you've ever had," she says.

"She is."

"And you like her a lot?"

"Oh, yeah. She's awesome. The prettiest girl I could ever get."

"How'd you two start going out?"

I take a sip. "Well . . . she pretty much instigated it. We rode the bus together for a couple of years, and she always sat with the kids in her grade, and me, I usually sat by myself."

"Why's that?"

"I don't have a lot of friends."

"Really? Wasn't your brother like Mr. All-American popular guy?"

"Yeah."

"Usually the younger siblings of a person like that reap the benefits and never lack for any friends or admirers."

"I know. But I'm not at all like Kenny was. We don't even look that much the same. I'm just a totally different person and never had girls crooning over me or dudes wanting to kick it with me. I've been a loner for pretty much my whole life."

"But you got a girl."

"I do. It was after I found out he died, when I started getting into Palahniuk. Like I told you, reading him got to me in a good way. I started working out, and all the noise and the chatter didn't get to me anymore. I got focused on this goal to get out here to see him and improve myself, and she noticed."

"So what happened?"

I take another sip and tell her the story.

a. jocelyn kramer

She's a grade under me and lives on a farm right off the highway just two miles from my farm and is on the same bus route as me. I'd known her for about four years and had always thought she was real pretty and all. Easily the best-looking gal on the whole bus, including the high schoolers. She has this long brown hair that she French-braids on the sides and ties together in the back, these tiny freckles on the tip of her nose, and she has a more tan complexion than me. And these light blue kitty-cat eyes. But we'd never really talked much to each other or anything like that. Then one day on the bus, I'm all bundled up in a scarf and this old blue Dysart-Geneseo stocking cap with a yellow fuzzy ball on top and this old brown peacoat I found on the sidewalk outside of the community building one night, and she came over and plopped down right next to me and said, "I really like your stocking cap." She flicked the fuzzy yellow ball. "Especially that."

I looked up from the book and thought she was the cutest thing ever. I truly did. My whole body got all tingly, and the butterflies in my stomach were all floating around, and I could feel my cheeks burning. I was totally surprised that she was sitting next to me. She was always sitting with the "cooler" guys from her grade, Brent Mitchell and Pat Werner, near the back of the bus. Once I thought about this, I became ready for anything. A practical joke, a spitball, a yellow sticky note on my back that said: *Kick me. I'm gay.*

I didn't say anything. Just shelled up into defense mode.

And she went, "I read an article about your brother in the *Dysart Reporter* last week. It was nice."

I remembered the article she was talking about, even though I hadn't read it. Three pages long. Started on the front page. All about Kenny's accomplishments and his football recruitment and our family. I guess there was a lot about me and how close the two of us were. It had gone straight into my mom's scrapbook of Kenny's life.

"Your brother seemed like a real good guy," Jocelyn said.

"He was." I looked away from her. "He was the best."

She smiled. "Are you shy?"

"No."

"You're blushing."

"So what?"

"So nothing. It's cute."

"What do you want?" I asked her.

"I'm not sure yet. It's just that I think you're curious all of the sudden."

"How's that?"

"You look different, Kade."

"Kaden," I corrected.

"Kaden. You look different. All the girls think so. Plus you're always reading these big books by the same guy. I've seen you read this *Fight Club* one twice in the last couple of weeks."

"Yeah, well, it's that good of a book. It really is."

"Have you seen the movie?" she asked.

"Yeah."

"Is it better than the book?"

"Not quite as good. But it's close."

"I thought the movie was kinda weird."

"Then you should read the book."

Jocelyn smiled again. I even think she winked at me. And I felt pretty good. It was like the first real conversation I'd ever had with a girl.

She looked past my shoulders and went, "Oh, crap. My

stop is coming up." Then she jumped off my seat and ran back to where she had been sitting and grabbed her school-bag and raced off the bus without even looking at me or saying anything to me.

As the bus pulled forward, I watched her cross the high-way toward her pea-green-colored farmhouse in that soft purple and white winter coat and stocking cap, stunned at how good I felt just by talking to a girl in that way. I remem-ber thinking how that couldn't have just happened. No way. That was too nice to be true.

My self-esteem was so bad that I figured there was something up. Something. I got real paranoid and started looking around as if I was about to be attacked. I looked for notes that might've been stuck to my body, kids giggling and pointing at me, but there was none of that.

Strangest thing ever, I remember saying to myself as I floated through the rest of the bus ride and the rest of the day and night on the soft cloud of my first-ever crush.

But the next day and the day after, everything went back to the way it was before. Both times of the day I saw Jocelyn on the bus she didn't even look at me, let alone say anything to me. She was back to talking and laughing real loud with her friends about other kids in their grade. She completely ignored me. It stung. For those two nights I sat in my room and tried to concentrate on the other shit I needed to do, but I couldn't. I felt really hurt. I couldn't eat. I wasn't hungry anyway. I missed my brother more than ever. He'd know what to say to me and how to help me. He'd know exactly what I could do to make those feelings disappear and never come back.

Those two nights were so miserable. Not even reading Palahniuk could get my mind off the girl. I took walks again outside with my German shepherd, Sam, to get away, even though I never really got away. I promised myself to never warm up like that again.

I'd learned my lesson, I reassured myself.

Until it all changed again the next day, on Friday. I stayed after school to do research in the library for this paper I was working on about hate speech and if it should be banned or allowed on college campuses.

It was almost seven, and there was a home varsity basketball game that night. My mom was picking me up at seven, and as I walked out of the library to go wait for her by the front doors of the school, I noticed that the girls' game had already started, so I stopped to peek into the gymnasium to check it out: to watch a game on the same floor that my brother used to dominate kids on. I saw one of the girls from our school make a three-pointer, and then the other team's coach called a time-out, and the band started playing.

I turned around and started for the front doors when I heard my name get called out. I turned back around and saw Jocelyn running up to me.

"Kaden," she said. "Hi."

I was confused. "Hey."

"What are you doing?"

"Going home."

Her face pouted, and she went, "Oh. All right."

"Did you want something, Jocelyn?"

She paused and swung her eyes around from me to the people walking by in our red and black school colors, then back to me. Her face got red. She said, "Do you not like me, Kaden?"

"What are you even talking about?"

"You've been ignoring me for the last two days."

"No, I haven't. You've been ignoring me. You've been sitting in the back of the bus with Brent and Pat, and you haven't looked at me since we talked."

"Kade."

"Kaden," I told her.

Jocelyn put her hands on her face and said, "I did my part. Girls aren't even supposed to make the first move, but I did. I approached you. After I do that, you're supposed to make the next move."

The tingly feeling came rushing back through me. "The next move?" I was blushing again. "You actually like me?"

Jocelyn shook her head and playfully hit me on the arm. "Duh."

"Really?"

"Yes."

Pause.

I was stunned.

And she said, "You've never had a girlfriend before, huh?"

"No."

"You don't know what to do."

"No."

"Here's a hint." She leaned forward and whispered into my ear, "Call me." She leaned back, smiling. "Tomorrow."

I swallowed the huge lump in my throat and went, "Okay."

"Promise?"

"Promise."

Her face turned even redder, and she giggled and then went, "Good," and ran back into the gymnasium, while I walked through the front doors of Union High School feeling like the goddamn champion of the world.

I got my first-ever girlfriend.

Caralie is smiling big. "That's so cute. I love it."

"And that's the story with that. I love her."

"I bet you do. She sounds terrific."

I take another sip. "She is. She's the most terrific girl in the world."

Pause.

"Besides you."

Caralie grins, and we finish our bagels.

* * *

Back in her car I ask her if she's talked to James yet.

"No, I haven't."

"So he has no idea that I bailed last night and could be anywhere right now?"

"Probably not."

And just the mention of James seems to stress her out. Her body changes at the sound of his name, and like that she's holding her head in her hand, her elbow pressed against the bottom of the window.

"Do you think he would even care?" I ask.

Eyes narrowing on the road in front of us, jaw clenching tight, Caralie bites the bottom of her lip and says, "That's a good fucking question."

Pause.

"No," she snaps. "I take that back. He does," she says in the most unconvincing way ever.

She turns up the stereo and lights a cigarette.

Gerry is standing in front of the Whip Pad when Caralie drops me off.

"Have fun," she tells me.

"Right." I smile and step outside. It's so warm out again.

Gerry's smoking a cigarette and holding a coffee; he's wearing royal blue–colored jeans, a white T-shirt, and Nike high-tops, and there's a white pick sticking out of his 'fro.

A huge grin on his face as I approach him, he laughs and says, "Look at you looking like a piece of shit."

"Thanks for that, man. I feel like one."

"Pale as Casper. Paler than you were when you got here, if that's even possible." He laughs some more. "Damn, Kaden, you musta went nuts after I saw you last."

"You have no idea," I tell him, laying him some skin. "Can I get a drag of that smoke?"

"Sure, man." I take three before handing it back. "So what's up with this gym?"

"The San Francisco Health and Fitness Club," he snorts. "It's more like a country club than an actual gym."

"Sounds nice."

"It is nice. We cater only to the most elite and rich in the city."

"Cool."

"Shit." He winces. "The place is asshole central. It sucks the most."

We hang there for a few more minutes and split another cigarette, and this bus comes rolling up.

"This is us. You got a buck fifty?"

"Sure."

"Cool. Let's do this shit, mang."

b. the bus ride

It's crammed, dirty, and smelly, people breathing their bad breath on other people. People coughing and passing germs and avoiding all eye contact with one another.

We get two stops in when two seats open up near the

back of the bus. Gerry and I scoop them up like we own them.

"The Muni sucks," he tells me. "I usually take my bike, but I got you with me."

"You don't have two bikes?"

"Used to," he says. "Used to have three, actually."

"What happened to the other two?"

"Sold the parts off of one, and the other one got jacked."

"Shitty."

He shrugs. "Happens in this city." He says, "So what the hell happened with the rest of your night? I heard you disappeared from the pad after James ditched you."

"Dude, I did some of the coke that James left, and I fucking lost it."

Gerry starts busting up.

And I say, "I've never done that shit before. I was already drunk, and then I did the blast, and it was like a fucking comet exploded under my ass. I was in another gear, another fucking dimension."

"That's how that shit works, kid."

"I know that now. I was mowing through the streets like a bulldozer. Called my girl's house back home, and her dad freaked out on me. I ended up in a park not too far from the Whip Pad, and shit was cool for like another minute, and then BAM!" I smack my hands together.

And Gerry goes, "You started crashing, huh?"

"Something. It was like this total reversal. All the sudden I started feeling like a scumbag, so shitty, and I got all depressed and cold and felt worse than I've ever felt before."

Gerry shakes his head, then adjusts his pick. "Damn, man. So that was the first time for you getting all fucked up like that?"

"Yup."

He takes a drink of his coffee and goes, "Man, I still remember the first time I got all fucked up like that."

"How old were you?"

"Fourteen."

"Shit," I snap. "Where'd you grow up at? How old are you now?"

"Twenty-eight."

"Okay."

"And I grew up on the south side of Chicago."

"What happened to you the first time you got all loaded like that?"

"I went to go see this hip-hop documentary, *The Show*, with some of my boys."

"I've seen that before."

"It's the shit," he says. "One of the best documentaries on rap." He takes another sip of the coffee and goes, "So before we got to the theater, we smoked a couple of blunts and sipped on some St. Ides. Even snuck a few cans of eight ball in. At that point I'd done some drinkin' and shit, smoked some trees, but it was after the movie when I ran into some kid I used to know from playground pick-up games in the hood. Said he had some new shit that'd get me all loose and weird."

"Coke?"

"Yessir!" He smacks his hands together. "He told me to try some, and fucking right it was the shit . . . the legit shit. Like I felt like Lawrence fucking Taylor looking for a quarterback to run over. It changed my life forever, and I ain't been back since."

"Fourteen. Damn, that's a lot of coke-doing."

"It is. The shit's a monster, man. Sinks its teeth into you real deep, but it's a good kinda monster to me. Like the cookie monster and shit. You feel good when you see him, but there's always a few times when you eat too many cookies and you get an upset stomach and feel like shit . . . always a few times. But that don't stop you from eating cookies altogether."

Pause.

"Ya feel me?"

"That's pretty awesome," I say.

"I know it is. And ya know what, I don't give a fuck who gives this shit, this life, a bad name. I have more fun than anyone I know. I know everyone in this city, can get into any show for free. I've had my photos on every major gallery wall here, and I'm doing what I gotta do. I still manage to live it up. My own American dream."

He holds out his fist for me to bump it, and I do and look

out the window as the bus comes to a stop. The corner to my right is more gnarly than anything I've seen yet. More harsh-looking people than the day before. Transvestites pushing carts, a half-naked black lady wearing a diaper, three ghouls creeping out of an alley down the block, and a busted man holding a garbage bag, cruising through a busy intersection, bringing the traffic to a halt, like he's hoping to get mowed down by an oncoming truck and put out of his misery for good.

"What's this neighborhood?" I ask.

"It's Sixth Street, man, The skid row of San Francisco."

"Looks rough."

"The aesthetic is, but at the heart it's not bad at all. There used to be some okay bars on this strip. It used to be kinda fun to kick it down here."

"See a lot of shit, I bet."

"Well . . . It's San Francisco. You'll see a lot of shit regard less of what neighborhood you're in, except for maybe the Marina."

"What's there?"

"The kinda people you'll see working out at the fitness club we're going to."

The light changes, and the bus moves ahead.

I say, "So how do you know my cousin? You're good friends and all, but you seem real different than him."

"I am. We're way different, but we also like a lot of the same shit."

"You're into hip-hop, right?"

"Oh, shit yeah, man. I'm working on an album right now."

"What do you rap under?"

"Lenny Drool. I got two albums out. But the one I'm working on is gonna be under Omar Getty. He's like Lenny's alternate ego. It's a totally different style."

"Like Kool Keith and Dr. Octagon."

"Like a lotta motherfuckers, but yeah, same as you said too."

"Nice."

"I'll play you some new shit I just recorded with this cat Nick Andre."

"That'd be awesome."

He tweaks the pick again and says, "I'm putting your cousin on a couple of tracks."

"I thought he didn't like rap."

"Shit . . . don't be fooled by his shit talking. He just don't get into much past ninety-six."

"That's what Caralie said too."

"But he does, even though he doesn't need to. That shit was the glory era, man. It's really all you need to listen to, but there's tons of good shit going on right now. But about James, he just loves to hear himself talk. He loves his rants. And he can rhyme real good and writes some killer shit."

"That's dope," I say. "But how'd you two meet?"

Gerry sits back and looks at the roof of the bus and rubs

his chin. "Partying and shit. And we were both fucking Ally for a minute too."

"She's hot."

Gerry lunges forward and rubs his hands together. "Yes, she is. Top ten hottest girls I've ever put my dick inside, man."

I'm really liking Gerry a lot, way better than James at this point. He's cool shit, not all agitated and in prick mode like James has been to me so far on this trip.

That Michelle girl pops in my head, and I ask Gerry about her.

"We used to go out," he says.

"But not anymore?"

"Nah. We fuck sometimes, and it's cool. She likes hanging around and getting loaded."

"It seems like everyone likes that."

"For sure everyone does, but her especially. She likes that I know a lot of people doing rad shit. Pretty big names in the city. She's kind of a ladder-climber in that sense, but I love that girl to death. . . ."

And I want to tell Gerry right now about how I saw her at James's and heard her get fucked by him. It's on the tip of my tongue. Like, fuck James Morgan. It was like, *How you going to say this guy is your awesome friend and slam his ex-girl?*

It's just about to spill from my lips, how I saw it all go down, when Gerry goes, "Your cousin and her get together now. She thinks James is the best."

My jaw drops.

Like, *What the fuck? You know about it and what . . . just don't give a shit.*

And I go, "That's pretty crappy."

He makes a face. "No, it ain't. You just gotta look at it in the right kinda light. That's the key to most of this, man. Transcending your one-track mind about relationships."

The bus roars past Third Street and is almost empty.

c. the san francisco health and fitness club

A whole city block of building next to the water. I follow Gerry inside, and he introduces me to a couple of dudes working the front desk. Dudes who look pretty beat up, actually, like maybe they slept in a gutter the night before or passed out under a car. They look the way I feel. Two sick and tired faces standing behind the front desk of the nicest health and fitness club in San Francisco.

"Lemme show you around," Gerry says.

"Cool."

The place is incredible, full of gorgeous, hard-bodied women, young and old. Cougars is what Gerry calls them.

There are five squash courts and one racquetball court. Two clay tennis courts on the roof, with a sundeck and chaise longue chairs. Place has a full spa, a huge weight room, a yoga center, two Olympic-size pools, and a massive cardio and cycling area. The men's locker room has leather chairs, big-screen televisions, a sauna, and two steam rooms.

Plus there's a café. The place truly is more of a country club than a gym.

I ask Gerry what he does.

"I work the garage," he says.

"Like parking cars and stuff?"

"Nah, man. I sit in a tiny-ass booth and pass out slips with the time each car pulls in written on it, and on their way out I collect them."

"That's pretty easy."

"It is, but it's also a bitch. Most of these motherfuckers treat me like a piece of shit. They don't like taking instructions from some black kid making minimum wage."

"Just doing your job, though, right?"

Gerry stops and grabs my shoulder. "You think that makes any difference to them? These people come from money. They've spent their entire lives doing whatever they want, whenever they fucking please, and they don't view what I'm doing as my job. I'm just an annoyance. Like a gnat floating around, waiting to take a bite out of them."

"So why work here?"

"Shit," he says, moving forward. "Fucking eye candy all day. Plus some of these people are good people to know. You can network with some pretty big ballers here if you play it just right."

And it's right here, at this moment, when I think about what a self-serving, slimy, impersonal matrix of coalitions people in this city weave together just to try and get ahead.

The word "hustler" takes on a new meaning for me.

We weave back through the lobby, into the basketball court. It's a full court with a scoreboard and shot clocks attached to the top of each hoop.

Gerry grabs a loose ball and throws up a shot from a couple of feet behind the three-point line, and the ball swishes through the net.

"Still got it." He grins.

"You play a lot?"

"Used to. Even played a year of college ball at a juco in Texas."

"Awesome."

"What about you?" he asks. "You play ball?"

"Nah, man. I never took much to sports. It's weird like that."

"How?"

"Because my older brother, Kenny, was awesome at sports. You shoulda seen him. He was great at everything, but especially at football and basketball."

"But not you?"

"Nope. I just watched him fuck other kids up."

"Huh."

We keep walking, and I tell Gerry these two stories about how great Kenny really was.

The first one is about this football game his junior year, when our school was playing the number-one team in the state, Aplington-Parkersburg. We were doing pretty good that year, and Kenny was the conference's leading rusher. It was a home game, and the score was tied at seven in the last quarter, and Union had the ball with about two minutes left. It was one of those third down and forever times, and the quarterback, Kenny's good buddy Matt Schwaggert, handed the ball off to my brother. He started up the middle, but there was nothing there, so he bounced to the left and tried to break it outside. That didn't work either, so he spun back around, breaking two tackles. Then he cut back all the way into his own end zone, ran back to the right, and did a spin move against another defender. And man, as soon as he popped off that spin move, my brother was gone. Officially, it was listed as a ninety-seven-yard touchdown run, but Kenny, with all that jukin', he'd probably run about a hundred and twenty yards total. And the whole place went nuts. I was sitting in the stands with my mom and dad, and everyone was on their feet in their red and black Union jackets and sweaters, screaming and jumping up and down. Everyone except my dad. Instead of reacting at all, he just sat there, emotionless. Although he may have faked one smile to the school principal, who was standing near us.

Union won the game that night, and a bunch of kids that went to the high school ran onto the field and celebrated; some of them even climbed the stinkin' goalposts like it was some college game and their school had just won the national championship or something. My brother got carried off the field that night on the shoulders of his teammates.

And the other story I tell Gerry is about this basket-ball game. Union was playing against North Tama, which was a rivalry game 'cause the towns are so close together. Union was down by eight points with just over twenty seconds left. North Tama had the ball and was taking it out of bounds, when Kenny intercepted the pass. He took one dribble to his left and fired up a three-point shot. It swished right through the net, and Union called a time-out. After the time-out was over, Union fouled one of the North Tama players. The kid had to shoot free throws, and he missed them both. Brad Johnson rebounded the ball for Union and passed it to my brother, who went between his legs twice, then behind his back, and fired up another three that hit the rim twice and dropped through with nine seconds on the clock. North Tama then tried to inbounds the ball, but the guy who caught it for them stepped on the out-of-bounds line, turning it over back to us. Union got the ball at half-court. Again it was Matt Schwaggert who got the ball to my brother. He threw a bounce pass to the near sideline, and Kenny got it and spun out of a double-team to his left. Then he took two hard dribbles and popped another three and sank the fucker right as the buzzer sounded, giving Union the one-point win and making Kenny the local news station's athlete of the week, where he was featured on TV.

Gerry and I finish the tour, and he asks me what I wanna do.

"Go swimming," I tell him.

"Cool. I got some extra trunks and goggles in my locker."

I go and change, and Gerry heads out to the garage to start his shift, and the pool is packed. All the lanes are full to the point where some people are doubling up in them. Each of the pools has a wider lane at the end, so I move into one of those and triple up. The lane I pick is being used by two older women, sixties, maybe seventies. I jump in and start breaststroking, and like halfway into my first lap I clip one of the ladies swimming by me, and she loses her cool. She screams something at me, and I ignore her. When I spin around to go back down, I notice she's gotten out and is in a bathrobe. Then she storms out of there.

I don't give it a real second thought. I just keep swimming. The water feels amazing against my sore and beat-up frame. I feel relaxed working my body like that in a positive way and all. I'm on my third lap when I see this guy in a shirt and tie waving at me, with the same old lady standing next to him with her hands on her hips.

I swim over to them.

"What's your name?" the guy asks me.

"Kaden Norris."

"Are you a member of the club?"

"No. I'm here as a guest."

The old lady makes a face and says, "He's not even a member. Classic."

"I'm a guest," I shoot back.

"Whose guest are you?" the guy asks.

"Gerry Jones's guest."

"My garage guy?"

"Yeah."

The old woman sneers at me and says, "He's not even a guest of a member. What kind of club are you running, sir?"

Gerry is exactly right about what he told me about these fucking people.

"So what's the problem here?" I ask.

"You can't triple up in a lane; that's the problem. You have to wait your turn."

"I didn't know," I say.

"That's fine. But I am going to have to ask you to get out and wait. She had the lane first."

"Okay," I say. "I didn't know me swimming was going to be such a huge deal."

"Don't get smart with him," the lady snaps.

I roll my eyes. I don't wanna fuck Gerry over, so I do what the guy says.

I get out and I'm like, *Fuck it. Over it.*

I dry myself off and change back to my clothes and head for the garage where Gerry is. And he wasn't lying at all. The booth he's sitting in is tiny, like a two-by-two box of glass with a small desk and stool.

Cars pull up and stop, and Gerry hands them a slip. They drive away. It seems like the easiest thing in the world, but Gerry seems agitated.

He says, "It's not that the job is tough, man. Like I told you earlier, it's having to deal with some of these attitudes. It's like people pulling in even though I'm telling them not to because the garage is full and I want them to wait outside so I don't have to suck in their car exhaust for five minutes. It's shit. I can't stand the attitudes."

"Just ignore them," I say.

"I can't. I'm trapped in this fucking box with nowhere to hide. Plus, it's not like all the people here suck. It's just some of them can really fuck up my mood. Like, shit, you're driving a Benz, coming to the gym at two in the afternoon, so your life ain't that bad. Relax. Take a deep breath and calm down, but that's the mentality you don't get when you've been given everything in life. There's a distinct difference in the attitudes I get from the people here who are self-made versus the people who inherited what they have and only earned anything through the value of their last name or bloodline."

I nod and can't really disagree with what he's saying, even though I've never experienced dealing with people in an upper class like the ones who go to this club. My own family is well off and all, but in Iowa terms exclusively. In San Francisco we'd be just another middle-class family.

A Mercedes SUV pulls up to the booth. Driving it is this incredible-looking blonde with big blue eyes and big tits, wearing a leotard. She smiles at Gerry, blushes, even, and Gerry's like, "What's up with you today, Jennifer?"

"Not much. Just here for my spin class."

I notice this huge rock of an engagement ring on her left hand.

"You're looking great today," Gerry says.

"Thanks. You're not looking so bad yourself."

Gerry cribs the time on her slip and hands it to her. "See you on the way down."

"Of course."

She drives up the ramp, and Gerry turns to me and goes, "I've banged that girl three times."

"Isn't she engaged?"

"So what if she is. Mr. Fiancé ain't giving it to her right. Doesn't know how to dick that fine piece of ass."

"Do you get a lot of action working here?"

"A fair amount," he answers. "Mostly middle-aged white women on the down slope of their marriages."

"Cool."

"For sure it's cool, man."

On his lunch break we go over to this grocery store across the street, and he grabs two dinner rolls and heads for the line, and I say, "That's all you wanna eat?"

"No. But I can't afford to eat anything else right now."

"I'll buy you lunch," I say.

"You ain't gotta do that, man."

"Yeah, I do. It's totally cool. I got money."

I get us two sandwiches and two sodas, and we walk down a block and eat in this sunny park.

The sun feels great. A perfect cure for the wounds I suffered last night. For most of the time we talk about hip-hop and music in general, but I'm still intrigued by the dynamic of James and Caralie's relationship. How two people who care so much for each other can treat each other like dirt. So I ask Gerry about it, and he asks me to be more specific and I say, "I just think it's bullshit. Their whole entire deal. It's like they obviously fight a lot, and they both cheat on each other. It's like they're just using each other."

"How so?" Gerry asks, leaning back on the grass and lighting a cigarette.

"I think he uses her because she's so young and beautiful and she makes him feel relevant."

Pause.

"Go on," Gerry snaps.

And I continue, "She uses him to live in that nice-ass apartment and because he gives her a certain level of credibility she probably wouldn't have otherwise."

"So you've been here two fucking days and think you've got it pinpointed down like that."

"That's how it seems to me, man."

Gerry lets out this short, cynical laugh, and goes, "Kade—"

"Kaden," I snap.

"Kaden, whatever. I know your cousin well. I've known him for six years, and he's helped me out a ton when I've run into problems. He's a good man, like family to me, and

I know for a fact that he loves that girl to death and that she loves him the same way back. Sure they argue and fuck other people, but that's because they love each other so much."

"Dude," I say. "I'm sorry, but that makes no sense at all to me."

Gerry puts his smoke out and says, "By the way you define love . . . probably not. Probably not even the way I would. But the thing is, you can't define a relationship between two people by randomly observing them for two fucking days."

"I still don't get it," I tell him.

And he goes, "It's like this, man. You do the shittiest things to the people you love the most. That's just the way it is. You always hurt the people you care about the most. And trust me, I know what you've been seeing, and I know what it must look like to you, but your cousin, he'd run through a brick wall for that girl, and that's a fucking fact. So what it really comes down to in the end is that their relationship is nobody else's business."

I roll my eyes and look away, thinking about how stupid it is what he said. And then Gerry smokes another cigarette and we walk back into the health club.

But I have no interest in staying there any longer. I'm fucking over it, and when Gerry disappears to the garage, I ask one of the guys at the desk how I can get back to the Mission, and he tells me to walk to Market Street and take BART and get off at Sixteenth Street.

"Thanks, dude," I tell him; then I bail.

d. the walk

By the time I get to Market Street, I have no desire to go underground and get on BART. It's too fucking nice out, and hoofing it seems like a better idea. Kind of explore the city while I have the chance to. So I move in and out of crowds of people and get to Post Street, where I keep moving down to what I think is the right way.

It's a powerful sight down here, looking at all these fancy department stores and people crowding the sidewalks. I cruise through Union Square, past five-star hotels and restaurants, but just as quickly as the glitter and gleam of the fancy downtown blocks arrived, they're replaced with a sudden scumminess. The harsh reality of another facet of the city. I'm in the Tenderloin again, and the high life of my day dissolves like some strange desert mirage. Thing is, I don't feel rattled one bit. I feel tougher from what I've already been through and keep walking. I even drop down a few more blocks to the deeper part of the Tenderloin, projecting as much confidence as I can, like I've been haunting these streets for years.

On O'Farrell and Leavenworth I make a right, my nostrils bombarded with the smell of rotting garbage, swampy ass-cheek whiffs, and Asian-food grease kitchens. It's a space that smells the way it looks, which I actually appreciate as I navigate deeper and deeper, past the bums and the crazy lady with poop smeared on her and the skeletons covered in droopy skin, eyes sunk in, empty faces, nobody home at all anymore.

Hyde Street. I begin to really take notice of all the graffiti covering some of the buildings around me. Real art done under the cloak of night by secret warriors fighting a never-ending war against the ordinary and the stale of everything else.

Most of the shit I'm seeing is pretty dope. Sick pieces spanning half walls, animated names in bright colors, a second-story mural of infectious creation. I've always been a fan of graffiti since the first time I remember seeing it done in a meaningful way. It was on the east side of Waterloo where I saw it, where these secret warriors turned an ugly brick wall of some long-abandoned warehouse into their own canvas. Every inch of it covered in paint and purpose. A surface brought back to life by the genius wit of some urban poetic assassins.

My dad hates it. He hates most anything that has to do with art, but especially graffiti art.

"It ain't art, son," I remember him ripping at me after I got into trouble for painting a middle finger on this giant rock in the middle of the playground at the Dysart elementary school. I received a week's worth of in-school suspension, and my dad was pissed.

He snapped, "Is that what you want to be growing up . . . a vandal . . . a felon . . . a bum? Because that's what those guys are, son. They're criminals, property destroyers, and I'll be damned if I'm going to let my son turn out to be some sort of super bum with a can of spray paint in his hand."

My mom never spoke up or said a thing about it, and my brother, he thought what I'd done was rad. His only thing was that I needed to be more careful about it.

He said, "One of the things that makes it so cool is that half the art is not getting caught."

Damn, I miss Kenny so bad.

Larkin and O'Farrell. A red light and a small park with children playing in it, the New Century strip club across the street from the park, two liquor stores and a bar and another strip club just up the block, and the Great American Music Hall, with this band Grinderman playing there tomorrow night.

It feels surreal to see children playing in a park twenty feet from two different strip clubs. It wouldn't ever be like that in Iowa, but then again the circumstances of growing up there versus here, that dramatic urban reality difference, they just can't be compared to each other at all.

Plain and simple.

The light changes to green. I cross the street and see this thugged-out white guy with a thick blond strip of moustache and blond hair pulled back into a ponytail, wearing this triple-X-size Raiders jersey and baggy black jeans. He's rolling up at me, and when I pass him, my eyes focus straight in front of me, because even I know that staring at people is a stupid thing to do in this neighborhood.

But then I hear him go, "Weed."

I spin around. "What?"

"Weed, man," he says.

"No," I say. "I don't have any. . . . I'm sorry."

"No," he says back as I'm turning away. "Do you need any bud?"

My first thought, my first instinct, is to keep walking away from him. That this whole thing will only lead to trouble. It's how I've been raised. Raised to ignore everything and never succumb to an impulse. It was all just a lot easier that way, the way I was taught how to live.

But the thing is, this trip I'm on is based around the idea of how I need to expand my horizons and broaden my scope and not fall into the trap of only one way of living. Walking away will spit in the face of my very reason for being in San Francisco, so I turn back around and go, "I could use some."

I've never smoked weed in my life, let alone bought any before.

"How much?" he asks.

I shrug. "Dime bag . . . I guess."

"All right, cuz. Follow me."

He leads me across the street, and my heart is slamming against my ribs. My palms are real sweaty, and my face is wet. We walk past one liquor store and then the other, an old black lady buying two pints of Royal Gate Vodka, then past a bar called the Olive, and into an alley where two bums are sticking needles in their arms.

I gulp down some spit and wipe my forehead. Stick my

chest out. A mural of two black kids holding hands with a rainbow in the background is behind the two bums.

The dude reaches into his pocket, and it takes me everything not to run away.

What if he has a knife?

A gun?

Brass knuckles and shit like that.

Am I ready for a fight?

I've never been in one my whole life. Fifteen years spent avoiding conflict and ignoring everything.

It's easier that way. To always be moving and avoiding.

I gulp again, and the guy goes, "Here."

My eyes drop to his hands. A big nugget of green in a clear baggie.

Relief.

"Ten bucks," he says.

Pulling my wallet out, I hand him the money and say, "Thanks," then wheel out of the alley with an adrenaline rush pumping through like I've never felt before.

I practically skip down the street.

My first drug deal, done in an alley in San Francisco with two bums shooting up in it.

"What I Did for Summer Vacation," a story by Kaden Norris.

On Eddy Street I turn and cross Van Ness. I pass a Burger King, chicken bones amassed on the sidewalk, and pass another intersection and walk into a liquor store. A beer sounds great. A nice tall can in a brown sack and the streets of San Francisco.

I buy a twenty-four-ounce Bud Light and some rolling papers and get no static at all.

Cracking the can open, I take a nice big drink, a victory drink, and then I keep moving, not caring at all where I am or where I'm going.

I pass by this near-empty park and two baseball diamonds, and I think for a second about popping under one of the trees in the park and rolling a joint. But I don't. I keep pushing ahead, noticing that the housing and the architecture are beginning to change.

Just a block up, all the houses become the exact same on the outside. They're all beige with red doors and bars on the windows. I also notice how I only see black people on the next block, all of them standing in their doorways and their yards and front porches. I hear rap beats bumping through windows and loud TV sets. I'm in a different neighborhood now is what this all is.

I just have no idea which one it is, and this uneasiness returns to me.

I take a drink and put my brave face back on. And on the next block I see these two pretty girls sitting on the bottom steps of a stoop with a boom box in between them.

One has on these real tight jeans, red Nike high-tops, a black Tupac T-shirt, and red lipstick, and her hair is pulled back.

The other girl has red strips of dye in her hair, and she's wearing tight white jeans with the knees ripped out of them. She's got on a pair of black Vans, and a black jean jacket with all these tiny pins stuck in it.

Both of them are so pretty, and I can't help but stare over at them and smile, while they stare at me walking by them.

And then the one in the jacket calls out to me like, "Hey, you."

Again I gulp hard and turn away and keep walking.

But she says it again. "Hey, you."

I look back and point at myself. "Me?"

"Yeah, you," she says.

"What?"

"Come here."

My face gets all red, and it feels just like it did the first time when Jocelyn called me out on the bus, like maybe I'm about to get ambushed and shit.

Fucked up bad.

I say, "Why?"

"Just because," she presses.

And her friend says, "Don't be scared now, dude. It's okay to stop and talk to other people."

"You're right."

I spin around and walk up a cement path that parts the small patch of green yard down the middle as the girl in the Tupac shirt says, "Whatcha doing walking around in the Western Addition all by yourself?"

I shrug. "Just doing some sightseeing is all."

"You ain't from around here at all . . . that's what you're saying?"

"That's what I'm saying."

"Where you from?"

"Dysart, Iowa."

Both of them crack the fuck up.

And the girl in the jacket says, "Iowa. What the hell is that shit? Fucking Iowa is where you're from. Ha!"

"You think that's pretty funny, huh? What do you think you know about Iowa?" I ask.

Tupac shirt girl goes, "Whoa, man. Don't get all snappy like that."

"I'm just saying is all."

And the girl in the jacket goes, "Well, what the hell you think you know about the West Addy? What you think you know about this?" she snorts, then cranks up the volume on the boom box.

And I smirk. I'm like, *Holy shit.*

It's Mac Dre she just turned up. "Not My Job" is the jam. And shit, what do I know about this?

I show them what I know right there.

I go, "It's like this, girls," and I start flowing with the first verse. . . .

"Dre rock the jewelry with the clear stones, get on a nigga head like some earphones. I finna spit it with a clear tone, get your attention, the biggest thing since the TV invention. . . ."

Both girls' jaws drop like some two-hundred-pound rock is sitting in the back of their mouths now, and I just keep on going until the song is over. Then I take a nice long pull from my beer and say, "That's what I know about Mac Dre, ladies."

"Who the fuck are you?" the girl in the jacket asks.

"I'm Kaden." I grin. "Kaden from Dysart, Iowa." I stick a hand out. "And you two are?"

"I'm Janet," the girl in the jacket answers. "From the Fillmore."

She shakes my hand, and her friend goes, "I'm Brandy from the Western Addition."

I shake her hand too and say, "Nice to meet you two."

Janet shakes her head. "That was the shit. I gotta give you your props."

"Why, thank you."

"That was from out of nowhere," she says.

"Thank you again."

My confidence is back and growing. Six months ago I would've pissed myself if two black girls had called me out on a sidewalk. I know it sounds lame, but it's the truth. There woulda been a huge puddle of mess at my feet if this had happened back in December. No question about it.

I go, "You two smoke weed?"

"You got some?" Brandy asks.

"I sure do."

They glance quickly at each other, and Janet says, "Let's go smoke that shit in the park."

e. the park

Starts out real rad. Janet shows me how to roll a joint; it's a fat one, and we smoke it and take swigs from my beer and take turns freestyling.

And I surprise them with my skills:

"Bud Lite forties running down my fucking throat, pretty girls laughing, loving my fucking jokes. Don't give a shit about the morning; I'll never feel all right, which is cool, it's not the point, no one needs to tell me I'm this tight."

We smoke another joint. And both girls are really into me. I swear to God they want to kiss my lips.

But no sooner than Janet kills the last drop of beer, our party in the park gets crashed in a huge way. By the way of three black dudes, all of them way bigger than me, much older-looking than me.

I'm just about to slap a verse out about blasting Biggie on a boom box in a cornfield when these guys roll up, one of them jumping in my face, growling, "What the fuck is this shit?"

My balls shrink fast, and I say, "Nothing. We're just kicking it."

The guy inches closer, his chest bumping into mine, his mouth up in my grill, and he snaps, "Who the hell do you think you are?"

Both girls try and calm the situation, but it's useless.

I say, "I'm no one, man. We're just having some fun."

"Those are my girls," the guys snorts. "No one has fun with them except me and whoever else I say."

And I'm like, "I'm sorry. I didn't know. My bad."

Then one of the other dudes goes, "Fuck this cracker up, Andre."

"No!" Brandy screams. "Just let him be. It's nothing."

"Shut up," Andre barks back.

"Fuckin' relax, man," I say. "Everything's cool."

This is when the third guy comes charging at me and pushes me.

I stumble back at first, but then slam forward and shove him back.

Then POW!

Andre throws a fist into the side of my face, and I drop to the ground and know what's coming, so I cover myself while the three of them take turns kicking me.

And it hurts real bad. And I can hear Brandy and Janet pleading with them to stop it.

But they don't. The slams to my body keep coming, one right after the other, second after second, feet and shoes sending shots of pain into my frame, and I can't do a thing to help myself.

The beating doesn't stop until some lady starts screaming that she just called the cops.

I feel a glob of spit hit my hands, and then nothing. I look up and everyone is gone except this lady in a purple jogging suit. She kneels over me and tries to help me up, but I knock her hand away.

"You need to go to the hospital," she says.

"Fuck that."

"You're bleeding."

I sit up. "I don't care, lady. I'm not going to the hospital."

I push myself to my feet, and it takes a minute for everything to refocus, and when it does, I see the blood on my hands, and I feel the sting of the wound where Andre's knuckles slammed against my face. My whole body is on the swell, the bruises, the first real ones of my life.

The future scars.

"You should really go to the hospital," the lady presses. "You don't look so well."

Pressing down on the bloody gash on my forehead, I say, "Just shut the fuck up. It's none of your business, lady! Leave me alone."

"Settle down."

"I won't settle down," I snort, then turn away and leave the park and stand on a corner until a cab finally stops and picks me up.

"I'm going to the Mission," I tell the driver. "Back to my cousin's apartment."

Then I look in the mirror and look at the driver looking at me. Looking at me like I'm the biggest piece of shit in the world.

f. the valencia street apartment III

I storm in and find James sitting on the futon with his face in his hands. There's a mirror with three huge lines of blast on it and two notebooks off to the side, open to pages that have been crossed out and scribbled over.

James jumps like he's all startled at me walking in on him. It's odd, actually. His eyes are red and swelled up like he's been crying, or pouting, or something along those lines. Plus he seems real agitated to see me there.

He jumps to his feet and goes, "What are you doing? You're supposed to be with Gerry."

I walk out of the hallway, saying, "Yeah, well, the gym sucked my white ass, so I left."

He notices my face. I can see it in the reaction on his own face. He does a double take and looks almost scared.

He goes, "What the fuck happened to your grill?"

"I got jacked up by some kids in a park."

"What?" he snaps, rubbing his face. "What fucking park?"

"I don't know what it's called. It was near the Tenderloin, though. In the Western Addition."

"Holy shit, asswipe!" he yells. "You got a death wish or something?"

"What?"

James steps toward me and says, "You go walking through the West Addy all by yourself and get into a fucking fistfight." He grabs my shirt and balls it in his fist. "Your fucking mom is going to kill me, man. She's going to cut off my balls and destroy me."

I rip my shirt away and say, "No, she won't. It's not even that bad."

"You're fucking joking, right? You got a three-inch gash in your forehead and blood smeared across your face."

I shrug and plop down on the futon. "Dude, relax."

"Fuck you, I won't relax. What are you gonna tell her? That you tripped down some stairs wasted on beers and loaded on the blast? Don't think for a minute I didn't hear about the little stunt you pulled last night."

"You stranded me in that hole in the ground."

He rolls his eyes. "So that means you do a bunch of coke and go run around the city like a fucking maniac, crying in front of a Popeyes Chicken on Divisadero."

"I guess it does."

"Fuck that." He leans down and does one of the lines. "Your mom is going to destroy me," he snaps, after popping up and rubbing his nose. "I'm fucked. She's gonna kill me."

"Dude, it'll be fine."

"How?"

"I'll tell her I got hit with an elbow playing basketball at the fitness place."

Pause.

"Hmmmm," James rips, holding his chin and looking at the ceiling. "That could actually work. I bet she'd buy that for sure." He leans down and kills some more coke. "Good thinking, man."

"I know."

"But you need to put some ice on that shit. Hold on."

He goes to the kitchen. My whole self is beyond

exhausted, more fucked up than ever. I hear him dump ice into a bag, and then he rolls back to the living room and hands it to me.

I put it on my forehead.

I say, "What was happening with you when I walked in?"

He lights a smoke and takes a seat at his computer. "What do you mean?"

"You looked like you were losing your shit. Like you've been crying for a while."

He doesn't say anything.

"Were you crying about your girl?"

He shakes his head and snaps, "Don't fucking talk about my girl."

"Hey, don't be a dick to me, man."

Again he doesn't say anything, even though I don't really care about what the hell is bothering him.

I go, "So what was it you were crying about?"

James flips his chin at me, then points to his left, at the four crates filled with notebooks. "Fifty-six," he says.

"What's that mean?"

"Those are how many notebooks are sitting in those crates, man. Fifty-six. That's how many times I've started my new book without getting past the first chapter."

I move the ice from my face and wipe the wet away, then put the bag back on it and say, "You told me last night that shit was going real good. That you were working hard on some new stuff."

His face bunches up like he just bit into a lemon. He looks at the floor, a line of smoke floating to the ceiling, and then he looks back at me with water in his eyes.

"I lied to you," he says.

"Why?"

"I don't know. I lie to everyone."

He wipes his eyes, and I bite down on my tongue. It's all I can do not to start laughing at him.

And he goes, "It's like I can't write for shit anymore. I feel stuck. Like my creative juices are dried the fuck up, and the only thing that comes out is shit." He takes the last line. "It's all fucking shit!"

He drops his head again, and I say, "What do you think happened?"

"I don't know, man. I just don't know. But I got nothing if I can't write. Not even Caralie makes me feel as good as the way I feel when I know I've fucking nailed it right on paper and written the greatest thing ever. No girl has ever made me feel as good as my best writing has. And it's the one thing I have that nobody else I know does. The thing that separates me. My success. No one else I know can match it, and now that it's all lagging, I don't know what to do. I'll lose my fucking soul if I can't get this shit turned around."

Wiping away the wet again, I say, "I mean, maybe you shouldn't party so much. Maybe all the drugs you do are messing with your creative flow."

James snaps his head up, and his eyes get eerily intense-looking, and he goes, "What the fuck do you think you know about any of this?"

"Whoa," I say. "I was only—"

He cuts me off. "What the fuck do you think you know about me or about writing at all?" He stands up. "You don't know shit about this. Nothing. That's all you know. Nothing."

"Sorry," I snort. "I didn't mean to—"

"Bullshit, *Kade*," he snaps, cutting me off again. "You did too know what you were doing, and it's crap that you did it. Don't think you can just waltz on in to my fucking city and act like we've been tight for years and shit. Trying to tell me what you think is going on. That's some fucking bullshit, kid. And nobody likes a bullshitter."

He smashes his cigarette in the ashtray and storms back into the kitchen.

My face turns more red. I really hate this motherfucker. Hate him enough to wanna go back home to Iowa and pretend like I was never here. My face is fucked, my body feels fractured, and the only thing I'm getting is shit on by some guy who hasn't done anything since like 2006.

What a fucking d-bag.

I take the ice off my face again and sit forward and stare at the cover of this *SOMA* magazine with M.I.A. on it, and she's hot. I'm getting a woody just looking at the cover.

James comes back in the room. He's holding a bottle of beer, and he sits back down at the computer and takes a drink. A big one. And then he goes, "I'm sorry about that. I shouldn't have snapped at you like that."

This catches me off guard, hearing him say that. "Okay."

"It's just that I'm totally strifed and shit right now. This lack of writing production is making me really agitated and miserable, and then you bring up the whole drug issue. . . . It just pushed the wrong button."

"Sorry about that."

"I know you are. I just, um, it's like I hear that crap from so many people, and it gets really fucking old and lame. Because a lot of the people who tell me that shit do it while they're partying with me. Or like the next day after they were asking me for drugs all night and doing them. And ya know, the thing is, it's not that I really like doing coke all that much anymore. It's just that I don't dislike it enough to quit. It's kind of like being a Rolling Stones fan still." He takes another pull and shakes his head. "Damn, you really did get fucked up. What the hell went down in the West Addy?"

And I tell it all to him. About leaving the gym and plowing through the Tenderloin and buying the weed and meeting Janet and Brandy and rapping some Mac Dre and smoking the grass in the park and then getting pounded on.

And James loves it.

He's like, "You're fucking crazy, man. That's the raddest

shit I've heard in a long time. Straight outta Iowa and you're here grifting up black girls, rapping Mac Dre, and having a showdown with their dudes."

"And ya know what?" I snort.

"What's that?"

"I coulda had both girls easily. They were that into me."

James kills the rest of the beer and goes, "That's awesome, kid." He reaches over the table and lays me some skin, then turns back to his computer and scrolls through the music. "You like Jonathan Richman?"

"Never heard of him."

"What?" He glares at me from over his shoulder.

"Dude, I don't know as much about music as you. I'm only fifteen."

"What the hell does that matter? When I was fifteen, I had over a thousand records and was DJing illegal warehouse parties. Age ain't an excuse."

"I think it is."

"You're wrong. Lack of curiosity is why you don't know shit."

"So play this guy, then. Stimulate my curiosity."

He does. "This song is called 'Hospital.'"

It's pretty good stuff. I like it. And James does a key bump and goes, "Listen, listen, listen." He wipes his nose. "Right here, coming up, one of the best lines ever in music." He puts a hand up. "Listen right now."

And the song goes . . .

"I go to bakeries all day long. . . . There's a lack of sweetness in my life. . . ."

"So fucking good," James rips. "What a fucking line. You like that?"

"It was okay," I say.

"Just okay . . . fuck that shit, man. You don't appreciate good music."

"Yes, I do."

"No, you don't. Because if you think that's just okay . . . there's no way you have a clue of what greatness really is."

"Whatever, man."

His phone rings, and he answers it. "You're here," he says. "Good shit. I'll be right down." He stands up. "I have to go."

"Where?"

"Out for a while."

I can barely believe it. After all of this shit that went down today, this asshole is ditching me again.

"You'll be all right, kid. Just keep the ice on your face."

"What the fuck am I supposed to do, though?" I ask.

"Get some rest." He opens one of the desk drawers and pulls out a prescription bottle and dumps out two pills. "Here," he says, holding the pills out. "Take these."

He drops them in my hand, and I go, "What are they?"

"Valium. It'll help with the swelling and help you fall asleep."

"Fine."

"I'll be back later."

I just nod and watch him slide his blue and black flannel on and then leave the apartment.

I look at the pills. I'm not sure I even wanna fuck with them, but then I think that if they make me feel at least one thousandth of a time better, then it will be worth it, so I get some water from the kitchen and swallow both of them, then set the ice bag in the sink and sit at James's computer.

I look through the music on it and find a ton of Jay-Z and play that song 'Lucky Me,' from the album *In My Lifetime, Vol. 1.* . . .

"*You think I'm freakin' these chicks, right? I try not to brush against they chest, get a lawsuit for shit like that. I feel trapped. . . .*"

It makes me think of Jocelyn. We talk about this album over the phone all the time. She loved it too. I'd first heard it after I found it lying in the parking lot of Gates Park on the east side of Waterloo, and I got so into it. I got Jocelyn to buy it, and it was over after that. We've made up verses to each other on paper to the beat and traded them on the bus and after school.

I miss her.

I get on the Internet and log into my Facebook and go straight to her profile and look at her pictures. It's the closest I can be to her before I go home. And I just miss her so much but don't know what to write her. Nothing makes sense for me to say, not even how much I miss her and that I love her, so I just look at her pictures again and again until the Valium comes rushing on. I go and lie down on the futon and put my head against the pillows and go backward in my head to the last night me and Jocelyn hung out.

g. friday, may 30th (last day of school)

I watched her get on the bus after school that day. Her skin was damp and shining from the sweat of the hundred-degree day. Humidity like a heavy blanket that you can never pull off of yourself. Inhaling the moist air. Heat waves and gas fumes. She was smiling at me like always.

In her hands she carried the random notebooks left over from the grueling year of school. She looked so pretty, too. She always looked so pretty, though. She was wearing a green mesh skirt that hung around her scuffed knees. A white shirt with the sleeves rolled all the way up her tan arms. A gold chain with a heart medallion. And a pair of flip-flops. Her brown hair was French-braided on the sides and tied together in the back.

She sat down next to me. "Hey," she said.

"Hey."

I didn't have any books or even a backpack with me. Only thing I had was the two cold cans of root beer that I'd bought from the vending machine at school before the shuttle bus took me from La Porte to Dysart, where I boarded the next bus for home.

"Here." I smiled. "This one's yours."

She took the root beer from my hand and tried to get

comfortable. As she moved, I could hear the sound of her skin sticking and unsticking against the cheap blue plastic of the bus seat even over the roar of the excited voices that surrounded us.

"Thank you," she said, after settling in.

"Why, you're welcome, Jocelyn Kramer." The bus started moving, and I nudged her and went, "You ready?"

"Yes."

"Okay, one, two, three," I said, and the two of us snapped our cans open at the same time.

So what if it was fucking cheesy. I really felt something for this girl.

We took drinks, and the bus chugged out of town. Flat landscapes far as the eye could see. Big tractors moving through the farm fields. Tiny farmhouses. Red barns. Bright sun. Clear blue skies. The faint aroma of hog manure blowing through the open windows of the bus.

I was wearing a tight Cincinnati Reds T-shirt. A pair of white Guess jeans that I rolled halfway up my calves. And my penny loafers.

Jocelyn wrapped her left hand around my right one. She held the root beer against her face and squeezed my hand and said, "I'm gonna miss you."

"I'm gonna miss you, too."

Jocelyn took another drink. "Are you nervous?"

"A little bit."

The bus rides with her were never very long. Her house

was the third stop. Still, those fifteen minutes every morning and afternoon were the best moments I spent all day. I'm being serious here too. They were awfully good.

The bus roared up to fifty miles an hour on Highway 21. Jocelyn rested her head against my shoulder and said, "So what do you think about tonight, Kaden? Are we still going to meet?"

"Yep." I took a drink and put my face against the top of her head. And I whispered, "It'll be so easy, too."

When we were on the phone the night before, Jocelyn had brought up an idea right before the call was over. She said, "What if both of us snuck out tomorrow night? We could meet up halfway, between the houses on Pheasant Road," which is this dirt road right off Highway 21 and Eighth Avenue, the gravel road I live on.

"I'd be into that," I told her. "What time?"

"My mom and dad always go to bed around ten thirty, when the news is over."

"Mine too."

"We could wait until eleven just to make sure and then do it. We both bring flashlights, and when we get to Pheasant Road, we start flashing them on and off so that we'll know that the other person is there."

"That's a great idea. Did you just come up with that?"

"During sixth-period study hall."

"You're awesome."

"I know," she said. "So what do you say?"

"Yes."

The bus zoomed past the Dysart Golf Course and all of its hills, and Jocelyn said, "I wish we could go somewhere far away together. Just me and you. Watching the world."

"That would be awesome. Leaving Dysart and all."

The bus began to slow down for Jocelyn's house. She lifted her head back up and gathered the notebooks in her arms and said, "Leave your house at eleven."

"Okay."

The bus stopped. "I'll see you tonight."

She stood up and started walking. A couple of kids yelled, "Have a good summer!"

She yelled, "You too!"

And I watched her cross the highway, and the bus started moving again.

I left my house at exactly eleven. I brought my backpack with me. Inside it was an extra jacket for Jocelyn in case she forgot one for when it started cooling down fast. I also put some beef jerky, some A&W Root Beer, a plaid blanket, and a flashlight inside of it.

I walked. I would've ridden my bike, but Jocelyn's dad had accidentally run over hers with a tractor about a week earlier, so she didn't have one to ride.

We both walked.

I wore a red La Porte City Rams sweatshirt and jeans and a navy Fila jacket.

It was so awesome out that night.

Perfect stars dotting the black blanket of sky. A pie slice of moon. I could see the blinking red radio-tower lights near the edge of town. The block of faded Dysart streetlights. Crickets chirped. Ditch weeds moved in the breeze. The big shadows of ancient buildings. The suffocated roars of semi trucks steaming down the highway on the other side of the cornfields.

The whole big walk to Pheasant Road took twenty-six minutes almost exactly. And that included a stop near the Bradfords' driveway, where I took a pretty big piss. I timed the walk on my Casio just in case I ever decided to do it again.

Along the way I thought a lot about the trip. I was getting nervous as fuck. I didn't know James Morgan at all outside of all the bad shit I'd been told about him from the mouths of certain family members. How he was a crazed drug maniac who fucked underage girls and burned bibles. How he always paid top dollar to have his girlfriends get the best abortions. How he hated this country and thought everything besides himself sucked.

I even talked to my mom about him. I said, "Truly, Mom."

I asked, "What do you really think about James?"

And she said, "I am letting you go out there by yourself, Kaden."

She said, "That should say enough."

She said, "What it all boils down to is that he's really just misunderstood."

She said, "You have nothing to worry about, Kaden. James Morgan is one of the most remarkable and wonderful and loving people you'll ever get to know."

She looked away from me and bit her lip. Her face bunched up.

And she said, "You'll do really great out there with him."

She sounded like she was sending me out there for good or something. It was weird. But I just attributed it at the time to her still dealing with the demons of losing her oldest kid in that stupid fucking war.

Pheasant Road. The moment I turned onto that half-mile slab of dirt and weeds and rocks, I turned the flashlight on and off. On and off. On and off. No response. I kept walking. People rarely ever drove on that road. If they did, it was usually farmers going from field to field or drunk high-school kids at two a.m. taking the back roads home to avoid the highway patrol. I remember Kenny telling me that sometimes, back when he was still in school, when the party he was at got busted or they needed to find a new place to have a keg, a whole big crew of kids would just drive to Pheasant Road and set things up. They'd sit on the backs of cars. The flatbeds of trucks. Lawn chairs. Blankets on the ground. The kid with the nicest stereo system would play the music.

He told me, "It was far enough away that none of the

houses around the area could hear any of the noise and a pretty safe bet that nobody would ever be driving down that road that late at night."

He said, "I used to drive girls out there all the time and pull my car into one of the field entrances and roll around in the backseat with them for hours."

Damn.

I missed my brother.

I was like six electrical posts down when I saw the blinking yellow light of a flashlight just up a little ways. It was Jocelyn. A gush of excitement tore into my body like I'd just inhaled a sack of Pop Rocks and a can of Jolt soda. I was moving fast as I flashed the light back at her. In such a hurry for really the first time ever in my life.

In front of me I could make out the curved block of a shadow coming at me. The shadow of Jocelyn Kramer. My girlfriend.

She flashed the light on again and then ran to me and threw her arms around me. I squeezed her back so tightly. Her hair in my face. Her hair that smelled like apple orchards and ocean water.

"We did it," she said, stepping back from me. "We both made it here."

The steel door of a cattle shed slamming somewhere in the distance.

In the shallow white light of the stars, I could see her pretty face. She was wearing red lipstick. She hardly ever wore lipstick. She was wearing a blue and green plaid jacket and a navy skirt with black tights on her legs.

"It's nice out," I said. "My mom told me it usually gets really cool at this time of night in San Francisco."

"It's weird that a place in California can end up being colder than a place in Iowa in the summer."

"Yeah. No shit."

There was a little nervousness between the two of us. We'd never been alone like that before then. With anyone. No one else around us at all. It was like, *Now what?*

Jocelyn kicked some rocks into the ditch and went, "What's in the backpack?"

"Snacks. A blanket. An extra jacket in case you forgot yours."

"Awww, that's sweet, Kaden. What kinda jacket?"

"One of those green Pioneer zip-ups."

"My dad has one of those."

"So did mine."

She laughed at my pretty bad joke. Her head tilted to the left. The corners of her lips arched. She crossed her right leg in front of her left one and put her hands on her hips. "Take the blanket out," she said. "Let's sit down."

I smoothed out a spot on the ground and laid the blanket out. Jocelyn sat hugging her knees. I leaned back. My hands pressed to the sides.

She said, "You're so lucky you get to leave."

"It's only for a week."

"Still," she said. "This ain't like getting sent to some summer camp in the middle of the woods, Kaden. You're gonna be in San Francisco for a week with your crazy cousin." She let go of her legs and planted her right hand on the blanket and looked at me. "I totally Googled him."

"You did?"

"Yeah. I read some interviews with him. He sounds like he knows how to have a good time. I read an article about him that claimed he was an egotistical maniac who wanted to devour anyone who tried to challenge him."

"My mom said he's just really competitive. That it just rubs people the wrong way."

"I wish I was doing something at least one percent of how cool that is this summer."

"What about that Iowa State volleyball camp in July?"

Jocelyn sighed. "Really? That's what you're gonna compare it to."

"Hey," I said. "Ames, Iowa, is pretty all right."

We both laughed. I got even more nervous. I wasn't sure really what to expect that night with Jocelyn. We'd never done anything besides hold hands before and one kiss on the cheek. We'd never talked about anything we might do once we met. I knew deep down inside of me what I wanted to do. I wanted to kiss her. Make out. But I wasn't sure if that's what she was thinking. I didn't know how to read girls. She was my first girlfriend. With each passing moment of an awkward silence or a knee or hand knocking together followed by nothing, I could feel the pressure starting to build. How my window of opportunity was closing. She was yawning. Girls aren't supposed to be yawning after they sneak out of the house to meet a boy.

I took a deep breath. Felt a mosquito land on me and bite my arm. I smacked it away and pressed my hand down.

Jocelyn slid her hand over to me again. Except this time, she rubbed her fingers gently over mine. She moved them back and forth, and then she maneuvered her hand underneath mine so that we were actually holding hands.

I got all tingly inside. I could feel a surge beginning in the crotch of my jeans. I gripped Jocelyn's hand hard. My palm was sweating.

So was hers.

When I glanced in her direction, she was looking in mine. Smiling. But I just didn't know how it all worked. I had no idea what to say.

It was thirty seconds that felt like five hours. I could tell she wanted me to do something. She looked like she really did. But there was something else holding me back. I was fucking scared is what it was. I was chickenshit as hell to even make a move. Afraid that I'd be turned down.

I loosened my hand from hers and went, "I could really go for a snack right now."

Jocelyn's shoulders dropped. Her body language transformed entirely. Boy, she looked so fucking disappointed.

She let go of me and fake-smiled and went, "Okay. That sounds nice, Kaden."

I was such a dumbass back then.

That whole other lifetime ago.

I grabbed my backpack and took out the two cans of root beer and the bag of beef jerky. The peppered kind.

"Picked this up at John's Quick Stop the other day," I proudly stated, as I started to open the bag. "It's probably the best beef jerky I've ever had."

Jocelyn sat Indian-style. Her elbow on her leg. Her chin resting against the knuckles of the fist she'd made. "That's really good, Kaden."

I struggled to tear open the seal. Seriously. The shit wouldn't open. I stopped and took a breath. I looked back at Jocelyn. She was so pretty. With the way the moonlight was slicing across her face, she looked like this perfect angel, but with a sad face. I couldn't do that to her. I said, *Fuck it.*

I said, "Ya know, I don't wanna eat any snacks."

"Me neither."

I dropped the bag. Everywhere on me began to sweat except my throat, which dried right up. My face felt like it was burning. I thought my nerves were going to paralyze me. I really did.

With my chest thumping I said, "I just . . . really . . . it's like . . ."

I paused.

Jocelyn dropped her hand, and she scooted closer to

me and put a hand on my knee. "It's like what, Kaden?" she asked.

"Can I kiss you?"

A smile wide as the sea cut across her face. "Yes," she said. "Please."

"Okay."

My first kiss.

That big moment.

One of the most important moments of growing up.

I leaned in to her. I could still smell her hair. I could smell her lips with that cherry-flavored lipstick on them. It was love, man. That's all anyone needs to know.

I rubbed my face against hers briefly. Her skin was soft. And then I moved my face right in front of hers and then I kissed her lips with mine.

I did it again.

My insides were going nuts. I remember being dizzy. For real. I pulled back. I remember hoping that Jocelyn wasn't going to be all grossed out. Like maybe if I'd done it wrong. I know it sounds pretty stupid and all, but I wasn't exactly this beacon of confidence like my older brother, Kenny, had been.

Jocelyn was still grinning. I licked my lips. Cherry awesome is what I tasted. And she said, "I've been waiting for you to kiss me for so long."

She leaned forward and we kissed again. A bunch of times. Our lips pressing together. The tiny smooching sounds. The small pockets of drool in the corners of our mouths.

Jocelyn leaned back. "This is really nice."

"It feels really good," I said.

"Do you want to try it with our tongues?" she asked.

"If you want to, then I do."

"I totally do."

"Have you ever done it before?"

"No! But I've practiced." She paused. "On my hands a few times."

"Like this," I said, putting the palm of my right hand against my mouth and rubbing my tongue on it. "Is that how you practiced?"

"More like this," she said. Then she did the same thing to her hand, except with more grace. And more passion. Like she'd really been practicing for a while or something.

I was laughing so hard.

She was too.

She dropped her hand and wiped the slobber off on the blanket. Then our eyes met in the middle.

It was insane how great I felt.

Almost criminal.

Pounding my hands into the ground, I lunged forward and grabbed on to Jocelyn's waist. I slammed my mouth against hers and slid my tongue inside of it.

It was easier than I thought it would be. Just slapping the muscle of our mouths together.

Slap. Slap.

Slap. Slap.

With my hand on her waist still, I began to push Jocelyn on her back. She didn't stop me. I pushed harder, and she gave way. I broke her body down like a piece of cardboard and laid her flat. I got beside her. My right arm draped across her stomach. Jocelyn tilted herself up on her right side.

We kissed for hours. It was everything that I'd ever wanted.

And more.

Sometimes we would take a break and lie there on our backs and look up at the nighttime Iowa sky, talking about whatever popped into our heads.

How bad Scarlett Johansson's CD was.

How all the kids we knew had taken their obsession with the movie *Juno* a little too far.

How awesome all cherry sodas were.

And then we made out a bunch more. Until three in the morning.

That was when Jocelyn got so tired and cold, and I told her I had to get home because I had to get up real early for my flight.

Before we left each other, I gave her both my jackets, 'cause she was shivering.

I told her, "This was the best night ever."

"I'm gonna miss you."

"I'm gonna miss you, too."

She hugged me again, and we kissed again, and before we walked away from each other, I told her, "Instant-message me when you get home. Please?"

"Why?"

"Because I wanna be sure that you made it there all right."

She pecked me on the cheek and told me to have a good trip.

I fucking floated all the way home. I snuck back into the house and logged on to Facebook, and there was already a message from Jocelyn. She was home too. And she'd also had the best night ever. And she wanted at least one phone call or a postcard from San Francisco.

It was the best I'd ever felt up to that point of my life. Easily. I couldn't even sleep well at all. The toxic mixture of how good Jocelyn had made me feel combined with all the crazy anticipation and nervous excitement about the trip had formed this lethal cocktail that was seriously fucking with my ability to pass out.

I even remember looking at the clock next to my bed at one point. The bright red digits said five twenty-seven, and the next thing I knew, I was waking up.

The clock said eight, and my mom was knocking on my door.

Tuesday, June 3rd

EVERYTHING ON ME HURTS. EVEN MY EYELIDS, WHEN
I open them, feel sore and roughed up. It takes a minute for
things to get into focus, and when they do, the first thing
I see is Caralie. She's sitting at the desk, looking like some
sweet angel in white with the way the sunbeams are pushing
through the windows above her, all through the room.

I groan and hold myself in my arms as I sit up. My throat
is dry and swollen-feeling again.

I hear some hip-hop that I've never heard before, and
whatever it is, whatever she's playing, is good and soothing
to my brain meat.

Leaning forward, I groan and cough. "I feel like a piece
of shit," I say, and then realize I've been wearing the same
shit since Sunday minus the puke that I scrubbed off at
Caralie's.

Caralie spins around in the chair, shaking her head.
"What the hell were you thinking, pulling that shit yesterday?"

"Huh?"

"James told me what happened to you, Kaden. Going

to the Western Addition by yourself and smoking dope in the park."

"So what?" I cough.

"You could've been hurt real bad," she snaps. "A lot worse than you were."

"Well, I wasn't."

"That's good. I just don't get why you even did what you did."

Rubbing my face with both hands, I snort, "What else was I supposed to do, Caralie? This whole trip has been a bunch of bologna so far. I haven't done anything, nothing, except get ditched by James and get wasted in a fucking dungeon. I mean, shit, I thought I might actually get a chance to do something meaningful beyond Chuck's reading while I'm here, but that's not what's happening at all. Not even close."

Caralie stands up. She's wearing skin-tight white pants, a pair of Nike Cortez, and a white wife beater with a black and white flannel wrapped around her waist. Her hair hangs straight and past her shoulders.

She sits down next to me. "That is what James thinks is meaningful and real. What you've seen and been a part of so far is the only way any of these guys know how to live. It's all real to them."

"So that's it?" I say. "Getting wrecked and treating people like garbage is the only thing they can do to make themselves feel real."

She bites her bottom lip and goes, "That's what makes

them feel liberated from the rest of the world. When they're in that mode, they don't feel the bullshit of the world or anyone else's, because they're too preoccupied with maintaining the needs of their addictions."

"That's messed up."

"That's what you're seeing."

"Okay, fine. That's all nice and dandy, I guess. But I wanna do something other than hanging out in the garage of a health club. I'm not having any fun. I got my ass kicked yesterday, my fucking face hurts, and really, I just wish I was with my brother. He'd know exactly what we could do that would be fun."

Caralie sighs. "Okay. How about this? You take a shower and get clean, and I'll figure out something that we can do today that'll be fun for you."

"Really?"

"Yes."

"Thank you."

She hugs me and kisses my cheek and tells me, "You'll look back on all of this one day real soon and be glad you were part of it."

"Right."

"You will," she insists. "The scars and the stories will last you a lifetime."

She lets go of me, and I go to the bathroom and look in the mirror. My forehead is a bump of blue and purple and black. I touch the lump and wince.

Fuck.

I take off my shirt and shorts. A huge bruise on my left side, bruises on my chest, and on the right side as well. A big scrape on the underside of my right arm, and a black and green dent in the middle of my back.

Man, I actually have to give it to those dudes; they worked me bad. But shit, both girls were into me. They liked me the best, so in the end I fucking won. In the end it took three motherfuckers to take me down after they found out that their girls were more interested in me than them.

I get into the shower with a smile. And just like yesterday was supposedly the best shower of my life, the shower I'm taking right now is at least ten times better, with the way the steaming hot water is healing my sore bones.

I get dressed in James's room, putting on a blue LA Dodgers shirt, a pair of dark Levi's, a pair of Chuck Taylors, and my Cincinnati Bengals jacket.

I walk back into the living room, and Caralie is back at the computer. "Watch this," she tells me.

I look over her shoulder, and she pulls up a video on YouTube.

"This will put you in the best mood ever."

"What is it?"

"A video by this band Beirut for the song 'Nantes.' They play it live on a sidewalk. I absolutely love it. Every time

I'm in a bad mood, I play this, and my mood changes in an instant."

"I wanna see it."

She plays it, and this guy in a V-neck sweater starts singing . . .

"*Well, it's been a long time, long time now, since I've seen you smile . . .*"

Caralie gets up and leans in to me and runs a hand through my hair and sings along. . . .

"And I'll gamble away my fright, and I'll gamble away my time . . .

"It's been a long time, long time now, since I've seen you smile . . ."

And she's so right. Because by the time the video is over, I feel a thousand times better.

I say, "That was some shit. I feel all right now."

Grabbing a hold of my left hand and squeezing it, Caralie says, "That's nice, darling. I know exactly what we're going to do today."

a. the embarcadero

We leave James's place in Caralie's car with the windows rolled down and the Weathermen bumping from the speakers. We drive down Valencia, and it's nice out, and I love this neighborhood. The feelings I have being in the Mission are so different from the ones I have being in the other neighborhoods of the city. I just like it better here.

It feels edgier than the other places, but edgier in a good way, not the edgy crack-cocaine, needle-sharing way of the Tenderloin, although I'm sure that's just as prevalent in the Mission. I mean edgy in this cultural sense. The Mission is this huge mix of Latin culture and black culture and white culture. And they all seem to go pretty well together.

The street art is way better in the Mission. The cafés look better, with all the girls in sundresses, tattoos, nice legs, pretty faces sitting around the tables outside. The used-book stores, small record stores, and rad boutiques. The fashion is more my style. The flannels, high-tops, rolled jeans, and beards. I like that look. I have since I started watching rap videos five years ago. The food is better. All the outdoor markets selling fresh produce, and the awesome taquerias. And again, the women look better in this neighborhood. And that's a fact. By far, the Mission is the best neighborhood in San Francisco.

I still don't know where we're going, and that's okay. I don't really want to. Just the idea that I'm going to be doing something different than what I've been doing is enough for me.

We stop and get Jamba Juices on Van Ness because my stomach is still raw, too raw for solid food, and then we drive on. All the way down Market Street to where the water is.

Caralie parks, and we walk up a block, side by side, and I ask her who was singing that song she was listening to when I woke up.

"This dude Lewee Regal. He's a good friend of mine and James's. Local guy. His stuff is sick."

"Oh, I fucking loved it. That song was dope. What's the name of it?"

"'Broken Ever Thus.' Fucking lyrics are amazing."

"They were good. . . .What was that line . . . ? 'Lately I haven't had time to think; it's hard to make time between the mistakes and drinks.'"

And Caralie goes, "'I haven't eaten in a couple of days, and I'm too lazy to bathe and I'm too shaky to shave.'"

"Fucking rad," I say.

"And he's lived that shit too," she goes.

"It seems like everyone here is living that way."

"They kinda are."

We sit down on the grass.

"Ya know, he might actually be at Ally's show tomorrow night. He knows all those kids."

"Cool." I sip the Jamba. "Is Ally's band any good?"

"I think they are. The whole lineup tomorrow is pretty sick. Any Lamborghini Dreams show is fun, plus we always party with those dudes afterward. They're getting pretty huge now. It'll probably be slammin' there."

"I've never been to a show before."

"Well, shit, this is the absolute perfect one to start with, then."

The noon siren goes off, a church bell chimes from somewhere else, and Caralie jumps to her feet.

"Come on." She smiles, grabbing my hands. "Hurry up."

I don't ask a question. I jump to my feet and follow her down a sidewalk and into the middle of this huge square block of cement.

Like twenty other people are standing around us; it's like we're all waiting for something. Caralie has a grin so big. More people come running toward us. It's confusing. Some of them are laughing, and others look like I do, clueless. The last chime sounds, and that's when I see the first one.

The first zombie.

It's a male, and he has on this olive-green suit that's covered in fake blood and is ripped to shreds. His face is smeared black and white with red around his mouth. A black wig clings and droops from the top of his head. And he's walking like some unoiled robot with a spell of spasms.

He comes at us from a grove of trees, a leather briefcase in one hand.

I look at Caralie. "What the hell?"

She points over my shoulder. I turn and look and see a girl zombie walking all fidgety from out behind this sculpture. She has green paint around her eyes, red all over her cheeks, a blond wig, and a peach-colored prom dress with red, black, white, and purple crap smeared on it.

I turn back to Caralie. She winks, grabs my arm, and then someone yells out: "Zombie crawl!" And like that, ten more zombies emerge from around building corners and the water fountains and from behind more trees. They're converging on the square like it's some maniacal scene in a horror movie.

I have no idea what this is.

It feels creepy and a little insane.

Then Caralie dashes away. She dodges from the square, and the first zombie I saw grabs her, smears paint all over her face and neck. When he lets go of her, she begins to walk like a zombie too.

It's happening everywhere. Everyone who gets touched by a zombie becomes a zombie. It's fucking nuts. There's at least a hundred people who've stopped and are looking on. Then the zombies converge onto them. Some people walk off, some back up even more, and the rest, they play along.

Me, I'm real timid as a person. I've never liked playing along with shit in front of other people for my whole life. I have never been able to loosen up enough to do things like this. I've always told myself that shit like this is stupid and not fun. When in reality it's just that I don't wanna look stupid and embarrass myself. I don't want other people to look at me funny and point. If there's anything I've picked up from my lame excuse for a dad, it's that.

I'm not shy as much as I'm too afraid of looking dumb.

But at this moment, today, something triggers inside of me. Maybe it's being around Caralie and the way she makes me feel: all good and pretty inside. Or maybe it's because I'm totally away from my comfort zone in Dysart, Iowa, and just rapped in the ghetto with two black girls yesterday.

Probably a combination of both.

It's just that when this girl zombie in a pink dress with red and black shit smeared on her grabs onto me and smears my face and jacket, I become liberated.

Within that single touch my body shifts into the zombie walk like I've been doing it for years, like it's all natural.

My whole sense of being opens up, and this enthusiasm that I haven't felt since I was a little kid in the arcade comes storming back to me. I go with it, and hobble with it. I twitch around with it.

I grab anyone without paint on them and smudge them. Then I move on. It goes like this for at least fifteen minutes. I even run into Caralie. We bump into each other and smear each other. She winks at me, and man, I'm falling for her. Like this crush isn't a crush anymore. It's definitely turning into something more than that.

The crawl lasts for about twenty minutes, and there ends up being close to a hundred people who take part. And when it's all over, all the zombies go back into normal mode and walk away like it's nothing. People disappear just as quickly as they arrived, and that's what Caralie and I do too.

She finds me, and I hug her and tell her, "Thank you."

I say, "I have never felt that free before. That was the best."

And she goes, "We ain't done yet, dude. I got some old school friends who wanna meet you."

"Where at?"

"Ocean Beach, mang."

b. ocean beach

It's so enormous and beautiful and emancipating, the rest of the world out there somewhere in the water. An endless sheet of blue draped in golden sheets of yellow, and I lean against a cement wall covered in graffiti and inhale the saltwater air and the smell of the sand.

"This is amazing," I tell Caralie, who's next to me, putting her flannel on because it's chilly here now.

"I know it is," she says.

"I've never been this close to the ocean before."

"Really?"

"I've seen it but never felt it. It's epic, man. Like the most powerful thing in the world, but it's not mean."

"I'm glad you like it."

"Thank you so much . . . again. You're really the best."

"Stop it." She grins, then checks her phone and looks back at me. "Let's walk. My friends aren't that far away."

She points to the right, and we go down some stairs and onto the sand.

"Take your shoes and socks off," Caralie tells me. "Feel the earth."

We both do and keep walking, and the sand squishes

under my feet and slides through my toes. It feels like there's some strange healing power being zapped up through my body.

According to Caralie, there aren't many people here, although it seems like there are to me. Every fifteen feet or so there's another pack of kids sitting on blankets, boom boxes blasting, cigarettes in their mouths, beers in hands.

Caralie's friends are like ten packs of kids down. There's five of them, three dudes and two girls, and all of them are Latin.

They're sitting on blankets next to the wall with a cooler full of beer in the middle and a boom box playing a mix tape of punk and rap songs.

An E-40 joint hittin' as we join the powwow.

And everyone is real happy to see Caralie, and she looks so, so happy to see them. And I don't know for sure, but it feels to me like she doesn't hang out with them much anymore.

My cousin's influence no doubt casts a long shadow over Caralie's other social life.

She introduces me around.

The girls are Cynthia and Maria, and they're both pretty.

Cynthia has dyed black and white hair and looks like a punk-rock prom queen. And even though she's wearing a black jean jacket that covers her arms, I can tell she has tattoos all over them, because she has some on her hands, one on her neck, and one on her chest, right above her boobs.

Maria is dressed more like Caralie. Tight black jeans, a blue hoodie, a red bandanna tied backward around her head, white slip-on shoes, and huge gold hoop earrings.

And I say, "This girl my brother used to see in high school, she was real hot, and she used to wear earrings just like that."

"Well, your brother obviously has some good taste in women."

"He did," I say.

The guys are chill too. Their names are Oscar, David, and Manny, and all three are wearing flannels and tight jeans and skate shoes. David has an SF hat flipped to the side. Manny has a black rag tied around his forehead, and Oscar is wearing a red beanie.

Caralie and I sit down on an extra beach towel that Cynthia pulls from a bag. Oscar flips open the cooler and pulls out two bottles of PBR and hands them to us.

I look at Caralie for approval, and she goes, "Go ahead, man. After what you pulled yesterday, you can obviously handle a beer."

"What happened yesterday?" Manny asks.

"You see the rock on my forehead?" I say.

"Who fucked you up?" says David.

"Well . . ." I twist the cap off my beer and take a drink. Then I tell them the story of Monday, and by the time I'm finishing, I'm getting high fives and hugs.

Caralie's phone buzzes. It's a text from James. "Him and

Gerry are over at Nick Andre's studio recording some tracks for the Omar Getty LP," she says. "They wanna know if you wanna go over there and check it out."

And right as I'm about to tell her yes, Cynthia cuts in and says, "My cousin Marco's having a barbecue at his house tonight if you two wanna do that instead."

Caralie looks at me and goes, "It's up to you."

"I'd rather go to the barbecue."

"Okay. We'll do that."

I take a drink and go, "See, now this is the type of shit I've been wanting to do since I got here. The zombie crawl, a fucking barbecue. It's like hanging out with James is kinda fun and all, but just watching him get ripped up day after day so far . . . I don't know. It's like . . ."

I pause.

And Maria goes, "It's like watching the worst episode of *Full House* at the same time of every day and night of your life."

I point at Maria. "Bingo."

Everyone except Caralie laughs, and I feel a little bad, since James and her are "in love" or some shit. But whatever. A spade is a spade, and you gotta call it when you see it, I guess.

I take another drink and ask Cynthia what kind of food they're gonna have at this barbecue. "Like some traditional Latin food and stuff?" I ask.

"No way," she says. "That would be like something we'd

do with my family and shit. This is gonna be burgers and hot dogs and forties, straight up."

"Nice," I say, as Oscar produces a blunt.

"You guys in?" he asks, looking at me.

"Sure. I like drugs."

"Good."

He lights it and passes it. The songs from the mix tape in the stereo change. It goes from rap to punk to rap to punk, and I know a lot of the rap ones. Rakim. Ghostface. The Knux. Eazy-E. But the punk ones I don't know so well. I've never been into much punk or rock in general. It's not in my blood. It's like the minute I heard good rap for the first time, I fell the fuck in love. But that ain't to say that the punk on the tape isn't good, because it is.

I like it a ton and ask what the songs are and who they're by when they play on the tape.

There's "Bloodstains" by Agent Orange.

"Rise Above" by Black Flag.

"Streets of San Francisco" by the Swingin' Utters.

"Gimme Danger" by Iggy and the Stooges.

"Skulls" by the Misfits.

"Suicide" by the Bodies.

"Anti-Manifesto" by Propagandhi.

A lot of stuff by the Bad Brains.

It's all good and nice to get schooled in another genre of music that actually shares a lot of symbolic similarities and ground with rap and hip-hop.

Another blunt gets lit, and I'm busy telling everyone about Iowa and my brother and why Jay-Z and RZA are the shit.

"I just love everything they do," I slur, and smile. "It's all fucking great."

I feel euphoric, almost, from the booze and pot, with the Pacific Ocean waves crashing twenty feet from me, seagulls screaming, surrounded by awesome kids and pretty girls.

The Grouch comes on, rapping, *"You ain't artsier than me 'cause you only read books, don't watch TV. You ain't artsier than me 'cause you shop at Whole Foods in open-toed shoes. . . ."*

And at some point, maybe around four, Manny pulls out a can of spray paint from his backpack and says, "Let's go hit some shit up."

"Word" is the general consensus.

And David asks me if I tag.

"A few times before," I say. "Got in-school suspension once for painting up a rock on school grounds."

"Cool, man. Let's do it."

We gather all the things and take them back to Maria's car, and then we walk like a half mile down on the sand to this giant cliff.

We post up in an area pretty far out of sight, and David hands me a can of red paint and says, "Go for it, my man."

Then he bounces a few rocks over to where Manny, Oscar, Cynthia, and Maria are, and Caralie stays with me.

"What are you gonna write?" she asks.

"I don't know. I'm not sure yet."

"What'd you put up that got you in trouble in Iowa?"

"A middle finger facing the elementary school I went to."

She laughs and shakes her head. "You're a fucking character. I like you a lot."

"I like you, too." Pause. "So any recommendations?"

"When I was younger I used to write 'Frumpy Mission Trolls.'"

"What's that mean?"

"I grew up in the Mission, ya know, and like five years ago the place just got taken over by these stupid scene girls who would show up at Delirium, on the whole block of Sixteenth and Valencia and Guerrero, and front a look and an attitude like they were so tough, and out hunting for some dick, and they would fuck any dude that could hold a conversation longer than two sentences. I don't know." She stops. Then says, "It's like, I know girls like that. They think they're flipping shit around, and they feel empowered by going out and looking for dick. And they think they're in control, but the thing is, when it's all said and done, they're still the ones taking dick. They're getting it given to them. They're still submissive in almost every way, so all that empowering stuff kinda flies in the face of what's really going on."

"Which is what?"

"That they're really just a bunch of fucking hos."

I smack my hands together and say, "Yes! That's the shit."

"It's the truth."

"I know what I'm going to write now."

"What?"

"Just watch."

Shaking the can, I hop over to the next rock and lean down and write: *Dickpig Sux*.

"There ya go," I say, winking at Caralie. "What do you think about that?"

"Fucking dope, dude."

c. the barbecue

It's in the deep, deep, deepest part of the Outer Mission. The Excelsior, or "the barrios, gringo" is how Oscar tells me, laughing when he says it. Which, despite Caralie's efforts to reassure me everything is cool, kinda rattles me. Because I have to be honest here, walking into this barbecue is not like walking into some scummy apartment with my cousin, full of white kids smoking weed and bumping the Temptations. It's a much different feeling than that.

The house is two stories and Victorian-style with a narrow set of stairs that are slam-packed with Latin dudes in wife beaters and flannels and jerseys.

I feel really on edge, and both Cynthia and Caralie sense as much and try to calm me down. Cynthia tells me, "This is my cousin's place. He's family. No one's going to fuck with you in my family's place."

And Caralie goes, "You're with me, Kaden. I run this

shit. You got nothing to worry about. Nobody fucks with one of Caralie Chavez's friends."

It helps a little, but not really. I'm apprehensive about everything I'm doing. Suddenly sober. Very conscious of things like not looking at anyone in the face for more than a second and staying out of people's way. Just keeping my head down and my mouth shut in general.

I'm the only white kid here.

I follow Caralie past the front yard and through this gate and into this long hallway that spills into a backyard also crammed with people.

There's two big grills smoking, the smell of cooked meat in the air, and rap blasting from unseen speakers. Near the grills is a fridge full of forties that reminds me of the "'G' Thang" video. There are four other metal tubs full of ice and forties and a table with potato salad and chips and salsa and beans on it.

As more and more people come up and give the girls hugs, I begin to ease into the environment a bit more. Besides a few cold stares and a few *What the fuck* expressions shot my way, I'm getting a pretty warm reception from almost everyone there. As warm as I can expect, I guess. And Caralie's right; she is running the show. Everyone likes her and knows her and is telling her how awesome it is to see her and how it's been too long.

And in a sense it's probably pretty true. I have a feeling that her relationship with James has probably strained her relationship with a lot of the people she grew up with.

We load plates with food. I have a hot dog and burger and beans, and I don't leave Caralie's side. I stand right up next to her while she talks with some friends of hers in Spanish.

After I'm done eating, I snatch a forty from one of the tubs and follow Caralie into the house, which is even louder and more crowded.

We go up a flight of stairs, me holding her hand so I don't get lost in the mix, and walk into a bedroom with like ten kids in it. All of them younger, like my age or Caralie's age.

Punk rock blasts from a stereo. A band singing in both English and Spanish.

"Who is this?" I ask Caralie.

"La Plebe," she answers. "They're from the city."

"It's really good."

"They're amazing. James really likes them a lot too."

A joint gets passed to me. I hit it and pass it along and look at all the cute girls in here. My age cute girls, even. And I take a drink and leave Caralie's side for the first time today.

I'm more comfortable in here. Another joint finds its way into my hands, and I hit it and pass it and go across the room to where these two girls are standing.

"Hey." I nod. "I'm Kaden."

They both giggle, and I blush. Look away before looking back and saying again, "I'm Kaden."

One of the girls laughs again, and her friend goes, "*Cómo está.*"

"Excuse me?"

"Cómo está," she says again.

I shake my head, and her friend laughs some more, and I go, "I'm sorry. I don't speak Spanish."

"Cómo está," the girl says again.

So I shrug and start to turn away, when she grabs my arm.

I look back at her.

"Cómo está," she says. "It means, 'Hi, how are you?'"

She lets go of me.

"So you do speak English?"

"Of course I do, mang. I was born here."

"So you were just fucking with me."

"Yup."

"What's your name?"

"Daisy."

"It's nice to meet you, Daisy."

I put a hand out, and she shakes it, and her friend says something in Spanish, which makes Daisy laugh, then walks away.

"What'd she say?" I ask.

"Nothing at all."

I hold my forty out. "Want a drink?"

"Sure." She takes the beer and takes two drinks and hands it back to me. "Thank you."

"You're welcome." I take a drink. "So how do you respond to *'Cómo está?'*"

"*Muy bien.*"

"Okay."

"*Cómo está.*"

"*Muy bien.*"

"See?" says Daisy. "I'll have you speaking this shit in no time."

I take another drink. "I'm down."

"So you know Caralie?" she asks.

"Yeah."

"How?"

"She goes out with my cousin."

"Oh," Daisy snorts. "James Morgan, the author."

"You know him?"

"Of him. He's kinda the reason Caralie don't come around much anymore."

"He won't let her?" I ask.

"I don't know. But I know her family and some of the guys here don't like him at all."

"Why?"

"'Cause he's a gringo."

Pause.

"Okay . . . ," I say.

"That's not how I think about shit," she says. "I don't care. I'm just telling you that there's a lot of old-school ways of thinking in this house."

I shrug and take a drink, and Daisy grabs the beer and drinks again.

"I figured when I saw you come in that it was something like that," she says.

"Something like what?"

"You being her man's family."

"Why?"

She smiles. "Um, look around you. You kinda stick out and shit."

"You're right."

"So you live here?"

"Nah, I'm just visiting."

"From where?"

"Dysart, Iowa."

"Iowa. What the fuck is that?"

"A state."

"I know that, silly."

"What's wrong with being from there? Have you ever been there?"

"Nope."

"So don't knock it until you have."

She gets red in the face. She's real cute, too. She has short black hair and a nose ring. She's wearing a black tank top, black jeans, and Adidas shoes.

She hits the forty again. "You're cool, Kaden."

"Thank you."

"You wanna go to the roof with me? It's got a view of the whole city."

"That'd be awesome."

"Follow me." She winks.

I trail her out of the room and down a hallway. We pass a bathroom, and there's a kid, not much older than me, probably, getting a tattoo done on his stomach by this fat old dude in a wife beater.

We move on.

Pass another room

Caralie is in it. She's talking to some guy who looks like he's in his thirties. He has a shaved head and is shirtless, wearing baggy pants. He has tattoos covering him. He has more than James does.

I stop, but Daisy grabs my arm and pulls me away.

"She used to go out with him," she tells me. "Before your cousin. But I have a sense that she's been seeing him again."

I don't say anything.

I'm just thinking, *What a self-serving scene this all seems to be.*

d. the roof with daisy

Like twenty other people are up there with us. Daisy pulls me to the edge of the roof. It's crazy. The whole city laid out in blinking neon. The Golden Gate Bridge towering over the water.

A sheet of fog is creeping in.

I turn to Daisy and say, "Thanks for bringing me up here."

"My pleasure."

"You're pretty awesome."

"I think you're pretty awesome too."

"Really?"

"Of course. Hanging out with all us *cholos* and *cholas* and holding your own. That's cool."

"All right."

"You wanna sit down?"

"Sure."

We sit on the roof's edge, and I say, "You should teach me that Spanish now."

"Okay." She takes the forty and takes another drink and goes, "*Soy malo y cabrón.*"

"What's that mean?"

"I'm a badass motherfucker."

I go, "*Soy malo y cabrón.* Is that it?"

"Yup."

"I am a badass motherfucker."

"Now try this," she says. "*Come mierda y muerte.*"

"*Come mierda y muerte.*"

"You got it."

"What'd I say?"

"Eat shit and die."

"Nice."

"Okay, now say this. *Tus pecas son lindas.*"

"*Tus pecas son lindas.*"

"Perfect. It means your freckles are cute."

"I'm glad you like 'em."

And everything is perfect up here. The way the day has turned out. Meeting Daisy and drunkenly attempting to learn another language.

I tell her about why I'm here and about Kenny and what happened to my forehead, and she seems blown away.

I even notice that she's clutching the inside of my arm, her head now resting on my shoulder.

My old life doesn't matter. Not up here with Daisy.

Caralie shows up.

She comes over to us and says, "Sorry to break this up, kids, but we have to get going."

"Why's that?"

"I have to work early tomorrow, and I'm driving and don't wanna get more fucked up than I already am."

"That's cool."

Daisy lets go of me and sits up straight.

"Well, it was really nice to meet you," I tell her.

"You too, Kaden."

I go to stand up, and she grabs me again and stops me. She puts a hand on the back of my neck and pulls me in to her and kisses me on the lips. She even slides her tongue into my mouth.

I kiss her back, and when she lets go, I'm fucking speechless.

"What?" She smiles.

"Nothing," I say, then kiss her again.

It's awesome. And I stand up after one more kiss, and Daisy says, *"Tu besas muy rico."*

"Sure," I say. "Whatever. Just take care of that body for me, girl."

She laughs and goes, "It means that you kiss good."

"Oh, cool. You do too."

e. caralie's pad II

It's just past midnight, and she puts on a record by some instrumental band that kicks ass. It's real melodic but epic.

"Who is this we're listening to?"

"This Will Destroy You. They're from Austin, Texas."

I sit on the couch, and she opens a bottle of wine and sits next to me and pours out two glasses.

"Cheers," I say.

"To what?"

"The best day ever."

"I like that."

We clank glasses, and she asks me about my mom and dad.

"What do you wanna know?"

"I don't know. I haven't heard you say a lot about them. What do you think of them?"

I hesitate and look at the floor.

"If you don't wanna talk about them, it's cool. We can talk about something else."

"No," I say. "I'm just figuring out how to answer that question in any kind of positive way."

"Oh."

"It's like I don't even think much about my dad at all. Fuck him. He's never been nice to me, and he was fucking hard on Kenny. Always making shitty remarks about how he wasn't good enough. The night Kenny told us he'd joined the Marines, we were eating steaks at the house, and my dad, he didn't even look up from the plate. He just shoved another piece of meat into his mouth and slobbered, 'Well, hopefully you won't quit that, too.' He's a prick. And he hates me."

"I'm sure he doesn't, Kaden," Caralie says.

"No, I'm sure he does. But my mom is cool. She used to do a lot of artsy-type stuff like make jewelry and design dresses for people. She used to look like a model when she was younger, but after my brother died, she just shut down. She wouldn't talk to anyone for the longest time, and when I did try to have any sort of conversation with her, it was like I was talking to a mannequin or something. There was nothing there. No emotions or expressions. She just, ya know . . . she just wasn't there. And it was so fucking hard to see her go from this outgoing social butterfly to this skeleton draped in skin. It hurt bad. It still does. But no one said shit about it the whole time."

Caralie lights a cigarette and says, "It's gotta be so fucking hard, though, dealing with losing your kid the way she did."

Pause.

"How did it happen again?"

Instant lump in my throat that I gag down. "It was just like the papers and my parents said. He got hit in the neck and bled to death."

"I mean, how do you cope with something like that?" she says. "How can you even make sense of something so senseless and brutal?"

I shrug again and swallow wine. "I don't know. But she's been getting better. Once she finished the scrapbook of Kenny's life and I came alive with this whole trip idea and started doing good in school, she started coming around. It's still not the same and won't ever be. I've already resigned myself to that. But at least she's been getting out and having real conversations with people again."

"That's good."

Caralie takes another drag off her smoke, and I ask her for one, and she gives it to me. "So what about your parents?" I ask, handing the smoke back to her.

"My parents," she sighs. "I barely ever talk to my parents anymore. Maybe twice in the last year."

"What happened?"

"Your cousin happened," she snorts.

"What about him, though?" I press.

"Right when I started seeing him, it was bad news. He was older and had a horrible reputation. And he's white. My whole family tried stopping me from seeing him. They grounded me and forbid me to talk to him. My older brothers even tracked him down one night at a bar and told him to stay away from me. They even threatened him with a gun, but he wouldn't stop. He kept calling, and I kept sneaking out, and then he finally offered to put me up here and take care of me. He told me that he couldn't let me go and that he'd never been with a girl who kept his attention like I did, so I did it. I moved here, and it seriously split me from my family. My brothers won't even talk to me."

"Can I ask you something, then?"

Caralie wipes her eyes. "Ask away."

"Has it been worth it? Not having those relationships anymore with the people who raised you and provided for you."

She squeezes her lips tight and looks at the wine in her hands and goes, "Ya know, I can't really say for sure anymore."

Silence except the music.

One, two, three minutes pass before she glances my way and says, "You wanna smoke some pot?"

"Absolutely."

She loads a bowl and then changes the music, putting on an Al Green record.

We take hits, and she kills her glass of wine, then takes a huge pull off the bottle and says, "Come dance with me."

I take her hand, my heart racing, and she pulls me to my feet.

"Put your hands here," she says, moving them to her hips. "And just sway with the beat of the music."

I do, and we get real close. She breathes in my ear, and it sends massive excitement through me.

I get hard.

She does it again.

And when the rush hits me, I put my lips on her neck. Nothing has ever made me feel like this before, not even that night with Jocelyn, and for a moment I have to pause everything because I'm scared of coming in my pants.

And when I finish holding the come back, I move my hands off her hips and run them up her sides and over her boobs.

"Whoa," she snaps, knocking my hands away. She steps back with her hands up. "This cannot happen at all."

"Why not?"

"Because you're fifteen."

"So?"

"Because I'm with your cousin."

Just hearing about James makes me snap. I say, "What does that matter at all? You don't think he cheats on you?"

She makes a disgusted face and barks, "That's absolutely none of your fucking business."

"He treats you like shit, Caralie. Like a fucking commodity. How does it feel? Getting treated like a piece of garbage."

"Shut up!" she hisses. "You are way out of line! I'm not going to fuck you, so quit being an asshole."

But I won't. I can't. I say, "And don't think I don't know about your ex that was at the party tonight. I saw you two. So spare me the 'James and I love each other' shit, because you're not supposed to hurt the people you love."

"You hurt the people you love the most, man."

"Bullshit. People really need to quit saying that shit to me."

Caralie rubs her face. "Kaden," she starts. "Cut the fucking crap. You have no idea what you're talking about, and I'm not gonna let you stand here, in my fucking apartment, and degrade my life. Who the fuck do you think you are to say what you said? You don't hurt the people you love? Don't you have a fucking girlfriend?"

My body goes numb. I put my hands over my eyes and shake my head.

And she goes, "Don't come here, to a place you've never been before, and judge the people who live here and the lifestyles they have. This ain't fucking Dysart, Iowa, little boy. And nobody out here wants to hear that shit!"

I'm a total fucking scumbag. I am. And I take a deep breath and fall to the couch and go, "Fuck!"

I go, "The one person who's been great to me since Kenny died, and all I do is piss you off and judge you. I'm fucking sorry. I don't know how to do anything right."

She rubs her forehead and goes, "Let's just kill this fucking night right now."

"You can't kill words."

"Well, let's fucking move past it, then. We had a great time, and it got stupid. It happens a lot in this city. We're wasted."

I wipe my eyes. "Okay." But I still feel like the biggest jackass in the world.

And then James walks in holding a beer. He looks at both of us and goes, "What the hell did I just miss?"

"Nothing," Caralie says. "How was the recording?"

"Awesome, baby. My tracks are great." He looks at me. "Gerry really wished you coulda been there, man."

"Well, I wasn't."

"No shit." He looks back at Caralie. "Thanks for taking him around today."

"You're welcome."

"And guess what," he says.

"What, James?"

"No coke today. I didn't do any."

She rolls her eyes and fakes a smile. "Good for you."

Looking back to me, James says, "Hey, kid. Tomorrow it's me and you." He pulls out two Giants baseball tickets. "Dodgers are in town. It's an afternoon game, so I figure we do that, then hit Ally's show. Cool?"

"I've never been to a professional game of anything before," I tell him.

"Well, see then," James snorts. "We still got time. The game, the show, the reading; you don't leave till Saturday. There's still plenty of time for more fun."

"I know," I whisper.

Caralie grabs James and says, "I'm really tired, baby. You guys staying here tonight?"

"If you want us to," he answers.

"That would be nice," she says, and they go off into the bedroom, and I make my bed on the couch and lie there, sweating, empty, listening to James fuck the shit out of her.

Wednesday, June 4th

CARALIE DROPS ME AND JAMES OFF AT THE VALENCIA
Street place around ten, then goes off to work. And even
though I know she didn't tell James what I pulled last
night, every time he glances over at me, I get more nervous and uncomfortable. On some low level I do feel like
a piece of shit for getting all creepy and weird on Caralie,
and I do feel a tiny bit bad for talking so much shit on
James the way I did. After all, he is putting me up out here
and hosting me. Plus, in all honesty I don't think the guy
really knows how to act any differently than the way he
has been. A guy like him, someone's who's been living this
type of insane life for over a decade, a guy like that just
ain't capable of putting on a straight face all the sudden
and acting like he has to give a shit. He probably does a
little bit. It just seems to me that he's so numb to the idea
of the family traces he sees in me, traces he's been trying
to disassociate himself from after he struck it awesome
out here.

But still, that ain't a total excuse for all of his asshole
behavior.

After we clean up and change clothes, James asks me if I'm hungry, and I am.

"Fuckin' starving," is what I tell him.

"Me too." He lights a cigarette. "I know this place a couple blocks down that has great breakfast burritos. We'll get some to go and eat at Dolores Park."

"I'm into that."

We leave and walk down to Sixteenth and make a right. There's a table set up on the corner with two girls handing out socialist newspapers, magazines, and letters. Two tiny old Latin women carrying bags and bags of fresh produce, an old black guy drinking a beer out of a brown sack, and two transvestites smoking cigarettes in front of a bar. One of them whistles at us as we're walking by. James looks at them, lowers his shades, nods, and goes, "Ladies." Then he slides his shades back over his eyes. "God, I love this city," he says.

We pop into this Mexican restaurant just across the alley from the bar we passed.

James throws his arms up and whistles. "Marcus! What's up, man?" He's talking to the guy standing behind the cash register.

"James," Marcus says. "It's good to see you."

"You too, man."

"Where's Caralie?" Marcus asks.

James leans against the counter. "She's working. Slanging coffee."

"On a beautiful day like this?"

"Hey, man. She's gotta earn her rent somehow." He smirks when he says that.

Marcus looks at me. "Who's your friend, James?"

"This is my cousin, Kaden. He's visiting me from Iowa."

"Iowa, huh? I don't know anyone from Iowa."

"Now you do," I say.

"So what can I get for you two?" asks Marcus.

"Two extra meaty breakfast burritos with everything and hot salsa to go."

"Got it. Ten minutes," he says.

We go outside to wait so James can smoke.

"So do you know everyone in the city?" I ask.

"No. But it fucking seems like it, huh?"

"Yeah."

"People know me. I only try and know people who are doing rad shit. That's it. I ain't got time for kids acting a fool and mouthing a part they ain't playing. I'll fuck a dumb chick for a night, but that don't mean I know her. I probably don't even know her name."

"Jesus."

"That's life, kid." He lifts his shades and rolls his neck around and then drops his shades back on. "How was the barbecue you guys were at last night?"

"It was good fun. A little intense being how I was the only white dude there. But I got over it. Talked to some cute girl on the roof and saw the whole city."

"Nice."

Pause.

"I'm gonna ask you something now, and I need you to be as honest with me as you can, okay?"

Holy shit.

I get real nervous. I can feel the color being sucked from my face.

"Okay, James." I gulp.

"When you were there . . . did you meet a dude named Luis?"

A sigh of relief. "I don't know. I don't think so."

"Shaved head. Big-time *cholo*. More tattoos than me," he says.

Shit!

The guy I saw Caralie getting fresh with when Daisy and I were going to the roof. And it's not a good situation to be in the middle of. James asking me about Caralie and Caralie asking me about James. It's awkward and lame. And my loyalties are completely with Caralie.

I shrug. "Shit, man. I don't think so. There were a lot of dudes with tattoos and short hair, man."

"Are you sure, Kaden?" he presses, taking his shades off and rubbing his face.

He looks real concerned, and I almost feel sorry for the guy, until that Michelle girl pops back into my head.

And I say, "I don't think I met him."

"Did you see her talking to anyone who looked like that?"

"I don't think so."

"Are you positive?"

"Yeah."

"Okay."

He puts his sunglasses back on and takes a deep drag of his smoke.

"What does it matter who she was talking to, anyway?" I ask.

"'Cause she used to go out with that Luis dude. And I think she started fucking him again."

"Why do you think that?"

"Just a feeling in my gut, man. I know she's been calling him."

"How?"

He looks at me, smoke driving from his nostrils. "Who do you think pays her phone bill?"

I don't say anything, and he drops his cig on the ground and steps on it.

Someone yells his name.

It comes from across the street. Some girl with black hair walking with her friend, wearing black pants and a white and red striped shirt and Nike Cortez.

She yells, "You small-dicked impotent fuck! You couldn't even get it up, bitch!"

James shakes his head and starts laughing. The girl who yelled high-fives her friend, and then James's face goes straight, and he lunges onto the street and screams, "You're a real fucking cunt, Emily! I didn't wanna fuck you. You're miserable and your cunt smells and you need to take that metal shit out of your face!"

"Whatever, bitch!" the girl yells back, flipping him off.

James jumps back on the sidewalk. "I bet our food's ready now," he says.

And that's it. I don't even press him on it. I follow him back in to pick up the food, which is on the house, and then I follow him to a liquor store on the corner of Sixteenth and he buys a six-pack of Pacifico beer. Then we hit the park.

a. dolores park II

It's not nearly as crowded as it was when I was there with Caralie. We sit at a table next to the playground. James doesn't waste any time. He's on his second beer before I even take a bite of my burrito. I've never seen anyone drink like him. I always thought Kenny was a big drinker until hanging with James. After what I've seen so far, the word "boozer" has taken on a whole different meaning.

He finishes the second beer and opens a third one, and I go, "My mom told me you liked to get fucked up, but shit, you drink all day, every day."

"Your mom's really one to talk," he snorts.

"What do you mean?"

"She loves her fucking booze too."

"Not really. Only after Kenny died. But she's cut back a lot in the last couple months."

"Trust me," James says, picking his burrito up for the first time. "She loves the sauce."

"Bullshit."

"I'm serious."

"I am too," I snap. "Before my brother died, she rarely touched the shit, other than a glass of wine at a dinner party every once in a while."

James takes a pull of beer, almost half of it, and says, "Well, I guess that's how you know her. But trust me, man, the Katherine I know loves to get down." Another pull. "Big time."

I'm getting real irritated with him. How the fuck does he know anything about my mom? It's fucking stupid to hear him talk about her. He has no idea what she's been up to. Not with the way he cut our family off years ago.

Dropping my plastic fork, I snap, "My mom is a fucking housewife who stays in most nights with my boring dad, and sometimes she teaches an occasional workshop at the community center in town."

James takes his shades off and sets them on the table. "How much do you really know about your mom's past?" he asks.

"Not a lot, I guess. What's there to know?"

"She was a wild child, man. A little hell-raiser."

"I don't believe it."

"How the fuck do you think she got knocked up with Kenny, dude? It's not like her and that d-bag dad of yours were dating for a long time and decided to get married and have a kid. Your pops was living in Chicago when they met. He was working as a legal rep for Monaco."

"What's that?"

"One of those bioengineering food companies." James finishes his beer and picks at his burrito. "A mutual friend introduced them, and they hooked up, but it wasn't like they were dating. He was her booty call. He was infatuated with her, but all she wanted was to fuck every once in a while when she was wasted. So they hung out like that maybe four times, and she got knocked up."

I feel weird listening to him talk about my parents hooking up, but I wanna know more. I ask, "How do you know this stuff?"

"I've kicked it with your mom before. She came out here with some friends a year after she had you. We drank a lot and talked a lot. I also got smashed with her at a couple of family reunions when I was in high school."

This whole thing is taking me aback. For as long as I've known, my mom has been this community-oriented, social-networker housewife of a lady. That's all. Not some boozer or a wild child or anything else for that matter.

Just my dad's trophy woman.

And I go, "So she got pregnant first, and then they got married. Is that it?"

"Yep," James says, chewing a bite of burrito.

I shake my head. I'm not really that hungry anymore.

I say, "I don't get it, then. If she was so wild and crazy, and if she didn't love my dad, you'd think she would've had an abortion or at least raised Kenny by herself. Not settle down and get married."

James opens his fourth beer and says, "This is how I know you don't know her that well, man. Your dad was in total awe of her. She was a stone fox."

"I know that. I've seen pictures. But that still don't explain why she did what she did."

"She got married because her parents forced her to."

"How? It was the eighties, for chrissakes."

"Because they were total religious freaks, man. Devout Catholic militants and shit, in the biggest and scariest way."

"What does that matter? You can't force someone to get married."

James looks at me hard and squints; then he rubs the bottom of his chin and goes, "You don't know, do you?"

"Know what?" I ask.

"That your mom was adopted."

"What?"

"You don't! Holy shit. You have no idea."

"No, dude. I don't."

"Your mom spent the first twelve years of her life in and out of foster homes before Grandma and Grandpa took her in. And they were rich. They sent her to the top private schools in Chicago and paid for her college until she got pregnant. And what happened was that your dad, knowing the kind of pressure it would put on your mom, went behind her back and told Grandma and Grandpa that she was pregnant and that he was going to propose to her, and they forced her, through the guilt of God, to say yes to him, and she did."

"Why?"

"Because she felt like she had to. They'd given her the world up to that point, man. So they did the service before Kenny was born, and then your dad's dad got sick, so they moved to Iowa to take over the farm for him."

I am stunned. Like, *What the fuck?* James isn't even my blood. Nor are my grandparents on my mom's side.

I rub my face, and James hands me a beer, and I pound it, watching the cars driving down Guerrero.

After I finish my beer, I smoke one of his cigarettes and go, "Why didn't anyone ever tell me this?"

James exhales some smoke and says, "Well, how the hell do you go about telling your kids that they were a huge fucking mistake?"

b. the baseball game

We take a cab to the stadium, Pac Bell Park, and it's the biggest place I've ever been in. Our seats are right along the third-base line, right next to the Dodgers' bull pen. James buys beers for us, and we settle in.

Baseball babes everywhere.

These three black girls in short shorts and shredded

Giants shirts are just a few seats away from us being loud and drunk and hilarious.

And James loves it. He keeps talking to one of them, and by the third inning he's putting her digits into his phone.

Me, I'm just sitting there getting trashed. The game is still scoreless in the fourth inning, and both teams have only one hit, and I'm bored. And I'm still rattled by all the shit James told me at Dolores Park.

I'm not his real cousin or my grandparents' real grandson, and no one has ever said a fucking thing about it to me or even to Kenny. My stupid family to the exact tee, keeping all the shit hidden in the deep dark.

James goes out for a smoke between the fourth and fifth innings, and when he comes back, he's got two more beers for us.

Handing me one, he sits back down and takes a drink and looks over at me.

"You look bored," he comments.

"It's a boring game, man. Baseball in general is pretty boring to me."

"You never played?"

"Nah. I've never really played any sports."

"Wasn't your brother like some huge-time athlete?"

"He was. Won a ton of awards in high school."

James gulps some beer, some of it spilling out of his mouth and down his chin. He wipes it off and says, "How did he end up in the military? I remember hearing at one point that he had a football scholarship."

"He did."

"Where to?"

"UNI."

"What happened?"

"It didn't work out for him there. He got on some of the coaches' bad sides and rode the bench and actually got out of shape. Then he got declared academically ineligible and ended up dropping out of school because he didn't wanna sit out a semester. After that he moved back home, and my dad never let him forget about it. He was always making these dickheaded comments to him about how he wasn't tough enough or good enough and not trying hard enough. He even called him a quitter once, and Kenny got so upset about it that he started crying and doing crunches in the basement outside of my room. Then he joined the Marines right outta the blue."

"Jesus Christ," James snaps. "What a fucking prick your dad is."

"I know. But the thing is, my dad was always talking about how much he regretted not being able to serve in Vietnam because of a bad knee that kept him out."

"That's what he told you guys?"

"All the time."

James shakes his head and clenches his jaw. "Man," he goes. "That ain't what happened. Your dad got out of serving because his dad was a close friend to a congressman who was able to get the paperwork lined up to make it look like he had a boil on his ass and wasn't fit to serve. Just like that fat piece of shit Rush Limbaugh."

"Are you fucking serious?" I snort.

"Totally serious. Your mom told me when she was out here once. She said that he did volunteer, but then Nixon announced a huge offensive a couple of weeks after he did, and like that your dad had a boil and was declared unfit to serve."

The blood drains from my face again. I say, "Kenny never knew any of that."

"No shit he didn't."

"That fucking asshole," I snap. "Why would he lie about something like that?"

"I don't know."

"There's gotta be a reason, James."

He shrugs. "Probably he did that because he thought you guys would respect him more. It's what fathers do, man. They lie to their boys about shit like war and heroism because they wanna look more masculine, as if killing a motherfucker in some third-world shithole is an accurate description of masculinity."

"Oh my God!" I'm furious. I say, "My brother joined the service because of my dad telling him shit like that. He's dead because of my dad."

"Your dad sucks."

"And so does my mom."

"Don't say that, Kaden."

"She does too. She knew all about that shit and kept quiet, and that makes her as bad as him. What the hell is wrong with her?"

"Nothing is."

"Bullshit! She married that asshole because she was *forced* to, even though she didn't want to, and then she goes along all these years with his stupid lies and crap. You suck when you do that. That means she's just as bad as him."

"But she's not," James snaps back. "You have to understand where she's coming from. And even more, what she came from. When you're treated like the piss and shit of the world for the first twelve years of your life and then get swept up by people with resources and wealth, you tend not to bite the hands that have literally been feeding you."

"That's so fucking weak."

James slams the rest of his beer and goes, "That's life, man. Ya know, it's real easy to sit here in this stadium, having never been in a foster home, having never been homeless and worrying if you might eat that day. It's real easy to sit here and judge the decisions made by somebody else who never wants to live like that again. You can do that, Kaden. It's real fucking easy. But let me tell you something."

"What?"

"If you do, if you hold your mom to the same standards

of someone who came from a nuclear and typical family and
was provided the world from day one, then you become just
as bad as the people who forced those impossible situations
on her and left her with no good choices at all."

He looks back to the field.

He says, "Your mom is an exceptional woman."

We leave the next inning, and the game is still zero to
zero.

c. an errand in the ghetto

James is so wasted. He's stumbling out of the stadium, curs-
ing at people and making phone calls. We hail two cabs but
don't take either of them, because the drivers won't let him
smoke inside the car.

I'm drained and angry and stunned still. Fuck my parents, the blood of my dead brother all over their hands.

The third cab that stops lets James smoke, and James
tells the driver to go to Fillmore and Eddy.

"A drug deal," I snort.

"You know me so well, man."

We end up driving by the park I got roughed up in, and
as we're cruising past it, I run my fingers over the lump, and
James taps me in the arm with his fist and says, "Tyson."

I ask him for a smoke.

"Stressed out a little," he says.

"What do you think, man?"

But he doesn't answer. He just hands me a cigarette and

his lighter and then looks out his window and tosses his smoke from it.

The place we stop at is this basement apartment with small bars on the only small window next to the door. James and I are the only two white kids around. He knocks on the door, and I look over my shoulder. Behind us are a group of eight straight-up thugs just grilling me and James from across the street.

But James doesn't seem to think anything of it, and even I'm not nervous about being here. There are just too many other things going on that I'm preoccupied with.

James knocks again, and this time the door opens, and this nerdy-looking black guy is standing there in a blue polo shirt and baggy khaki shorts and black-rimmed glasses. He has two lines shaved into each side of his head.

"My man," James says, giving the guy a hug.

"It's good to see you," the guy shoots back. "It's been too long."

"Like three weeks and shit."

"Like I said. Too long." He looks at me. "Who the hell is this powdered-up kid?"

"This is my cousin, man. He's visiting from Iowa."

"What's up, kid? I'm Damien."

"Kaden," I say.

He shakes my hand and tells us to come inside. And at first his pad reminds me a little bit of the Whip Pad. It has a long and narrow hallway with a low ceiling and shitty lighting. It's real smoky inside too. But that's where the similarities end.

There are no other doors going down the hallway until the very end. One on the right and one on the left. Black power posters and portraits of black liberation leaders cover every inch of the walls.

And the place smells really funny in a really bad way. It smells like burning rubber and melting trash.

Loud seventies R&B music blares from the room on the right. The room we follow Damien into. The craziest fucking room in the world. It's off the fucking wall.

A big round table in the middle of the room, and every inch of it is covered with semiautomatic guns, bricks of cocaine, and pills. A bottle of tequila and a shot glass sit in the center of the table, and just as it is in the hallway, the walls of the room are covered with black power and black liberation art. Sitting side by side next to the table are two caches of more guns, and there's a giant aquarium full of tropical fish.

It's more than a little nerve-racking to be in the room, ya know, with all the drugs and guns just lying there in the open.

James nudges me as we cross the room and goes, "Pretty wild, huh?"

"I'll fucking say, man."

And I'm thinking, *What is James Morgan even doing in a place like this? In the ghetto with weapons and a drug-dealing black power enthusiast.*

And that's when the obvious hits me in the face.

Like, *Duh, Kaden.*

Like, *The guy's a cocaine addict, so it doesn't matter who he's with, as long as they have what he's in search of . . . the white monster.*

We follow Damien to the table, and he picks up these three Polaroids sitting there and hands them to James.

"Holy shit," James says. "That's Gil Scott-Heron."

"That's Gil Scott-Heron sitting in my apartment an hour ago, dude."

"No way."

"Yeah, man. He called me this morning and told me he was in town and wanted me to cook up some rock for him."

And that's what the smell is. Crack.

And James says, "Fucking rad, dude. I love that guy."

"Who's Gil Scott-Heron?" I ask.

"A soul and R&B singer from the sixties and seventies," James answers. "He was the guy who did 'The Revolution Will Not Be Televised.'"

"I know that song."

"You better," Damien quips. "You motherfucking better, man."

We sit down at the table, all these pounds of coke and these weapons just inches from my face. If only my mom, hell, anyone from Iowa, knew what I was doing at that exact moment, I wonder if they'd even believe it with their own eyes.

Damien picks up the tequila and shot glass and pours

himself a drink and slams it, then passes it to James, who does the same, and so do I.

And James says, "I was in Santa Cruz a few years back for this music festival, and I was waiting in line for a beer, when this gnarly dude who reeked like piss came up and asked me for money. I told him to scram and didn't think anything of it, until like two hours later I see the same guy on stage singing. It was Gil Scott-Heron, and he was fucking killing it!"

"That's my nigga," Damien snorts, then picks up a pipe and smokes it. And it's crack, I figure, because it smells just like the rest of the place does.

James does another shot of tequila and goes, "So let's get down to business. You say you got the killer shit right now."

"You bet your ass I do. The stuff I got right now is hands down the best shit in the city right now. It's melt your face off type of shit. Stuff ain't stepped on at all, man. It melted down at ninety-six degrees."

James's jaw drops. "No shit. I love the sound of that."

"Here," says Damien. He scoops out two big spoonfuls of the blast from an open bag and dumps them on a mirror, then slides the mirror and a straw in front of James. "Try it and see for yourself, man."

James picks up a razor blade off the table and starts chopping the pile up. He makes it real smooth, not a single chunk, and then he makes two lines and does them both.

"Whoooooo!" he yells. "Damn. Shit. That fucking went down. Fuck! Whooooo! I'm dripping already." He shakes a fist in the air. "Yes! Yes! Yes, Damien! Whoooo!"

"I told you so."

"Face-numbing shit."

"It is, dude. But be careful with it. It's heart attack Jack, know what I mean? Not too much at once now."

James looks over at me. "Try some," he says.

"No way."

"Come on," James goes. "Just do a little."

"No."

"Please?"

"No."

Damien takes another hit from his pipe and starts getting real fidgety.

"Just a little bit of a line," James presses.

"I don't want it."

"Whoa, whoa, whoa!" Damien interjects, his eyes huge, his hands in the air. He looks at James. "Your boy cool, motherfucker?"

"He's my cousin."

"I didn't fucking ask you that," Damien snaps in a real freaky type of tone that sends a chill up my spine. "I asked you if he was cool, asshole."

"I just don't want any, Damien."

"Are you fucking cool, man?"

"Yeah. Relax."

"Fuck relaxing!"

"Just do a little," James presses, a slight quiver in his voice.

The pressure is on. I rub my face and say, "Fine," and Damien starts to calm down a little.

James makes another line, and I take it, and it fucking hits me like a motherfucker.

Deep breath after deep breath after deep breath I'm taking. My heart feels crazy, and my sweat is coming off hard.

Damien starts laughing. "Your boy's fucked, dude. Look at him; he's fucked."

"You okay?" James asks, while doing another line.

I'm nauseous. "I'm cool," I say. "Totally fine." My heart is hitting so hard it hurts. "Just gotta take a shit."

But it's not cool. I have to puke.

"Where's the bathroom?" I ask.

Damien points at the door we came in through. "Just across the hallway, kid. Through the kitchen and shit."

"Thanks."

I fly in there and look in the mirror. My face is white and wet, and I'm breathing tough, trying to hold off the puke, but I can't. A second later I'm hunched over the toilet barfing, the whole day pouring out of me, three times over, until there's nothing left and I'm done.

Wiping my mouth, I walk to the sink and wash my mouth out with water and then go back into the room, still high but feeling much better.

James and Damien are looking at these maps when I sit back down. Actually, Damien is showing them to James. They're floor plans of banks in the city, and even James looks slightly uncomfortable as Damien flips through an entire stack of them, every layout of every major bank in this guy's hands.

It freaks me out pretty good. I don't wanna get caught up in anything gnarly. Robbing banks and being an accessory and doing a stint in Folsom. Fuck that. But I play it cool. Every time Damien looks over at me with those scary eyes, I tell myself to be chill, and there's only one way to do that.

I grab the tequila and pound a big swig from the bottle and ask James for a cigarette.

"Now that's more like it," James says. He looks back at Damien. "See, I'm teaching him the way."

"Maybe you are."

The floor plans eventually get put away, and Damien doesn't say exactly what they're for, but I've got some pretty good ideas.

We each take another shot of tequila.

And I'm blitzed and stare at Damien as he dumps probably a gram's worth of coke into one of his hands and swallows it, then chases it with tequila.

"Just like they do it in Mexico," he snorts.

"You're a fucking savage," James tells him.

Damien smacks James in the back. "Things are changing," he says. "My perspective and vision is turning. Most of these fools who dabble in the distribution business, they wanna stay under the radar and be anonymous. But not me."

"Not you," says James.

"Nope. It's like with me, I wanna expand and shit. With me, I want the Bank of America to know that I'm fucking alive."

James bursts into laughter, and Damien takes another hit from his pipe.

"Shit, man," James gasps, wiping his face. "On that note I'll take two balls."

"Two fifty," says Damien.

James hands him the money and starts in about the show tonight, and I reach out and touch one of the guns

Damien jumps in the air, and he pulls a fucking gun from his waist, points it at me, and cocks it.

"Fuck!" I scream, and fly back in my chair.

"Don't shoot him!" James yells.

"What are you doing, man?" Damien snaps.

"Nothing," I blurt.

"Damien," James says. "Don't shoot my cousin. Fuck! Just be calm!"

"He touched a gun, author scumbag!" His bottom lip twitches. "Why did you touch a gun?"

"I don't know!"

"Why did you do that?"

"I don't know," I say again.

"Just tell him why you did it, Kaden," James screeches.

"Because I've never touched a gun before," I say.

"You're making me nervous," Damien snaps.

"You're making me nervous too," I say.

"Just put the gun down, Damien," James pleads. "You can't shoot him."

Damien winces and rubs his face on the top of his arm.

"You make me fucking nervous," he says again. A single tear runs from his right eye. "I don't like to be nervous."

"Okay," I plead. "I'm sorry. I didn't mean anything by that."

"See," James says. "He's sorry."

"Are you really?" Damien asks.

"Completely," I say.

"Don't shoot him," James says.

Damien takes a deep breath and puts the gun down. "I don't like to be nervous," he says, another tear falling from his eye.

"I know you don't," says James. He looks at me. "And now you do too, right?"

"I do."

Damien sits back down, and James does another line, then hands Damien the money and calls a cab.

Twenty minutes later we're on our way to the Whip Pad, and I'm thinking, *Really? Are you fucking kidding me with that shit?*

d. the whip pad III

James and I sit in his smoky room, and he plays me bands he
loves, who I've never heard before.

400 Blows.

Mouth of the Architect.

Times New Viking.

The Heartless Bastards.

Big Business.

Replicator.

The Altarboys.

XO Skeletons.

Get Dead!

He's still partying tough as fuck, but I need to take a
break. I'm exhausted from the day and from the sun and the
family shit and that Damien dude.

He asks what's wrong when I refuse his offers of beer
and more coke.

"I need to rest."

"Why? Party's just starting," he says.

"No, it ain't, man. I need to relax for a little bit. I just had
a loaded gun pointed at my chest by some dude who's been
up for days smoking crack."

James lights a cigarette and says, "That was nothing,
man. When I was nineteen, I lived in Chicago for a minute,
and one night I was over at my homey Raja's pad, drinking
it up with some kids, and these three fucking gangbangers
busted into the house holding motherfucking Uzis. They

were looking for some cat named Dante, but there was no Dante that we knew around, but they didn't believe us, so they fucking decided to kidnap me."

"What?"

"Yeah, man. They fucking grabbed me by the neck and dragged me outside and threw me in the trunk of their car after telling everyone in the house that they'd let me go once they talked to Dante."

"So what'd they do with you?"

"Not much. Drove around for a few hours. I could hear their rap music and smell the blunts they were smoking."

"Were you scared?"

"Fuck, yeah."

"What happened?"

"They finally figured out they'd gone to the wrong house, so when they realized it, they took me out of the trunk and bought me pizza and beer at a Godfather's, and we kicked it for a while, and they took me back to Raja's."

"My God, dude. You've done it all."

"Not quite, man. I still haven't slayed Lindsay Lohan's meat pit or drank wine with the dudes from TV on the Radio."

"Right."

I yawn and stretch my arms. It's five, and I lie down on his bed and close my eyes, listening to James play a record by this Will Oldham guy, and then I'm gone. Fast asleep.

e. my dream II

I dream of my brother again. In the dream, him and I are sitting on the edge of a cliff, and there is nothing in front of us. The edge of the world. And our legs are dangling over the sides, and we're sharing a jar of peanut butter. We aren't saying nothing for the longest time. Just passing the peanut butter back and forth, the wind howling, the sky dark and endless. I start coughing in the dream, and Kenny puts an arm around me and tells me not to worry.

"I'm gonna come back," he says.

"From what?"

"Everything. I'm gonna come back and do everything differently."

When I wake up, I hear James and Caralie, and Caralie is telling him how she wants to start her own fashion line, making and selling the clothes herself and putting on shows.

"That's a great idea, baby," he says.

"You really think so?"

"I do. You'd be so great at that."

"I think I would be too."

"And you know I have your back, baby. If that's what you really want to do, then I'll support you a thousand percent. Whatever you need."

"I know you will."

"I'll sink my last dime into making you happy, baby."

"I love you, James Morgan."

"I fucking love you so much, Caralie Chavez."

I close my eyes again and drift back to sleep.

When I wake up again, James is shaking me. I sit up. "Hey, man," he says. "We're leaving for the show soon. You need to clean up?"

"Yeah."

I wash my face and take a shit.

Back in James's room both him and Caralie are drinking beers and still doing coke. I haven't seen Caralie snort the monster yet. For a second I was thinking that maybe she didn't do it, but the notion is dismissed with a quickness as I watch her slam three monster rails.

James hands me a beer, and I open it, and he goes, "You wanna hear one of the tracks me and Gerry laid down yesterday with Nick Andre?"

"For sure, man. Omar Getty stuff, right?"

"Omar Getty and Murray Jitters," he says.

"That's your emcee name?" I ask.

"Yup."

I notice Caralie roll her eyes, but I say, "Fuckin' tight, man."

James looks at Caralie. "See, baby," he snorts. "It's a damn good name."

"No, it ain't, James."

"It is too." He looks at me. "Tell her, Kaden."

"It's not bad, Caralie."

"It's horrible," she says, shaking her head.

"Whatever, babe," James snaps, and I sit down next to Caralie on the couch, and she puts an arm around my shoulders, and James starts the track on the computer.

"The song's called 'You're Just a Ho.' I do the second verse."

There's an intro with real slow and classy music playing and Gerry saying, "*This song right here, this song is dedicated to all the girls who made it possible. This song goes out to all you Mission trolls, all you Delirium rats, just lurking tough and thinking you're all hard 'cause you fucked like half the dudes at the bar. . . . Hey, it's cool; there's just something I need to tell you all. . . .*"

There's a record scratch, and then the beat starts bumping. It's a sick beat. Like some east-coast alternative, Def Jux–style beat.

And then Gerry comes back with the first verse.

"*I see you coming like a mile away, strutting with your girls, thinking about your play. You got a twinkle in your eye and a bounce to your step; you think that you're a playa and you think you have that rep, but the rep that you have isn't that of a playa, it's the rep of a slut smoking cocks and gettin' slayered. You and your crew think you're hunting for some dick, talking tough, playing rough, like a dude with some boobs, but here's a little something I think you outta know: At the end of the night you're still just a ho.*"

Second verse with James:

"*All right, stop. . . . I know what you're thinkin': You got to the bar and you caught some dude peakin', you walked up to him and you bought him a drink, and you told him to his face he had the dopest ink, you told him you were horny and you told him he was cute, you told him you were single and you told him you had loot, you played your little game and he played right along; then you smacked his ass and you thought of this song. You thought how it was bullshit, how the lyrics were all wrong, but you're the one TAKING dick, the point of this song. And here's a little something I think you outta know: When that dude leaves in the morning, all you is is just a ho."*

There's a chorus of Gerry and James singing "ho" a bunch, and then it comes back to Gerry for verse three:

"You find all your friends and you gab away, talking shit like a fool 'cause you about to get some play. Never mind the way the dude's already forgot your fucking name, doesn't matter, you're the shit, sippin' forties, spittin' game, so you'll take a cab and take his hand and lead him to your room: a box of condoms, scented candles, you've been planning this since noon. But here's the thing you don't get every time you do your thang: On your knees, on your back, choked out, YOU'RE getting banged. So here's a little something I think you outta know: You never had the power, and you're just a fucking ho."

Another chorus of hos, and the song ends.

"Nice," I say, smiling. "That's pretty dope, dude."

"Ain't it. Fuckin' Nick's pounding out an even tighter version right now for us. Dude's the shit producer."

"What's his label?" I ask.

"Slept On Records."

I look at Caralie. "What'd you think?"

"Remember what I told you at the beach yesterday . . . about hos?"

I nod.

"Then you already know what I think, dude."

I take a gulp of beer.

"So how did you like the baseball game?" Caralie asks.

"It was boring," I answer. "So we left early, and that's when all the crazy shit went down."

James shoots me a look of panic, and Caralie goes, "What happened?"

James is shaking his head, and I'm saying, "We went to some dude named Damien's crib, and he pulled a gun on me."

Caralie whips a look to James, her eyes big, her mouth wide open, and she goes, "James Reuben Morgan."

"What?" he snaps.

"You took him to that gnarly tweaker's crib. What were you thinking?"

"It's fine. Nothing bad happened."

"He got a gun pulled on him! You should've known better than to take him there. That guy tried to kill me once."

"Oh, no, he didn't. He was just kidding around. Just like today, he was just having some fun."

"No, he wasn't," I snort.

"Goddamn it, James," she says. "What the hell?"

James stares at me, shaking his head, and no one says anything for a minute until I go, "So Reuben is your middle name?"

Caralie starts laughing.

"Yeah. And what about it?" James asks.

"Nothing," I say to him. "Nothing at all, fuckin' Reuben."

He flips me off, and I start laughing.

f. bottom of the hill

It's this hole-in-the wall dive way out in what James says is
the Potrero Hill part of the city. He also says it's one of the
best places to see a show in the city, and that if a band wants
to make it in San Francisco, they have to play and draw well
at Bottom of the Hill first.

"What other places are good to see shows in the city?" I
ask him in the cab on the way there.

"The Hemlock is rad. That's probably my favorite.
Annie's Social Club is pretty okay. Lots of punk shit there.
El Rio and the Elbo Room are tight. The Independent is cool
too. Great American Music Hall. 12 Galaxies was the shit
before it closed."

"You go to a lot of shows?" I ask.

"All the time, man. Sometimes it seems like it's the only
thing worth going out for these days."

It's nine, and the bar is packed full. The show is sold out.
But the three of us are on Ally's list, so it's no problem getting in. Although James does tell me, "Even if we weren't on
the fucking list, which I always am, but even if we weren't,
I'm James fucking Morgan and I can get whoever I want into
any show I want."

"Cool, man," I say. "You should clean off your nose. There's coke all over it."

"Good," James says. "I'm surprised you even think I give a fuck about that."

"I was just saying."

"I don't give a shit."

"Okay."

And like two seconds later I look over my shoulder, and he's wiping his nose with his shirt.

It's a steam box inside of here. And I'm filled to my head with excitement and anticipation. Adrenaline surges through my veins. I've never felt this much energy in one place before, not even at the ballpark. Well, except maybe at Damien's. But that was a different kind of energy. A much more disturbing and homicidal kind of energy.

I follow Caralie, who once again has attached herself to James's hip, toward the bar, sliding as gracefully as I can through this thousand-pound mass of beards and tattoos and stockings and high heels.

When we get there, I wedge myself in between James and this incredibly hot girl in a Dead Kennedys wife beater with a black she-mullet.

"What are you drinking?" James asks me, not even looking at me but over my head and at the girl in the beater, who's smiling at him.

"Whatever you're having, man."

"Got it."

James orders two PBRs, two shots of whiskey, and a vodka tonic with a lime for Caralie.

He holds his whiskey up. "Toast me, man."

I clank my glass against his and say, "What are we toasting to?"

"This Kentucky Brown, Chuck Palahniuk, and your brother."

"Cheers to all that," I tell him.

We down the shots and turn from the bar, and I look to the stage. That girl Bailey Brown is walking around it with the rest of her band.

She looks incredible, too. She's wearing a tiger-print tank top, extra-small-looking brown shorts with thin white stripes on the sides of them, a huge gold chain with a cross on it, and a pair of white knee-high snake boots.

As the three of us move in closer toward the stage, Bailey looks out in the crowd and waves at James, and I watch Caralie tense up real bad. I see her shoulders tighten and her back stiffen and her muscles freeze.

For his part James notices it too. He leans over and kisses her cheek, whispering something into her ear that makes her laugh. Then he kisses her again, and she loosens right back up, like she never even saw James and Bailey acknowledging each other.

I gaze through the crowd and notice those two Bacon girls standing all by themselves in the far corner by the merch tables, holding drinks. And that Omar Getty song pops into my head like that. . . .

You're just a ho . . .

James seems to know everyone again. All sortsa kids come up to him and Caralie, chatting and shaking his hand, trying to embrace him in any way they can.

Once more it feels nice to be part of the James Morgan posse.

Bailey straps on her blue guitar, which has a My Little Pony painted on it and a pink fuzzy strap. She strokes a couple of chords and checks into the mic a couple of times. Then she starts tuning some more, while a massive crowd begins to trickle inside from the smoking area out back.

It's shoulder to shoulder kids in no time, and I trail James and Caralie around a wall of backs and over to the right side of the stage, where we plant ourselves less than a foot from it and the band.

It's like nothing I've felt before. One more brand-new experience to chalk up.

Baseball game.

Crack basement.

Loaded gun pointed at my face.

Metal show.

And that's just nine hours of a day.

Awesome.

Bailey wraps her hand around the mic and says, "How y'all doing tonight?"

Three hundred drunk people roar back.

"Awesome," she says. "We're Bloody Flowers from right here in San Francisco, and this first song is called 'Bad Bitch.'"

She glances at the rest of her band, and the drummer counts off, and they fly into a song.

They sound great.

I mean, I don't know a lot about anything other than hip-hop, but they got this whole heavy-as-fuck metal punk-rock chorus thing going on. I can't put it into context that well, because I don't have enough of a music background to know what context to fit it in. Except Complete Awesomeness.

It's definitely that.

They play seven killer songs, and halfway through the third one a decent-size pit breaks out that even James jumps into. And at the end of the set I find the set list, which reads:

Bad Bitch

Pussy Reaper

The Way I See It—Part 1

Your Cum Is Brown

Pissed My Pants

Gross Dude

Broken Condom Solution

Which has a chorus that goes:

"You knew it fucking broke before you even finished, so don't take it like a joke when I make you fucking fix this!"

I'm soaking in my sweat and the sweat of a hundred people, and James goes, "How did you like that?"

"That was badass, man! I'm glad we're here!"

"See," he says. "We're just getting started, kid." He puts an arm around my shoulders and pulls me and Caralie out back.

We ascend up a flight of stairs and into this room with about twenty people inside, including Gerry, Ryan, and Reed.

And Gerry practically tackles me. "Dude," he snorts. "Fighting three-on-one in the park and shit. You're nuts, junior."

"I had to."

"Look at your forehead, man." He turns to Ryan. "You see this shit?"

Ryan looks at me and holds up the rock horns. "You got some fucking stones between those legs. I heard about your adventure. Destroy!"

I put my hand out and he smacks it. "Destroy, man," I say back, and ask him for a cigarette.

He hands me one.

"Why the hell you leave the gym like that?" Gerry asks.

"'Cause I'm in San Francisco, Gerry. What the fuck do I wanna be doing in a gym on vacation?"

"You shoulda told me you were bailing. I kinda freaked out when I couldn't find you. I mean, I can't be responsible for that shit, like you dying out here."

"I didn't die, man."

"I know. You just got busted the fuck up."

"Shit, who cares now? It's like *Fight Club*. You don't wanna die without any scars."

"That shit ain't real life," Ryan chimes in. "It's a fucking book."

I look at him. "It's real life to me, man."

Ryan makes a face. "Okay, dude," he snorts, then walks away.

I look back to Gerry. "I heard the rough mix of the ho song earlier."

"What'd you think?"

"It's sick. So fucking hilarious."

"Your cousin can rap, huh?"

"He was great. For someone who talks so much shit about it, he's pretty okay doing it."

"He talks shit just to hear himself talk."

"That's basically what Caralie says too."

"She should know," Gerry says. "She knows him the best. I actually feel sorry for that girl sometimes. Having to deal with all that ranting and raving all the time."

"No shit." I'm grinning.

"You feel me?"

"Oh, yeah. And I've only been here for a few days."

James comes over and hands me a Budweiser bottle and says, "Hey, I wanna introduce you to some people."

"All right."

I follow him across the room to where these two guys are standing against the wall, and James goes, "This is Rodney and Michael from Lamborghini Dreams."

"What's up, guys," I say, opening my beer.

"This is my cousin, Kaden," James continues. "He's visiting me from Iowa."

"Iowa, huh," says Michael, who's wearing a black T-shirt, an N.W.A. baseball hat, white jeans with a bandanna sticking out of a back pocket, and a pair of black cowboy boots. "We're from right around there."

"I know that," I say.

I look at Rodney, who is covered in tattoos and is wearing a 400 Blows T-shirt, cut-off jean shorts, black Nikes, and a pair of black-rimmed glasses.

"Hey, man," I say.

"What's up, kid? How you doing?"

"I'm all right," I say. "Had a gun pulled on me a couple of hours ago."

And James snorts, "Hey, man." He smacks me in the back. "Just chill out with that shit."

"It was a fucking gun," I say.

"Ha," says Michael. "He ain't going back to Iowa the same kid, is he, James?"

"He's fine."

Michael looks at me. "Your cousin's a crazy motherfucker. He showed up in Vegas with us last year, and we played a show, and the next morning before we drop him off at the airport, he slams two strawberry milks and eats a Popsicle to cure his hangover. Then we drop him off. Twenty minutes later I get a call from him saying that he's in trouble. Apparently, he gets in line and can't find the e-ticket he booked, and while he's trying to figure it out, he pukes on the floor. So he walks over and sits down, and someone from the airline asks if he needs help, so he tells them what's going on, and they go to look up his ticket. When they come back, they're like I got good news and bad news for you, and he says just hit me with it, and the airline person says the good news is that you did book a ticket leaving Las Vegas, but the bad news is that the ticket was for the day you actually booked it, a whole week before. So he has to buy another ticket, and when he's in line again to check in, he pukes on the luggage of these old people behind him and then runs to the bathroom and throws up for a few minutes. When he's walking back out, he's greeted by an airport security official and an official from the Department of Homeland Security. They take him into a room and start interrogating him, because when he ran off, he left all his bags unattended. After a few minutes of questioning he stops them and says, 'Hey, here's the deal. I'm from Illinois and live in San Francisco, so you can either send me back to Illinois, to San Francisco, or put me in jail, but I am not going back out to the Strip.' They ended up releasing him, and four hours later he got a flight to Oakland. Fucking hilarious."

I look over at James and go, "What the hell is wrong with you?"

James shrugs and starts shaking his head. "I have no idea, man. I mean, really, I just can't remember what the fuck went wrong." He shrugs again. "I just don't know."

And Michael goes, "You have any coke on you, James?"

James snaps out of it. "Of course I fucking do. It's a Lamborghini Dreams show. The whole point of coke is to be at your show."

"That's fucking right," Rodney smirks.

James digs out one of the grams he bought earlier, and I look over at Caralie. She's next to a table getting bombarded by Ryan with some kind of intense story. His arm is flapping above his head, and his voice keeps getting louder, and she looks totally perturbed that she's been trapped by his nonsense.

James hands the coke to Michael, and he does two key bumps and then hands the stuff to Rodney, who only takes one, and then Rodney hands the coke to me, and I do a bump, and then I hand it to James, who does three.

Swiping his nose, Michael goes, "Your cousin is the greatest living American novelist, man. You should be proud to be his family. There ain't two contemporary books out there better than *PieGrinder* and *Dickpig*."

And James goes, "Ya know, I really fucking appreciate you saying that."

And Michael goes, "And you're fucking awesome, man.

Thank you for supporting us and helping us out. The interviews and the shout-outs. It's been great for us."

"Well, I fucking love the band, man. You guys are putting out some great shit, just fucking killing it. It's an honor to be friends with you guys."

Michael high-fives James. The cocaine bro-fest. And I have to take a shit. Or just fart. I'm not sure what. Just that I need to leave the room and hit the can. So I smudge my smoke out and start for the door, when Reed gets a hold of me.

"Where you going, man?" he asks, his eyes all crazy and fucked up, kinda like Damien's were.

"The bathroom."

"Ya know," he starts, "I used to play tennis when I was younger and was good at it, but then I stopped playing."

"Okay."

"It's those kids, man."

"Which ones?"

"The ones who kept playing. Those kids are the real freaks, man."

"What are you talking about?"

He pulls me into a corner and goes, "I see the way you look at Caralie. How you stare at her from across the room with your mouth open."

"What?"

"Don't fuck with me," he snaps. "I see it."

"Okay."

"Don't even think for a minute that you're going to fuck her."

"I don't."

"Because you won't. She's in love with your cousin. So knock that stalker staring shit off. Capeesh?"

"Whatever, man."

"Don't be fucking around."

He lets go of me, and I roll back inside the bar downstairs and get in line for the guys' room, which is like six dudes deep.

While I'm waiting, Ally comes up and goes, "Hey, piss in here with me."

"Huh."

"Just come on," she says, and takes my hand and pulls me into the girls' room, where there's only one toilet. "Hurry up and do what you need to do," she says. "And when you're finished, you can watch the door for me while I change."

"Don't you have a van for that?"

"Yes. But there's like eight people getting loaded inside of it right now. Please just do this for me."

"Sure."

I walk to the toilet and know I can't drop a load or even fart for that matter. It would be too embarrassing and obvious. So I slide my penis over the waist of my jeans instead and push a small trickle of clear from it. And when I'm through, Ally unzips her backpack and says, "Just stand by the door and make sure nobody gets in here."

"What are you worried about?"

"Tons of dudes rolling in. This city is known for it."

"Dudes hanging out in chicks' bathrooms?"

"Yeah," she says, pulling clothes from the bag. "They come in groups at a time and do coke, and I don't want a bunch of fiendy punk kids crashing in here by the fives while I'm changing."

"But I'm in here."

"So."

"I'm a dude."

"You're a sweet kid," she says, grinning. "You're still innocent."

Deep inside, I want to be all, *No, I'm not. I'm way past innocent.* But I can't, because I'm not. Not yet, at least.

So I go, "Okay, fine."

"Turn around now."

I do, at first, until I cheat. I peek over my shoulder, because I can't help not to. Because Ally is such a fucking fox, and I see her reflection in the mirror, topless, her pale skin and boobs all nice and perky. Her nipples hard, and I can't take my eyes off them. It's only the second time I've seen a pair of boobs in real life.

Ally looks in the mirror, and I snap my head back around, acting like I haven't seen a thing, but she knows better.

She says, "So how was the show?"

"What are you talking about?"

"Did you like my tits?"

I'm busted and real high on the blast and come clean. "I guess so," I say.

"You guess so . . . That's fucking it?"

"Yeah, I mean they're nice. Real nice, actually."

"Your cousin loves them," she says.

Pause.

I bite my lip.

"You can turn around now," she says. "It's cool."

I do.

And she goes, "How do I look?"

She's wearing a short white skirt, a shredded purple top, and black boots.

"Like a stone fox," I say, stealing one from James.

"Well, that's sweet of you," she says. "You do have some of your cousin's charm."

"I think I've picked some up."

"Nice." She opens her purse and pulls a wallet from it and some coke from the wallet. "Come here," she says. "Do some of this with me."

I don't hesitate. I walk to her and can't believe how eager I am to do this shit now. How easy it is to say yes as soon as I feel good.

Ally scoops up two hits with a straw that's cut at an angle and does them. Then she gives the coke to me, and I take two bumps. I can tell it's different shit than what James has. It's way worse-tasting and not nearly as pure.

I hand the bag and straw back to her and look at her

face. She's looking at me funny, a half smile going on, her eyelids even fluttering.

It feels kinda awkward. "You okay?" I ask.

"Fuckin' fabulous," she says. Then she puts her right hand over my mouth and slides her fingers down my chin. "Do something for me, Kaden."

"'Kay," I stammer.

She grabs my right hand, takes my index finger and dips it into the coke, and says, "One of the things I love to do before I take the stage is get my pussy real numb."

"'Kay," I stammer again.

"So will you do it? Will you get my pussy numb, Kaden?"

"Yeah."

"Good," she says, then lifts her right leg and slams it against the sink, directing my finger between her legs, against her pussy. "Move it around," she snaps.

And I do. I run my finger up and down and in circles and inside of her while she moans and licks her lips.

"Do you like feeling my pussy?" she asks.

"I do."

"I know it," she says. She grabs my hand and yanks it from her pussy and shoves my own finger into my mouth. "Taste me," she says. "Taste my pussy mixed with cocaine. Does it taste good?"

"Huh-huh," I groan, the words muffled, slobber running down my chin.

"How good does it taste?"

"Great." More drool.

She pulls my finger out and lets go of my hand. "God-damn," she moans, looking in the mirror and fixing her hair. "Time to play a show." She leans in and kisses me on the cheek. "Thank you for that," she says. "I appreciate your help."

"You're welcome."

She kisses me again and leaves the bathroom, and I can't breathe.

I look in the mirror, my cheeks red, and I can't really comprehend what the hell just actually happened. How Ally, one of the hottest girls I've ever laid eyes on, just let me stick my finger in her pussy with cocaine on it and then taste it. It's remarkable. What can actually transpire in this city. Easily the best place ever.

I splash water on my face and leave the bathroom and watch Ally's band destroy it. I even jump into the pit for a few songs and fall down twice, only to get picked up again so I can continue in the madness.

Lamborghini Dreams are exceptional, by far the best band of the night. They're really heavy and loud, and I can see how much they don't give a shit about nothing except kill-ing it live. They play songs called:

"Fuck Your BMX."

"Tight Jean Resentment."

"Me and Bill Shatner Backstage."

"My Drug Heroes."

"Jewelry, Electronics, and Firearms."

It's actually more than exceptional. It's phenomenal. Even kids who seem like they've seen a decade's worth of shows are walking out after it's over talking about how that was one of the best live shows they've ever seen. That Michael dude played three drum solos that were at least three minutes long. And by the time it's all through, none of that shit from Dolores Park and the baseball game is even registering. I'm on a whole different level. This is my new fucking life.

I go out back and find James and Caralie at a table all by themselves.

"That was so fucking sick," I snort, taking a seat across from them.

"I've probably seen the Dreams play fifteen times before, and that was easily the best set I've ever seen them do," says James.

"You say that after every time you see them," Caralie snaps.

"Well, obviously, babe. They keep getting better and better."

And I say, "All I know is that was the raddest thing I've ever seen. Thank you for bringing me here."

James and I bump fists, and he goes, "I'm stoked you liked it, man."

"Can I have a cigarette?" I ask.

James pulls his pack of smokes out and hands me one and goes, "Your mom is gonna destroy me for all the shit I've let you do out here."

"No way," I say.

"Yeah, she will."

"She'll never even know."

"Dude," James says. "Anything you've done that she hasn't done is a big fucking lie you're telling yourself. She'll know the second she sees you again."

"Well, screw it," I say after lighting the smoke. "This is real life. I'm loving all of this, ya know. It's like this is how to really live life."

Both of them laugh. Then James kisses her lips, and Michael and Bailey roll down the stairs and stop at the table.

"Where you guys going?" James asks.

"To Ryan's, man," Michael answers. "You guys coming?"

James and Caralie answer at the same time. He says, "Yes," and she says, "No."

And Michael goes, "James, you have to hang out. We ain't gonna be back in town for at least nine or ten months."

"We'll be there," James says. "Don't worry about that."

"See ya there," says Bailey, and then they walk off.

Caralie rolls her eyes and pushes James off of her.

"What?" he snaps.

"You told me we were gonna go home after the show," she whines.

"No, I didn't."

"Yes, you did, James. Don't fucking lie to me."

"All I told you was that if there wasn't shit going on later then we would do that. But the Dreams are staying in town, so we should go to the fucking party. They're my friends."

"And I'm your fucking girlfriend."

"No shit."

"I don't wanna go."

"Then don't fucking go, Caralie."

"And what," she snaps. "Let you go hang out with a bunch of girls you've put your dick in before."

James slams his hands on the table. "Give me a fucking break with that shit. Why are you trying to pull this crap?"

"Because you said we could go home after the show!"

"Well, I'm not. You can. But I'm not, and I'm taking Kaden to the party. I'm gonna hang with my friends who are in town, so if you wanna go, then fucking go. But I'm not gonna ruin the night for Kaden."

Caralie and I trade a quick look, our eyes saying to each other something along the lines of, *Yeah, because that's been the problem so far. Caralie being stupid and going off by herself.*

James grabs her arm, pulls her in to him, and kisses her forehead. He whispers in her ear. She smiles.

Smiles!

And I sit there, stunned by how he can get her to stop

being angry with him and act like there was never a problem in the first place.

He kisses her again, and she looks in his eyes, and he says, "Just come with us. It'll be all right."

"Okay," she says.

"Yeah?"

She nods, and he passes her some coke, and she does five bumps and smiles.

g. after party

There's over thirty people here, and Faith No More is blasting from Ryan's room. A heavy cloud of cigarette smoke looms above everything. The stench of shit and garbage is everywhere, and I'm a fucking wreck.

On the way over James and I did a half g in the cab.

I get to the top of Ryan's stairs, and some guy with a curly black Afro hands me a PBR. I open it and can't even drink. It's like the first night, when I ended up in the park. Just a sip of beer makes me gag, and I don't wanna drink any more of it. I can't, anyway. I just wanna do more coke and smoke cigarettes and yap the night away. I get into a heated conversation about the war in Iraq and stick up for my home state even though there's no real reason to anymore; I'm over it, in love with San Francisco. I get into a fight with some jackass who's trying to tell me that Akon is more relevant than Jay-Z. And I also stick up for some guy named CC DeVille, even though I don't know who he is, and I think

I win the argument, 'cause the guy I'm arguing with flips me off and calls me a *chester* and walks off. I rap about Palahniuk with two girls in the bathroom, and they both seem to like what I'm talking about, and both of them say how they think James's books are only okay, and they both throw out some ways in which they would fix them. Me, I do a bump and couldn't agree more with them, even though I haven't read his books. On this drug you don't have to be honest about shit. On this drug you just have to be able to bullshit and sound like you might know what you're talking about. Like this, when I make up a fake band called HoneyJar 3, and this chubby girl with black hair and a nose ring tells me how she owns every one of HoneyJar 3's albums, that she even saw them at Thee Parkside last week and made out with their bass player. "It was amazing," she told me. "I have to tell you, those guys love me, too. I can get you into any show for free now. Just lemme know. I'm so glad you like them too."

"They're the best."

"HoneyJar 3 is so legit."

I clank her beer with the can I'm not drinking and tell her how much I like her necklace.

I lurk around the kitchen and walk into a bedroom down the hall from Ryan's room. Michael from Lamborghini Dreams is in here with Bailey and Reed and a handful of other kids. And the room is a fucking disaster. Piles of trash on the floor and piles of clothes next to the trash. There's empty boxes and a beanbag with a hole in it and bottles of wine and empty coke baggies everywhere. There's a stench, too. It's musty and rigid.

Michael is sitting on the edge of the bed holding an acoustic guitar. Next to him is a mirror with massive white lines cut across it. They look like white middle fingers.

"Hey," Michael snorts. "It's James Morgan's little cousin."

To everyone here that's still who I am. Not Kaden Norris so much as the author's cousin. James Morgan's relative.

"What's going on, man?" I ask.

Bailey is all over him.

And Michael goes, "You wanna hear something?"

"Sure."

"It's this song I wrote a few nights ago."

"Is it any good?"

Everyone in the room laughs.

"Are you kidding me with that weak shit, kid?" he snorts. "It's the fucking best shit. Sit down for a minute and listen to some greatness."

"Yeah," says Bailey. She winks and goes, "Stay in here and listen. It'll be worth it."

"It'll change your fucking life and shit, man," Michael grunts.

"Right," I say, and stand next to Reed below this giant Ghostface Killah poster. And Reed looks even more messed up now. I want to tell him to just go home and go to bed and sleep it off, but before I can, he goes, "This room is real messy."

"I know it is."

"I'll give you a line if you let me watch you clean it."

I shoot him a look. "What the fuck did you just say, man?"

He looks over his shoulder and whispers something to himself.

"Reed."

"Oh, yeah, um, I need to find my Pepsi can."

He leaves, and I look at Bailey and ask her for a cigarette. She gives me one, and I say, "So play the fucking song already."

Michael points at me. "Right, the song." Then he begins stroking the guitar and sings, "There's a place in my head that I think is superawesome; it's a place that I've known since my strung-out days in Austin. It's a place where I go when I need to see some beauty, where the creatures are exotic and the kids are never moody. It's a place in my head where the special creatures roam, a place in my head even funner than my home. . . . Unicorn Kingdom, my island in the sea; Unicorn Kingdom, only place I wanna be."

He stops playing, says that's it, and goes right for another line. Everyone there starts clapping, even me, because that song was pretty much the shit.

Michael puts the guitar down and actually pats himself on the back, and then he lifts the mirror and does another line. "I fucking miss Eazy-E, man. I really do. That guy is a hero and shit. One of the dopest heroes."

He passes the mirror to Bailey, who kisses his neck, and

I leave the room. I'm on the prowl for Ally, but I can't find her anywhere. I even ask one of the guys in her band where she is, and he tells me he thinks he saw her here earlier but that maybe he actually didn't, that maybe he was still thinking about the show. Or before the show. Or in the van or something.

So I try Ryan's room, no dice, and as I'm ducking back out into the hallway, I see James heading into another bedroom with that Ellen chick from Bacon.

I can't believe it.

No fucking way, man.

And I follow them into the room. They're sitting on a couch, and James is holding another bag of the blast.

"What are you guys doing?" I ask, trying to be as annoying as possible.

Ellen shoots me a nasty look. "What the hell are you doing in here?"

"What are you doing in here?" I ask.

"I asked you first," she snaps.

"Hey, goddamn it," James cuts in, and smacks her arm. "That's my fucking cousin. Be nice."

"So you're gonna let him stay," she snorts.

"Duh, he's my cousin. He's allowed anywhere I am."

She rolls her eyes. "Whatever."

"Whoa," James snaps. "Don't get that cunt attitude with me. I'm just giving you a bump, that's it, because you've been asking me, hounding me all night for one. I mean, I have no qualms with putting this shit away right now if you're gonna keep acting like a cunt."

Pause.

"So what's it gonna be?" James asks. "You gonna be a cunt or are you gonna knock that shit off for a bump?"

She runs a hand through her hair. "A bump, I guess."

"That's what I fucking thought," he snaps.

But just as James is lifting a hit of blast to her nose, Caralie bursts through the door and flies at fucking James, smacking all the drugs out of his hands. The baggie spills all over the floor, and there's nothing left in it. Then Caralie smacks Ellen across the face, and then she smacks James, yelling, "You stupid fuck! What's wrong with you?" And then she bolts back out of the room, and James chases after her, leaving me and Ellen inside.

Ellen's red. She looks shaken. She rubs the side of her face and then sees me looking at her and says, "So what? Do you have any coke on you I could have?"

"Fuck you," I say. "Ya know what?"

"What?"

"Your rhymes suck, and you have way too much shit pierced in your face. You ain't nothing compared to Caralie. You're pathetic."

"You're pathetic," she snaps, trying to get back at me.

"Yeah," I snort. "Good one." Then I flip my hand at her and leave the room, as she drops to her knees and puts a finger over a chunk of blast lying on the floor.

* * *

James and Caralie are in front of the apartment building, and it's pretty ugly. Caralie is swinging at him, crying, totally out of control. And James is yelling at her to quit. He's trying to grab a hold of her, but he can't. He can't stop her from coming at him. It's back and forth, back and forth, until she does a fake swing that makes James flinch. When he does, she goes into a full swing, and her knuckles crash into his face.

"Damn you, Caralie," he spits, then spins around and grabs a full beer that's sitting on the sidewalk and chucks it at her legs. "You bitch!" he yells.

The can misses, and Caralie charges at him again. This time he's able to grab her, and the two of them struggle for a minute until she finally breaks loose. And when she does, she trips over her own feet and slams to the ground.

I've seen enough of this shit. I run in between them, shove James in the chest, and scream, "Why the fuck do you two keep on doing this shit to each other?"

They both stop.

I say, "Just quit this relationship already. You two suck at going out. My God. You're miserable, and it's been fucking up my whole trip. I came out here to get away from shit like this, but here I am again, stuck with two people who can't stand each other. Both of you suck! Thanks for nothing," I finish, then bolt down to the corner and cross Haight Street, up to Oak.

I see a cab stopped at a red light and hail it. I have the driver take me to the Whip Pad. I'm hoping Ally is there. I stand out front and knock for almost a half hour. No one answers. Not one sound from the other side of the door. It's a lost cause altogether. It's getting colder, the air frigid, and I can't bring myself to go to a pay phone and call either James or Caralie. Or even go back to James's pad on Valencia. So I walk to Alamo Square and find a place to lie down under a tree, next to a bush, just far enough out of sight where I'll be hard to see in the morning.

It has to be around five, maybe even six, and I'm so fucking cold. My teeth are chattering, body shaking, and I slide my arms out of my sleeves and hug my body. I try to think about good things. I think of Ally and what happened at the show. I even try to masturbate to the visuals I'm recreating in my head, but I can't get my dick hard. I can't even feel my dick, actually. So I stop touching myself. Just another disappointment on a day during a week of disappointments. A whole lifetime of them, actually. I'm at a loss of where I stand in this world, what my place is, if I even have a place. And by the time my eyes finally begin to get tired and heavy, the sun is starting to come up.

Thursday, June 5th

I WAKE UP, AND THERE'S A BLACK FRENCH BULLDOG licking my face. The heat is intense, and the owner of the dog is yelling, "Lady, come here! Come here now!"

I look the dog straight in the eyes and pat her head, and she licks my face again before running back to her owner.

My body aches. My insides are sore and sensitive and feel like they're bleeding. Sweat and dog drool cover me from my neck up. My throat feels like I drank a whole jar of sand.

I sit up and lean forward against my knees and rub my face. I need water in the worst way. Looking around the park, I feel pretty much like a scumbag. Watching all these people out and about, all cleaned up and dressed, enjoying the day. Girls in bathing suits lying out on towels. Dudes hitting on them. A family of four having a picnic on a blanket not twenty feet from where I sit. Me sitting hungover, strung out, and stinky.

It's a horrible way to feel, until something hits me, and I think hard about what happened the night before. This perverse and gnarly pride overcomes me. It's a type of pride

I think only acknowledged in guys like James and Gerry and Ryan and Michael.

In girls like Ally and Bailey.

It's the pride that comes with being proud of living a certain way and staying true to what you like to do and the best style that accommodates that life. A pride of not giving a fuck about the way other people think about how you live. And this is really legit to me, because there is a huge difference between someone like James and your basic drug-abusing, asshole, drunk hipster d-bag. James is accomplished. He's been able to do some pretty amazing things in his life and is now reaping the benefits of those things while managing to do it all his way, on his own terms, with nobody else's help. So with all that said, all the hard work he put into achieving those successes, he's also managed to live a full life and has been around so much absurd and crazy shit. And he never backs down to anyone who disparages his way of living. And he's well served with rich material and stories for the rest of his life, which is something I've heard him say numerous times since I've been here.

He says, "Life is about accumulating a group of stories so rich and interesting that they'll serve you well beyond the time that whatever career you have has ended. That's what this day-to-day shit is really about. The accumulation of amazing stories and having the bruises and scars to show for them."

The difference seems very real to me now, sitting in the park. It's the difference between talking about how you picked a donut off the ground on a Friday night and ate it, or talking about being in some Western Addition basement apartment with some tweaked-out black nationalist and a pile of semiautomatic weapons and pounds of drugs.

So it is within this context of hopped-up nihilism that I find my pride this morning. The pride that comes with knowing and realizing that I can take care of myself. And that I can hang with the likes of a James Morgan and a Gerry Jones. And these adventures are going to serve me and help me slam into the future, not destroy me.

I mean, just one week ago, I was nervous about getting on a plane by myself. Now fast-forward six days, and I'm waking up in a park in San Francisco after finger-banging the lead singer of a hardcore band.

I'm way more stoked than ashamed.

Jesus Christ. This is the real shit!

As I'm leaving the park, still unaware of the time, sweat seeping from my pores, I notice a small can of black spray paint sitting under a tree and walk over and pick it up. It's still full. I shove it into my pocket and leave the park, walking down to Divisadero.

Water and food is what I want. I turn up toward the Independent and see that the Cool Kids are playing later that night. I move past the Independent. Across the street is Lilly's Barbecue, and it smells really good, but I don't think I can handle barbeque right now, so I walk on, past the Fly Bar, and across the street to Eddie's Cafe.

It's nearly empty, and the menu is taped to the window. It looks all right, so I go in and sit at the counter. The clock on the back wall is reading three. An entire day almost gone. I wonder if James and Caralie are freaking out about where I am and who I'm with. Do they even care? I'm sure Caralie probably does, but I think the real question is do I care if they care, and in this moment I don't have an answer to that.

I chug three glasses of water and a cup of coffee before my eggs and bacon get served. I suck that up with a quickness and drink more water.

It's four when I leave Eddie's. Since I've been in San Francisco, I haven't bought anything except some beer, some food, and some cigarettes. And that's just not enough for me. I remember some kids talking the night before at Ryan's about some killer record store just a couple of blocks away from there called Amoeba.

It's supposed to have everything you need as far as music is concerned. From mainstream shit to the EPs of little-known punk bands who broke up a decade ago. Since I've been turned on to so much new music during the trip, I want to take some of it home with me. As much as I can. So I head to the store and decide to have a bit of fun on the way.

a. the streets of san francisco II

By fun, I mean cutting through alleys and writing shit on the sides of brick buildings. The first alley I cut into, I find a nice bare wall, and I slide the paint out as discreetly as I can and shake it up. I spray:

The world is yours.

That Aesop Rock song "Daylight," maybe my favorite song ever, is slamming on repeat in my brain. . . .

"Yo . . . Put one up to shackle me, not clean logic procreation; I did not invent the wheel; I was the crooked spoke adjacent. . . ."

On the next block I see these two black kids sitting on a stoop, smoking. I stop and bum a cigarette from one of them, and I keep on moving on. I hit a trash can and write:

Lewee Regal.

Then I hit another alley and find another big spot and tag three words:

Coke. Pussy. Numb.

Aesop still pounding in my skull. . . .

"And I'm sleeping now—wow—and the settlers laugh; you won't be laughing when your covered wagons crush. You won't be laughing when the buses drag your brother's flags into rags. You won't be laughing when your front lawn's spangled in epitaphs, you won't be laughing . . ."

With the sun barreling down, the sweat and wet all over me, I hit another alley and tag:

Chowder Breath.

In the next alley, I drain my weasel.

"And I'll hang my boots to rest when I'm impressed . . . ," says Aesop.

For an hour I zigzag from street to street, through one

alley and the next, up two fire escapes, and through the window of an abandoned building.

Every time I stop, I write something different:

My Nikes are cooler than yours.

Swamp Donkey.

Fuck Wavy Gravy.

Aesop still slaying....

"This origami dream is beautiful, but man, those wings will never leave the ground without a feather and a lottery ticket; now settle down...."

There's one alley I roll into that I can't hit, because there is maybe the best thing ever in it. The only piece on a whole side of bricks, and it says:

My Grandma Has Fake Teeth, But Her Smile Is Real.

After I see that, I'm done. There's nothing I can even dream of that is more awesome than this. So I retire the can of paint next to a Dumpster and move the fuck on.

The sky is purple and I'm cooling down.

"All I ever wanted was to pick apart the day, put the pieces back together my way...."

b. amoeba music

Totally fucking wow in here. I'm blown away. Rows after rows after rows of every kind of music. It seems like I could spend a whole week in here and still not see every piece of music they have.

I lose myself.

It's impossible not to.

From memory I search for the albums by bands I want to buy, and most of it's metal and punk, because that's the stuff I got turned on to, the stuff I have nothing of back home in Dysart.

I get a lot of albums too.

Black Rainbow by 400 Blows.

White Drugs by The Bronx.

Bangers vs. Fuckers by the Coachwhips.

Hell Songs by Daughters.

Out of Africa by Triclops!

Living in Darkness by Agent Orange.

Pieces of a Man by Gil Scott-Heron.

Return to Cookie Mountain by TV on the Radio.

Present the Paisley Reich by Times New Viking.

Machines Will Always Let You Down by Replicator.

Head For the Shallow by Big Business.

And *The Master's Bedroom Is Worth Spending a Night In* by Thee Oh Sees.

I even scoop up a few DVDs:

Gummo.

The Dreamers.

American Hardcore.

The Weather Underground.

And *There Will Be Blood.*

I end up killing over two hours in there, but it doesn't feel longer than thirty minutes. I could've spent another ten hours without blinking. It's like that.

At the register I ask the girl ringing me up how to get back to Valencia Street, and she tells me to take the 33 bus that picks up on Haight and Cole.

I tell her thanks and walk to the bus stop, and the flashing time on the store window says eight o'clock.

c. the valencia street apartment IV

There's an envelope taped to the outside of the door. I rip it open and walk inside.

Read the letter.

Hey, asshole. You need to come to the Whip Pad as soon as you read this. What the hell? Little fuckface motherfucker running off like that. Get a hold of me as soon as you read this and come to the pad!

I shrug off the asshole tone of the letter and clean up instead. I go into the bathroom and make a bath and put in the Gil Scott-Heron CD and relax.

The CD is the truth.

I'm so stoked I picked it up.

When I'm done bathing, I change clothes. I put on that blue and gold flannel, a pair of black jeans, and a pair of Nikes. Then I go into the kitchen and dig through James's fridge and find just enough stuff in there that hasn't already expired to make a turkey sandwich with tomatoes, pickles, and mustard. Then I fill a glass with water and sit down at the computer in the living room.

I log on to Facebook and go to Jocelyn's profile and type her a message:

> Hey, Jocelyn. Jesus Christ. I don't even know where
> to start other than with it's been the craziest week
> of my life. Everyone I've met out here is fucking
> crazy. They're insane. But in mostly good ways.
> It's like the most intense group of people I've ever
> been around. Their lives are full of madness and
> absurdity. So much outrageousness! Like James,
> now he's done some pretty stupid and shady
> things to me while I've been here so far, and
> sometimes I can't stand him at all. I've cursed at
> him and hated him at so many different points this
> trip that it's stupid that I should even be talking
> to him anymore. But at the same time he's also
> been an amazing host in a real fucked-up kinda
> way. He's taken me to some pretty rad places and
> introduced me to what he calls "his new family,"
> who are basically the most insane but legit group
> of kids ever. The things that I've seen and been a
> part of are things that are almost unbelievable. It's
> all been so absurd that I can barely believe what
> I've been through as I type this.
>
> It's such a different way of living out here,
> Jocelyn, and I'm not sure I'll ever feel the same
> about being back home again. And I wish you

were out here with me. You could've met James's girlfriend, Caralie. She's absolutely amazing. Her and James get into a lot of fights. Big ones. And they do a lot of things to hurt each other in really bad ways, but man, she's been great to me the whole trip.

It's a strange dynamic with James and his circle of homeys. They all kinda treat each other like pieces of shit sometimes. But it's only strange if you only think about it in terms of black and white. The way people treat each other in this city. But all families are capable of doing terrible things to each other. And that's what James and his friends are . . . they're a dysfunctional family. My own family now. And with some of the shocking things I've learned this week about my mom and dad, it's become obvious to me why so many kids show up here and never go back home.

Anyways, I miss you a lot. I love you, Jocelyn. And I can't wait to see you right away when I get back to Dysart.

Kaden

Before I click the send button, I think about what I've just typed. I think about if I'm being a hypocrite and scumbag myself for having made out with Daisy and finger-banged Ally.

A big pile of shit for telling Jocelyn that I love her and how I wish she was with me but then not to have given a second thought about fucking around on her with two other girls.

The thoughts make me uncomfortable and sick to my stomach. I do feel guilty, and I end up doing what guilty-feeling people do.

I lie to myself and dismiss my actions.

It's different with me. I'm different. My situation is nothing like James and Caralie's.

I tell myself this until I'm convinced. Then I send Jocelyn the message, finish my sandwich, and leave the apartment.

Two blocks down on Valencia I find a pay phone and call James.

He's real fucking pissed off. He says, "You little shithead! You need to come to the Whip Pad right now. Caralie and I have been out looking for you all fucking day!"

I say, "Sorry, dude," even though I'm not.

And he goes, "So not cool, man. So not rad to disappear like that. We thought you might be dead."

"Well, I'm not."

"Just get the fuck over here," James snaps, then hangs up.

"Dick," I say, slamming the phone back down.

It's like, *Who the fuck does he think he is to tell me not to disappear?*

And here I am once again.

Here I am, back to hating James Morgan.

d. the whip pad IV

It's dark and quiet when I get out of the cab. The door to the Whip Pad has been propped open with a can of paint. I walk inside. The hallway light is on, but all the doors are closed except James's, which is open just a tiny crack. I move down the hallway and notice six cans of Campbell's Chunky soup stacked in front of Reed's door. What a strange fucking kid that Reed is.

I can hear Caralie crying as I approach the room, and when I get to the door, instead of banging through it I stand in the hallway and push my face into the crack of it.

Caralie is sitting on the end of the bed, face in her hands, and James is sitting beside her.

I listen.

"Why are you being like this?" James is asking.

She looks at him. "Are you joking?"

"No."

"Because we failed, James. We lost your fifteen-year-old cousin twice! He's been off by himself at night two times already, and we had no idea where he was. That's a huge fucking deal for me. He was missing, James. What the hell does that say about us?"

"You're putting way too much stock into this, baby. I just talked to him. He's fine."

"But that's not the point right now. He was gone. We had no idea where he was. We fucking lost him twice!"

"You're overreacting."

"Is that what you would say if you lost our child twice? If our kid ran away from us because we were being shitheads and acting horrible?"

"Well, we don't have kids, baby. And I would never lose my fucking kid."

"You don't even care that Kaden was gone!"

"Whatever, Caralie."

"He's seen the worst side in people on this trip. He came out here all innocent, and he's had to witness all this bullshit. He's been drinking and doing coke. He got his ass kicked after he disappeared."

"That shit's good for him. That's life."

"He's probably all messed up now," she says. "He hates us, and he hates this trip."

"No, he doesn't. He's been having a fucking blast."

Caralie sits up straight and runs her hands over her face. "He's not, though. He even said so last night. He thinks we're like his parents. That we're selfish, and that hurts me because he has so much anger built up for them."

James is shaking his head. He looks really agitated with her.

And she goes, "He's going to go back home, and nothing will be different for him. His dad is still going to suck, and they're going to hate each other forever."

"Goddamn it," James barks. "You don't know about any of it."

"About what?" she presses.

"Nothing we can do out here is going to help him have a better relationship with his fucking dad."

"How do you know that?"

James squeezes his forehead and twists his neck around.

"How do you know we can't help?" she snorts.

"Because that's not even his real dad, Caralie."

My body goes numb. My heart drops into my gut.

"What?" says Caralie.

"His mom had an affair. She had multiple affairs, and she got pregnant with Kaden. That's why his dad has always been such a dick to him. That's why he was a dick to Kenny. Because he blamed all the affairs on her getting pregnant with Kenny and marrying him at such a young age."

"And he doesn't know, does he?"

"Of course not."

"Who's his real dad?"

"I don't know," James says. He rubs his face again.

"His mom has been lying to him all these years. What a bitch!"

"Don't fucking say that about her."

"She fucked around on his dad and got pregnant, and that's why his dad gives him shit. She's a whore."

James jumps to his feet. "I said don't say that shit about her. You don't know."

"Know what?"

"She's a great fucking person."

"Obviously she's not. She's been screwing up his whole life."

"She's one of the best people in this whole fucking world!"

Caralie rolls her eyes. "How can you say that?"

"Because she's amazing."

"Jesus, James. Did you sleep with her or something too?"

Pause.

James squeezes his forehead.

"James," she says.

"Huh?"

"Did you sleep—"

"Yes," he snaps. "I slept with her numerous times. When I was sixteen."

A fury like I've never experienced in my life builds inside of me. The thought of James Morgan's hands on my mom's body, his hands inside of her, his dick inside of her pussy, makes me wanna strangle him and break his face open.

I step back from the door and walk down the hall and grab a can of soup from the stack in front of Reed's door and walk back down.

I catch my breath and wait for a second.

I listen to Caralie go, "Are you his fucking dad?"

"No," James snorts. "The dates don't match up at all."

Caralie shoots to her feet and slaps James across the

face and says, "You sick fuck! You slept with your own aunt!"

James grabs her arms. "You don't understand, baby. She's not really my aunt."

And this is when I storm into the room like a fucking soldier. Caralie yanks her arms loose and steps away from James, and I chuck the can of soup at him, hitting him on the left part of his face.

Blood starts pouring from the cut, and I yell, "You sick asshole! You fucked my mom and knew this whole time I ain't my dad's real son. Fuck you, James Morgan! Fuck your shitty life!"

"God! Fucking hell!" James hisses, with a hand over the gash on his face. "Just hear me out."

"No," I snap. "I won't hear you out. Everything is a lie. It's all one big fucking lie!"

I turn and split and slam the door shut, running out of that shitty basement with my fists balled, my insides on fucking fire.

e. mission pool

Betrayal is the only thing I feel, sitting on the roof overlooking the pool with my arms hugging my knees. Everything that I've known for my whole life has been pulled out from under my feet. My life, my existence, is a lie built on a lie built on a lie. My brother was only my half brother. My dad isn't my real dad. And my mom is a slut who slept with her own nephew. Never mind that they aren't blood. She fucked another member of her family.

Confusion and bitterness rack my brain.

A knife in my back twisting deeper and deeper and deeper.

For my whole life I've been lied to by the people who are supposed to be the most honest with me.

I begin punching the roof until my knuckles are scraped and bleeding. But I don't feel any pain. Not tonight.

A loud thud against the side of the building.

I look over my shoulder and see Caralie's head pop over the ledge. She pulls herself onto the roof and slides down next to me.

"I thought I'd find you here," she says.

"How did you know?"

"From the first day you were here, when I showed you this place and you said that this was where you'd come if you were feeling awful about something. I checked here last night but didn't find you."

"I didn't come here last night."

"Well, I figured it was still as good of a place to start as any."

"Shit," I say, looking back at the water. "I can't believe you actually remembered me even saying that."

"Why is that?"

"Because for my whole life, nobody besides Kenny has ever listened to anything I was really saying."

"Well, I did," she says, and grabs my hand. She drops it right away. "What happened, Kaden?"

"I beat up the roof."

"Are you okay?"

"No!" I shout. "I'm not okay at all. How could you even think I could be? My life is a fucking lie!"

I stand up.

"What are you doing?" she asks.

I look down at her. "I'm going swimming," I snap, then take off everything except for my underwear and drop the clothes onto the cement around the water. "See ya." I grin and jump into the pool.

It's a perfect feeling, the way the water feels against my body.

Popping back above the surface, I say, "This is the best part of the week. Right here."

I watch Caralie get to her feet and undress down to her bra and underwear and drop her clothes next to mine.

"Watch out," she says.

I move to the far side of the pool.

"Here I come."

She jumps in.

When she shoots back up, she wipes the hair from her eyes and goes, "It feels amazing."

"I know it does."

"Whooo," she says.

"Where's James?" I ask.

"He took a cab to the hospital to get stitches. That gash was gnarly deep. It looked real bad."

"Good. He needs to feel some hurt from all this."

"I know."

"I'm glad he's in the hospital, Caralie."

"Me too."

"Really?"

"Yes."

I splash some water over my face and say, "I just don't know what to think anymore. He slept with my mom, and my dad isn't my dad. What the fuck is that all about?"

"I'm so sorry you had to hear all that, Kaden."

"Don't be. I'm glad I heard it like that. I've been lied to enough, and it's about fucking time I started getting some truth."

I swim right up to her and I grab both her hands.

I say, "Do you wanna hear something else?"

"Yes."

"How I told you my brother died isn't the way it really happened. I lied to you about that."

"Why?"

"Because I didn't wanna talk about it or think about it. Because that's what my parents told me the truth was, but it isn't. He didn't die that nicely."

"What happened to Kenny, Kaden?"

Tears fill my eyes, and my throat tightens.

"It's okay," she says. "You can tell me."

Pause.

"What happened to your brother in Iraq?"

I wipe my eyes and look Caralie dead in hers. I say, "He got separated from his unit during a gunfight and was captured by insurgents. And those bastards, they held him for two days and tortured him. They snapped off his fingers and cut off his balls before slitting his throat and leaving his body on the side of a road like a piece of fucking garbage. And I didn't know about it at first! My parents hid that from me too. And you wanna know how I found out?"

"Yeah," Caralie whispers, tears running down her face.

"I overheard my uncle Jimmy and my cousin Mark talking about it the day after the funeral. That's how I had to find out about how my brother really died. My best friend ever!" I slam my right hand into the water. "My parents are liars. People are fucking liars. They try and keep the truth away from kids, and it only hurts everyone even more. And I miss him so much! It hurts me so bad how much I miss my brother, and it's not fair. And I just . . ."

Pause.

"I just don't know what to think about anything anymore."

Caralie puts a hand against my face and goes, "Shhhhhh."

I knock her hand away. "Don't even try to tell me things are going to be fine," I snap. "Because they're not. They never are. It's not going to be all right. Not anymore."

"I won't tell you that, Kaden. I won't lie to you."

"I don't know what to fucking do."

And Caralie takes a deep breath. "Come here," she says, and pulls me into her arms. She puts both hands on my face and moves me right in front of hers.

"I feel so lost."

"I know you do," she says, then lunges at me and slams her mouth against mine. She does it again and again, and I don't know what to think. I don't need to think about it. I want it with her so bad, and I kiss her back, and she moves my hands up the sides of her body and onto her tits.

I squeeze them, and they're so soft and perfect, and she kisses my neck, running her tongue all over it, while she backs into the side of the pool, pulling me with her. My chest is pressed hard against hers. She pulls my underwear down to my thighs and tells me to do the same to hers.

I do.

Wrapping a hand around my dick, she says, "Just stay inside of me, okay? Don't pull out until you're finished."

"Okay."

Then Caralie puts my dick inside of her.

My back tenses, and it feels more amazing than I ever thought it would feel. Me being inside of a beautiful woman. Our skin smacking together. It overwhelms me, and I can't hold my come.

Probably a minute after we started, I come inside of Caralie Chavez. I'm no longer a virgin. Add yet another first to my trip.

Letting out a huge sigh, I squeeze her and kiss her shoulder, my tears all dried up, and then she kisses me again and I slide myself out of her and go, "Was that any good?"

"It was great," she whispers. "Just perfect."

We fish our bottoms out of the pool and dress in silence under the California sky. And then we climb back on the roof and jump over the ledge, back into Dolores Park, and I follow her to her car.

"Where are we going?" I ask her.

"To my apartment."

f. caralie's pad III

No words were spoken during the ride here, and I'm beginning to feel stupid and awkward about everything. I feel like it was a horrible experience for her and that I was a horrible fuck. The self-doubt is destroying me.

Inside her place I start to make my bed on the couch, but she stops me. "Will you sleep in my room with me?" she asks. "Please?"

I nod and follow her in there. She walks over to the iPod sitting on her dresser and hits play, and this amazing music starts playing.

"Who is this?" I ask.

"My Morning Jacket. The Z album."

"I like it."

Caralie smiles, and I watch her undress down to nothing, and then she turns off the lights and slides under the sheets.

"Come on, Kaden," she says, patting the space next to her. "Just lie here and hold me. That's all I want you to do now."

"Okay."

I strip down to my underwear and scoot up beside her and drape my right arm over her warm, soft body.

Friday, June 6th

THE SOUND OF A CLICKING LIGHTER AND THE SMELL
of cigarette smoke is what wakes me up this morning. I lift
my head off the pillow and see James sitting in a chair at the
end of the bed. His legs are crossed, and he's wearing a black
T-shirt, a pair of jeans, and sunglasses.

I can see the bruising on his face and the bottom part of
the stitches poking out from under his shades.

"Shit," I snort. "Shit."

Caralie pops up and jumps when she sees him. "James,"
she says. "What are you doing here?"

James shakes his head and smiles, but it's not a friendly
one. He uncrosses his legs and snaps, "This is my fucking
apartment, Caralie. What am I doing here? What the fuck are
you doing here with this punk motherfucker?"

It's about to get gnarly, so I rip the sheets from my body
and get out of bed and start dressing, when James goes, "In
my own fucking apartment, kid. You lie in my bed with my
girl."

I don't say anything.

I'm fucking shaking.

Caralie sits back against the headboard and covers herself with the sheets.

Twisting out his smoke in the ashtray, James says, "She's not yours, Kaden. She's mine. She's my fucking girl."

"You fucked my mom, asshole!"

James stands up and points at me. "Go. Get the fuck out of this apartment right now!"

"Or what?" I shoot back, taking a step toward him, thumping my chest with my fist.

"I'll fucking show you what, man," he snaps back, then comes at me and grabs my shirt and throws his arms around my neck, putting me in a headlock. "You need to get the fuck out of here before I break your fucking neck."

Caralie screams for James to stop, and I try to take a swing at him, but my reach isn't long enough to connect.

"Are you gonna leave?" he barks.

Whipping the blankets off of her, Caralie jumps out of bed and tries to pull James off of me.

And here we are, the three of us. The one-time goldenboy author, his naked girlfriend of three years, and me, the pasty white high-school kid from Dysart, Iowa. A tremendous trio locked into a titanic struggle in the middle of a bedroom on a Friday morning in June in San Francisco.

What a party!

Caralie bites James's hand, and he yells out and lets go of me. But before I can step away, he shoves me in the chest. I go flying backward and lose my balance and fall to the floor.

"James!" Caralie screams.

"Shut your stupid mouth, Caralie," he snaps back.

I jump back to my feet. "I hate you, motherfucker! You're nothing to me. My brother was thirty times the man you are!"

"Just get out, man," he barks back.

But I can't. I won't. I'm not finished. I say, "You're a fucking child, James. You're a thirty-something child just fading into obscurity."

"I said to leave!"

"You're a bum, James."

"Leave!" he yells.

"A loser."

James lets out this big scream and charges at me. He pounds a fist into my chest so hard that it knocks the wind out of me.

I can hear Caralie crying as I gasp for air, my right hand pressed against my chest, and then James grabs me again and says, "Just go, Kaden. Leave."

"Fuck you," I gasp, still struggling with him. "You're nothing anymore."

James's grip around my body tightens, and he drags me out of the bedroom and down the hallway and then throws me out of the apartment.

"Get the fuck outta my sight!" he snaps.

The door slams shut.

"Oh, yeah!" I scream at the shut piece of wood. "Just to let you know, your books suck too, motherfucker!"

a. the valencia street apartment V

I take a cab there and grab all my shit. There's no fucking way I'm going to crash here, no fucking way, but I don't know where to go. Anger is seething out of me, clouding my head. My last night in San Francisco, and I don't know where I'm going to stay. The only things I know are that:

1. I hate James Morgan.

2. My entire family life has been made up.

3. As much as I want to fucking destroy and murder James, I still want to say good-bye to the kids at the Whip Pad. They've been too awesome for me to allow my beef with James to get in the way of me thanking them and seeing them one last time.

4. I need to give James the finger one last time.

After I double check to make sure I have all my things, I open up this shoe box full of spray paint that I looked through earlier in the week and grab a can of red.

Shaking it, I look around the living room for my target and find it on the wall above the futon.

I hop onto the futon and take down the James Spader piece. I take a quick eye measurement. Then I shake the can again and start spraying. Three minutes it takes me to finish. And then I step down and look at what I've written:

Dickpig Sux Balls, Brah!

I smile wide and drop the can on the floor and leave the Mission in a cab.

b. the whip pad V

The front door is propped open again. N.W.A. is bumping hard from Ally's room. I get my shit inside and walk into her room. It's her and Gerry sitting in there sharing a blunt.

"What's up?" I say.

"Hey, there." Ally smiles.

And Gerry's like, "What's happening, homey?"

They're both so high, like they've been smoking all day.

I sit down on the futon next to Gerry. He puts an arm over my shoulders and moves the blunt in front of my face. "You wanna hit this, mang?"

"Nope."

"You sure?"

"Yeah. I just stopped in to say bye to you guys."

"I thought you were leaving tomorrow," Gerry says.

"I am."

"But you don't wanna hang out at all tonight?"

"I got the Palahniuk reading," I say. "And then no, I don't wanna hang. You two are fucking rad, I love you guys, but James is a d-bag and I hate him."

"What happened?" Ally asks.

"What didn't? Shit got crazy. The guy's out of control. He's a liar and a backstabber."

Gerry laughs and hands the blunt to Ally, who's sitting

in the chair next to the coffee table. He says, "We're all fucking liars, kid."

I shake my head and say, "Yeah. But the shit you probably lie about isn't really on that large of a scale. It's like you lie about scoring with some chick; you tell a story that happened to somebody else like it happens to yourself. You tell people you did a tour or started a band back in the day even though you didn't. Things like that aren't that big of a deal. What James did is bullshit on every level, and what I did back to him makes it basically impossible that me and him will ever be tight."

"Damn," Ally says. "What the hell happened?"

"I'm sure he'll tell you guys everything, but I don't wanna go into the details about it. I'm tired of thinking about it right now. I just wanna find a place for the night and see Chuck read and get outta here."

"Where are you gonna crash?" Gerry asks.

"I'll figure something out. I've done pretty good being on my own so far. It shouldn't be a problem." I stand up. "Anyway, it was nice meeting you two."

Both Gerry and Ally stand up, and Ally hugs me and whispers into my ear, "That was some moment on Wednesday, huh?"

"Yeah, it was."

She steps back. "Ya know, you seem older than you seemed earlier in the week when you first came here with Caralie."

"I feel older."

"You should," says Gerry. "You've been through some shit."

"I know. It's like the day I got here, it seems so fucking long ago. It's crazy how many things can happen during a week."

"That's the deal with this city, man. It fucking puts you through the wringer. Everything happens here. That's why I love it. That's why San Francisco is the best."

"I had a good time."

Reed walks into the room. "Do you guys know what happened to my soup?" he asks.

We all shake our heads no.

"Fuck," he snaps. "I had six cans in front of my door, and now there's only five. One of them is missing."

"Don't know what to tell ya," says Ally.

"Motherfucker," he snorts, then leaves the room.

"Anyway," I say. "It's been awesome."

Gerry and I bump fists, and then Ally hugs me again and kisses me on the cheek.

"All right, guys," I say. "I'm out."

"Later," they both say.

I grab my stuff and walk out of the Whip Pad with a heavy heart. The insanity and greatness of this little gem in the heart of the Lower Haight and its amazing group of inhabitants. If there's anything to be pulled from any of this, it's that I'm a better person for having spent time with Gerry Jones and Ally.

Setting my things on the sidewalk, I run through a list of all the possibilities for the night and remember seeing this place called the Harcourt Hotel that had a room vacancy sign in the window when I was walking through the Tenderloin earlier this week. The rate said sixty bucks a night, and I have about a hundred and fifty left and my fake ID, so I hail a cab and have it take me to the intersection of Sutter and Larkin streets.

c. the harcourt hotel

It's not a very nice place at all. The air is stale and thick, and it smells like swamp ass and BO. I stand at the front desk and hit the help bell, and this fat old man with makeup on comes out of the back room.

"I need a room for the night," I tell him.

"How old are you?" he asks.

"Twenty-two."

"You have an ID?"

"Yup."

"Can I see it?"

"Sure." I take it out of my wallet and hand it to him.

Two transvestites with no makeup and unshaved legs walk through the lobby.

A very young-looking mother with a baby boy emerges from the elevator.

The man hands the ID back to me and says, "With tax the room will be sixty-five dollars."

"Sounds good."

I hand him eighty, and he hands me change and a set of keys. "Third floor," he says. "Room three thirty-eight."

"Thanks."

"Checkout is eleven a.m."

I nod and take my stuff to the elevator and ride it up to the third floor. The walls are beige, and the hallway floor is covered with pink carpet. This lady with black sores on her legs and arms walks out of the communal bathroom, which I have to share with everyone else. The same stale air as the lobby.

My room is at the end of the hall. I walk in, and it's not so bad at all. It's actually nicer than any of the rooms in the Whip Pad. It's pretty decent-sized, with white carpet dotted with a few red stains, a queen-size bed with this wicked headboard shaped like a mermaid, and windows that look out into a small space between buildings. There's no TV. There is an old wooden dresser and a dusty mirror on the wall.

I drop my things on the floor and take a deep breath. I'm worn out and tired, and my chest hurts from James's fist. I stand in front of the mirror and wipe some dust away and pull my shirt up. There's a bruise on my chest, and I touch it and run my fingers around it. I drop my shirt. Everything that happened comes crushing back into me. I can smell Caralie on my skin still. I can taste her skin in my mouth. I can't believe I had sex with her. It's a little surreal, to think

I'm not a virgin anymore. My first time doing it, and it was with the prettiest girl I've ever laid eyes on. My cousin's girl-friend. My cousin, who's not really even my cousin.

I move across the room and sit on the bed. An image of Jocelyn and me on that last night in Iowa holding hands while we stared at the stars slams through my head.

Jocelyn Kramer.

My girlfriend.

I cheated on her, but it's only making me feel a little shitty. Almost like it's not that big of a deal. I am no saint, that's for sure, but it's different in my head for me versus what a guy like James does. The difference being that I actually feel something for Caralie, a feeling that no girl has ever been able to give me, whereas James just fucks random girls who mean nothing to him, who aren't anything near Caralie's level, and he does this just to get his rocks off. Just to prove some bullshit point about how fucking cool he is. Or something like that. The point here is that there is a dif-ference. In my head what I did wasn't at all that bad. Yet still, there's an undeniable feeling of guilt rushing through me.

I run my hands through my hair and look at the floor.

More crushing thoughts going on.

For the first time I have a moment to take in all the things I found out and really think about them, and it's hard. The truth is so fucking hard here. It's clean but hard, and some of the shit leaves me not knowing how I should feel about it.

Shit like who my real dad is. On the one hand I'm a little in love with the idea that Steven, the man posing as my biological father this whole time, isn't at all biologically related to me. I feel relief and liberation, like there's no way I'm going to be such a d-bag like him when I'm older. But on the other hand it's like I've been fucked from day one. Me having to bear the incredible brunt of Steven's anger and jealousy, born out of the affairs my mom was having, which themselves were born out of some notion of a forced marriage and a forced first-born child. I try and put myself in Steven's shoes. I think about how hard it must have been for him to look at me and see anything but betrayal, broken promises, and how his wife is a ho.

I think, *How do you ever come back from that? It has to be impossible. You can never come all the way back from that sort of deception and ever really trust anyone again.*

But this doesn't mean I'm letting that fucker off the hook. He could've done things differently. Instead of being such a prick to me, he could've done the best to amend the situation by being honest about what happened and making decisions that he felt were truly in everyone's best interest. Like divorcing my mom and coming to terms with the fact that she was never in love with him and that she absolutely had lashed out at their joke of a marriage by screwing other men, one who happened to be her stinkin' nephew.

The whole scenario blows my mind. How a grown woman with a child could bring herself to have sex more than once with her sixteen-year-old nephew. Never mind that they weren't blood. Family is still family and shouldn't fuck other family members, plain and simple. The thought of those two together, James Morgan at sixteen and my mom at whatever age, hooking up secretly at family reunions and gatherings, rolls off my brain. Like what, did they sneak upstairs after Christmas lunch for a quickie in the bathroom? Or was it bailing in the garage and balling in the backseat of a car while the rest of the family played dominoes after Thanksgiving dinner?

I smash my fist against the mattress and continue thinking about the two of them and how that revelation of what transpired all those years ago does shed some light on things that now make more sense. Things like my mom getting a huge kick out of leaving those signed copies of James's books lying around the house. How she always talked so glowingly of him. And the way she got so emotional at the thought of me being in San Francisco with him when I first brought up the idea back in January, as if she was sending a huge part of herself to the coast to continue some strange, lost, beautiful lifetime love affair with him.

I look up and stare at the wall across the room.

Still thinking.

And what it comes down to right here, at this moment, is that Kenny was a mistake that drove my mom into a brutally unhappy marriage with someone she didn't love at all, which drove her to have affairs, one of which ended with another unwanted pregnancy, which led to me being on the receiving end of Steven's nasty resentment and feeling of total rejection.

Like, *Whoa.*

Like, *What an amazing family!*

I'm dizzy and nauseous all over again.

I need some fresh air and something to eat.

I leave the hotel and walk a few blocks to this corner store and pick up some chips, a root beer, and a sandwich. On my way to the checkout counter I pass a display of notebooks and pens, and I scoop up two of each and go back to the hotel.

While I eat, I start writing down my trip. I don't know what it's going to be yet, just that it has to get out of me and on to something else. I do this until six. Then I grab my copies of *Fight Club* and *Choke.*

There's still a book reading I have to see.

Despite everything, I haven't lost sight of the real purpose behind my trip.

d. the chuck palahniuk reading

Down in the lobby I ask the clerk where Books Inc. is, and he tells me it's real close.

"Just walk out and take a right and go two blocks up Sutter to Van Ness; then make a left and go four blocks down."

"Thanks."

It's nice out. The sun is still high and glowing, and the people I pass have good energy. They seem happy. It's a happy city. And truth be told, I don't wanna leave San Francisco tomorrow and go back to Dysart. I've fallen in love with this place, the beauty of it and the buildings and especially the girls. The culture is real here, and there's so much of it. I've only experienced a small sliver of it.

I don't wanna go back at all. But I am. The next morning, and I'm very sad about this.

There's at least a hundred people already waiting to get into the store. I walk to the back of the line, past a group of maybe twenty guys dressed as waiters and a group of people dressed as Shannon McFarland and Brandy Alexander from Chuck's book *Invisible Monsters*.

I've almost fucking made it. I'm this close to finishing off the last request of my dead brother. My dead hero. And I can only hope he knows somehow what I'm doing, knows that I've experienced more in the last week than any kid I've grown up with has experienced in their entire lives up to this point. I'm proud of myself for having done this, having gotten to San Francisco in the first place. My whole other life before I got Kenny's letter I'd never set a goal, and here I am, two thousand miles from home, having done what I needed to get myself to this reading.

Parking myself at the end of the line, more people converging on the store, I flip open *Fight Club* and go to my favorite part of the book. The part where Tyler Durden creates Project Mayhem at breakfast the morning after the narrator pounds the fuck out of Mister Angel Boy. My favorite lines at the very end of the part. My favorite lines right here . . .

"I'd do the Elgin Marbles with a sledgehammer and wipe my ass with the Mona Lisa. *This is my world, now. This is my world, my world, and those ancient people are dead."*

I pop my head up from the book and breathe. After all these times I've already read it, it still gets me fucking jacked. Inspired. And I think, *Goddamn! What if I could do something like that with my story. This story! Write something so powerful and cut glass with my own fucking words! How fucking righteous and empowering that could really be.*

I want to read on. My mind is racing, but as I'm putting my face back in the book, Caralie pops up beside me and looks the best she's looked at any point during my whole visit.

I'm not lying at all.

She's wearing this black skirt that hangs to her knees, a pair of Chuck Taylors, a black tank top that says SWINGIN' UTTERS on it, and a white bandanna tied around her neck. Her hair is pulled back. A few strands hang down each side of her face.

"I figured I might find you here," she says, smiling all big.

I try and put on my tough kid act. I say, "Obviously. This is the whole reason I even came out here, isn't it?"

Pause.

"Isn't it?" I press.

"Yeah," she says. "It is."

"And I made it."

"I know you did."

How I really wanna be is proud. I wanna stand here, just inches from her face, and be proud about how I fucked her last night and how I'm better than anyone else in the line I'm standing in because I had sex with her.

Thing is, I can't. I can't think of her in those simple terms of a trophy girl I won over and conquered. I know that her fucking me had more to do with James than anything else. It's the truth, straight up. If James hadn't said what he said about my mom, and if he didn't have a massive history of wiping a bunch of stupid chicks who can't even touch Caralie, then I wouldn't have gotten to do what I did last night. There would've been no way my dick would've ever made it inside of Caralie Chavez's pussy.

It's the way it is.

And I am well aware of this obvious fact.

Closing *Fight Club*, I say, "What happened after I left this morning?"

"We talked."

"What'd you tell him, Caralie?"

"It doesn't matter what I told him."

"Yes, it does matter."

"No, it doesn't," she says. "Not to you."

I sigh. I'm getting over it. I say, "You don't have to fucking be here. I don't need you to hold my hand anymore and tell me how James doesn't fucking mean what he does and says. I've heard all that shit before. I've been listening to my mom stick up for that asshole posing as my dad for as long as I've lived, and I'm over it. So goddamn over it."

Caralie shakes her head and rolls her top lip back. "Ya know, dude," she starts. "If you wanna be angry, go ahead and be; I'm not gonna blame you for it at all. You have every right to hate the piss and shit out of this world. But just do me this one favor, man."

"What's that?"

"Quit spitting the attitude in my face. Seriously. I've done as good as I could by you this whole fucking week. And ya know what?"

"What?"

"Last night was very special to me. It meant a lot."

"Did you tell James that?"

"Nope."

"What'd you tell him, Caralie?"

She doesn't say anything.

"What'd you say?"

"I said it was a huge mistake, Kaden. I told him I wasn't thinking in the right frame of mind."

I shake my head, although I have no real reason to be bummed or irritated by her answer, and I say, "That's pretty fucking typical for somebody out here."

She makes a face and snorts, "Tomorrow morning you get to board a plane and leave here. You're fucking gone from us, and what happened at the Mission pool, that's over for you as far as anything except memories go, but that's not how it's going to work for me. James is the only thing I've known for the last three years. Those ties are deep. This is my whole life we're talking about. Everything, Kaden. And it's a lot more complicated than you wanna make it out to be."

"That's bullshit."

She crosses her arms with the same attitude she stuck up for me with all week and goes, "Jesus Christ, dude. If there is one thing I figured you would take away from this week, it's that sometimes you have to do and say whatever needs to be done and said in order to get the fuck by. It's not all black and white, Kaden. You should've figured that out. This whole thing is about getting by however you have to, and that means I had to tell James that what happened between us was a big fucking mistake and that I wasn't thinking right when it went down, because I don't have anyone other than him to fall back on. I need him."

"The more you try and justify living like that, with that horseshit philosophy, it makes me feel even better about thinking the way I do about it."

She undoes her arms and says, "Are you gonna tell your little girlfriend in Dysart that we fucked in the pool?"

Pause.

"No," I groan. "But that's different."

She reaches over and puts a hand on my arm and says, "See."

She says, "You've already started doing it, Kaden. It's always different when it's you, and that's a human-nature fact of life. Your situation is different, and you're always better than the people you say you don't wanna act like, even though you're acting just like them."

Knocking her hand away, I go, "Well, you can go ahead and think like that, Caralie. But I know what I'm all about. So this whole conversation is pointless to me. I know who I am."

"Well, good for fucking you, man."

"Isn't it?"

Pause.

We both look away before looking back at each other.

And she goes, "See. This is what I didn't want to have happen tonight. I didn't wanna come down here to argue with you, Kaden."

I roll my eyes, even though I believe her.

And she says, "I didn't at all. I came here because I want to be here when you finally see this thing through. Your brother wanted to be here with you, but he didn't get the chance, and now you're doing this shit for both of you. And that's so awesome to me. You came out here all by yourself, and now you get to see your writing hero read. I'm just not gonna miss it."

I smile. "Thanks . . . I guess."

"I'm being serious here. I'm fucking elated to be with you right now."

e. the chuck palahniuk reading II

The doors open at six thirty, and we file into the store. There's over two hundred people now, and we all go to the back, which has been cleared out. There's a big table with copies of *Snuff* on it at the far end of the room, and Caralie and I find a spot as close as we can to the table and wait. It's finally about to happen, and I imagine my brother sitting Indian-style on the floor in his letter jacket and Cubs hat, a stack of books next to him, the biggest smile in the world on his face. I imagine him lying in a bunk in Iraq after spending eighteen exhausting and terrifying hours moving through the desert streets, reading one of Chuck's books, and being happy for the only time that day.

Caralie nudges me. "This is so exciting." Her smile is big and warm and awesome.

"Do James's readings get as big as this?"

"The one he did when *Dickpig* came out was."

"Really?" I'm actually bummed to hear this.

"Your cousin has a huge following. His books are best-sellers."

"But they're not as good as Chuck's."

She nods. "I agree. But James still has his fans. Lots of them. They love him."

"It's how you two met."

"That's right it is."

One of the bookstore employees emerges from a door holding a microphone and begins to introduce Chuck. She calls him the most important living satirist, a true literary prankster, and one of the most important writers of his generation, who has inspired hundred of thousands of young kids to pick up books and start reading again.

She says, "Ladies and gentlemen, please give a warm welcome to the one and only Chuck Palahniuk."

The store erupts with cheers as Chuck walks in and takes the microphone and thanks the woman who introduced him and everyone for coming out.

It's an incredible feeling, to be in the same room with someone who's changed the way I look at everything, my whole fucking life.

He asks us if we're ready to hear him read, and we cheer even louder. Then he kicks off his shoes and sits on the table in between stacks of his books and starts reading.

One sentence in, and I've already been swept into another place altogether. Into Chuck's fiction world, and nothing else matters at this moment. Everything I've gone through falls to the wayside as I watch the man who helped redefine my life read for an audience of hundreds in a San Francisco bookstore.

He finishes about forty minutes later, then answers some audience questions. And then starts to sign.

When it's my turn, I hand him the books, and he mentions how worn they look, and I tell him I haven't put them down since I got them.

He laughs.

And then I tell him about Kenny and how he was the one who got me into the books. Chuck seems very moved by the story and thanks me for sharing it with him.

When he's done signing the books, I go, "Do you know who James Morgan is?"

"The author?"

"Yeah. Him."

"Of course I do," Chuck says.

"Well, he's my cousin, and he sucks, but I think that you're the best, man."

f. the streets of san francisco III

It's almost nine and dark now, and the wind has picked up. Caralie and I are standing in front of the bookstore.

"Where you staying tonight?" she asks me.

"I got a room in some piece of shit hotel in the Tenderloin."

"How?"

"The fake ID. Thing's worked like a charm this whole trip."

Once again a perfect smile parts her lips, and she scoots closer to me and goes, "Seriously, and I'm not trying to be corny at all, but you've grown up a lot out here, dude."

"You really think that?"

"I absolutely do. You look ten times more confident than you did when you first got out here. You got this feeling about you now that you know how to handle your shit and take care of business, and that's fucking dope. You ain't fifteen anymore. That's for fucking sure, dude."

"I don't feel fifteen."

She hugs me and goes, "You don't have to stay at some roach coach either. You can stay with me."

"Fuck that!" I snap. "Are you nuts?"

"Not at all. It's not a big deal."

"Bullshit it ain't. Fuck that idea, and fuck James Morgan. I'm staying in the hotel and catching a cab to the airport, and that's that. I ain't trying to get hassled and beat up by some out-of-control cokehead. I'm over that piece of shit."

Caralie looks worn out after that rant, and she should be. She's been put through a lot.

I sigh. "Hey," I say. "You wanna walk me to my door?"

"I'd love to."

We start up the block, and a huge gust of wind rushes past us. I see Caralie shiver. She wraps her arms around herself.

"Here," I tell her. "Wear my hoodie."

"I'm okay."

"Just put it on, Caralie," I say, and take it off and give it to her.

She puts it on, and we stop at a red light.

"So what do you think is going to happen with you and James?"

"I don't know."

"You think you'll split up?"

"Maybe," she says. "We didn't get that specific this morning. We just yelled and screamed to the point that it became nothing more than noise. It became pointless."

The light goes green, and we start walking again, and I say, "I'm real sorry about all of that. I mean, I'm sorry for you, I guess."

"Don't be," she snaps back. "I don't need anyone to feel sorry for me. James and I are both adults. We just need to take a hard look at our situation and the decisions we've made ... even if we don't like it."

"But you do, Caralie. That's the thing. It's James who acts like a goddamn twelve-year-old all the time. He doesn't deal with his own demons and all the fucked-up shit they cause. He just lets everyone else around him pick up the pieces and patch him back together."

"He takes care of me, Kaden. That says a lot."

I shake my head. "So that's the whole reason you're gonna be with him. Because he pays your rent and he'll pay for school when you go back."

She doesn't say anything.

And I go, "If that's true, that sucks, because the minute he feels like it, he's gonna drop you for another eighteen-year-old who makes him feel young and energized like you did. And then you're gonna have nothing to show for yourself. You're gonna be twenty-four and have nothing but a few memories to prove the worth of the last six years of your life. I mean, think hard about that. Don't stay with James because he pays your bills; stay with him because you love him and you think you can work things out with him."

We hit another red light on Polk and Sutter, and she turns to me and runs a hand down my face and goes, "You got a decent sense about you now, Kaden. And that's a great thing to have. You're smart. You still might not get how things really work, but you can read people, and that's a good thing to have."

"It's all from this week," I tell her, crossing Polk. "All the crazy shit that's happened really opened my eyes. It feels like it did the first time I read Chuck. This place has transformed my entire fucking world."

She giggles and says, "So you did have a little fun, then?"

"A fucking blast." We stop in front of the hotel. "There was some bullshit, but I needed an experience like this. I've never had anything else in my life except these sugar-coated moments. This trip was the best thing I've ever done, and I made it happen for the memory of my brother, and I'm stoked about that."

"That makes me happy to hear," she says. "So . . ."

A long pause.

"I guess this is it."

"I guess so."

"Come here." She grabs me and squeezes me tight and then kisses my lips. "You're awesome," she tells me. "I feel honored to have met you." She kisses my lips again. "Are you sure you don't wanna stay with me? I have cable and a clean bathroom."

I smile. "This is fine. It's kind of fitting, actually. Me spending my last night in San Francisco in a Tenderloin hotel room. And to be totally honest with you, it's better than the Whip Pad. There's no fruit flies or rotting garbage piled in the corner."

"That's good to know, Kaden.

"It's pretty all right, actually."

We hug again, one last time. Then she gives me my hoodie back and smiles and says good-bye.

And I stand there watching her, watching the greatest girl in the world walk to the end of the sidewalk and disappear around a corner and into the San Francisco night.

g. jocelyn kramer II

I do not go back into the hotel right away. There's something I need to do. I find a pay phone and call Jocelyn. What Caralie said to me earlier about being honest with her and about thinking things are different for me stung. She was right. Who am I to think I'm not the same as James when I did what I did to Jocelyn this week? For me to think anything different is a load of shit and puts me in the same place as my mom and James Morgan and all of those who've been lying to me my whole life. What I did to Jocelyn is fucked up. I don't regret it. But I have to own it. I have to take responsibility for it. I can't make an excuse for it, and I can't lie to her and then look her in the eyes the same way ever again. I probably won't be able to anyway, but she needs to know. I am not James Morgan.

She answers this time.

"Hey," I say.

"Hey."

Thirty seconds of silence.

"What's wrong?" she asks me.

"I, um . . . I—"

"Kaden, you sound sad."

"I do?"

"Yeah. What's wrong?"

"There's this thing—"

"I can't wait to see you tomorrow," she says, cutting me off.

"Can't wait to see you."

"I got your message. It sounds like your trip has been amazing, and—"

"Jocelyn," I snort. "Listen to me. Listen to this."

"What is it?"

I start tearing up. "I fucked a girl out here and made out with another one and finger-banged another one."

More silence.

"And I'm sorry that I hurt you, but I'm not sorry that I did it."

"Is this a joke, Kaden?" Her voice is cracking.

"It's no joke, Jocelyn."

"Why are you telling me this?" She's crying now.

"Because you have to know. You have to. It was a shitty thing to do, but I don't regret what happened, and I love you, and I need you to know that."

"Fucker!"

"Jocelyn."

"You don't love me. You can't love someone and do that to them."

"But you can! And I did."

"Oh my God!"

"Listen to me," I say. "I'm a different person now. I'm not the same as when I left. Too much has happened. I know too many things now, and my life has been a sham, except you and my brother."

"What are you talking about?"

"I'll tell you everything when I get back."

"I don't wanna see you!"

"You can break up with me. That's fine. But I need to see your face and tell you everything when I get back, and then that can be it."

"You're breaking my fucking heart."

"I'm sorry."

"But not for what you did."

"No. I'm just sorry that I hurt you."

She hangs up.

And I say, "I love you."

And then I hang up and wipe the tears off my face.

h. putting kenny to rest

I go back to the hotel and climb out my room window and shimmy up the fire escape all the way to the roof. It's brilliant again on another roof. The lights and the buildings and the shadows.

I walk to the edge of the roof and inhale the bay air.

One thing left to do.

I take out my wallet and slide Kenny's letter from it. I cuff it in the palm of my hand so tight and think about how much it changed my life. The way the words on those pages have made me a better person and opened my eyes to something bigger. Even more than with the Palahniuk books, this letter was the beginning of everything, the driving force behind everything, and it's time to let it go, I've thrown myself into everything it asked me to.

More tears slide down my face as I open the letter and pull out some matches.

The last communique of a dead hero. America's finest. The greatest person I will surely ever know.

I hold the letter in my outstretched hands, and then I light the corner of it on fire.

It burns slowly but surely.

And once the flames are halfway up the pages, I let it go and watch it float and fall into ashes in the street below me.

Saturday, June 7th

I WAKE UP TO SOMEONE POUNDING THE SHIT OUT OF my room door. I glance at the clock next to the bed. Seven a.m., and there's more pounding. I'm a little nervous. I can't even imagine who it is.

A strung-out crackhead at the wrong door. Or maybe a wastoid who wants to beat the shit out of someone.

I get out of bed and walk to the door in my underwear and look through the peephole.

James Morgan is standing on the other side in a T-shirt and a pair of sunglasses.

And there it is. A little bit of both crackhead and wastoid.

"What do you want, James?"

"Let me in, man."

"Have you slept yet?"

"Yes. Let me in."

"I don't have nothing to say to you," I bark. "Not a single word anymore."

"Kaden, let me the fuck in now. I just wanna talk to you before you leave. Please. I'm not gonna do anything evil. I just wanna talk."

Shit!

I kinda have to. I gotta leave in an hour and a half, and I have a feeling that James will just stand there and wait for me. Smoke a few cigarettes, do some blast bumps, and run down to the store and grab a sixer and just wait for me.

I say, "You promise not to hit me?"

"Duh."

"Do you promise, man?"

"Yes, I promise. Now let me in."

I undo the chain lock and door lock and pull the door open. And when I do, I put both fists in front of my face to block any potential swing, but James just walks by and says, "Put your fucking hands down, dude."

I do.

And he goes all the way to the other side of the room and says, "Shit. It's nicer than the Whip Pad."

"I know." I follow him. "Caralie tell you I was here?"

"Yup."

I stop about five feet from him. "So what is there left to say, James?"

"A lot." He points to the bed. "Sit down."

I sit on the edge of it, and he sits on a chair next to the small desk by the windows, then leans forward and lights a cigarette.

And this is it. A whole week in San Francisco boiling down to one moment. Me sitting in my underwear on a bed at seven in the morning and my cousin at a desk, the two of us in some ghetto hotel room.

"So what do you have to say to me?" I ask.

James exhales a thick line of cigarette smoke and goes, "Whatever you think you know about any of what you heard the other night, you don't know jack."

"You slept with my mom. It's disgusting. My mom is a ho."

"No, she's not, Kaden, and you wouldn't say something like that if you really knew what it was like for her."

"'Like for her'? Are you kidding me? What does that even mean? She made those choices all by herself, and then I find out that I've been bearing the shitty repercussions of those choices my entire life because I'm some bastard child. It's bullshit. She's a ho."

James slams a fist against the table and snaps, "She's not! You don't even know, man, so don't judge."

This pisses me off. I go, "Ya know, I'm so sick of everyone out here telling me that it's so not cool to judge people by the piece of shit things they've done to other people. My mom cheated on Steven and got knocked up with me, and that's why that asshole hates me. It's her fucking fault, James!"

He jumps to his feet and smashes his smoke out on the carpet with his foot. "I know why you think that, and I understand it, I do. But what I'm saying is that you don't know shit about any of it."

"So fucking tell me already," I bark, getting to my feet. "Quit telling me how I don't know anything, and start telling me something. Christ!"

James turns to the window and moves his shades onto his head. He sighs. And he says, "What happened between me and your mom wasn't just some random fling because we were hammered one night and realized we weren't really related." He looks back at me. The gash from the soup can looks horrible and sore. "I'm gonna be honest with you. It was on a much deeper level than that. I mean, damn, she was something else, kid. Even with a family, she still had that something about her that I was in complete awe of."

"So what?" I snap. "You two were in love? What the fuck?"

"No," he says. "It wasn't like this true love thing. It was more in the way we understood each other. We've always had this strong bond between us."

I roll my eyes. "And how's that?"

"First off," he snorts, "she was stunning. Why she was ever fucking Steven in the first place is beyond me. Even she never understood why she'd started in with him. But once you get beyond that, it's insane how fucking amazing she was. Wild and sexy and elegant. She's so smart, too. She knows about rad music and amazing art. Plus, she was so talented. Did you know that she had her paintings on gallery walls in New York and Berlin by the time she was nineteen?"

"She did?"

"Yeah. She's an amazing woman and was totally ambitious, stoked on school, and then she got knocked up, and it was over."

I rub my face and say, "I still don't understand why she decided to marry him and have a kid if she was giving up so much."

He lowers his shades again and sits back down and tells me to do the same and says, "This is when you have to put yourself in her shoes, man. This is that moment, the time, when you have to think about spending the first twelve years of your life in and out of foster homes. Your first twelve years alive, and you have nothing, no stability, nothing, until one day this very well-to-do but devout Catholic family adopts you. For the first time ever you're wanted, and you do good for yourself. You work your ass off and go to school, and they foot the bill for all of it. But then you get pregnant and proposed to by a man obsessed with you . . . who can take care of you. I mean, what are you really gonna do? Have an abortion and spit in the face of everything the family that took you in fundamentally believes in? Are you gonna say 'Fuck off' to the guy who knocked you up and raise the kid on your own? No. She did what she had to do. She knew what it was like to grow up with nothing, to be treated like the shit scum of the world, and she wasn't going to do that to Kenny. She made the best decision for him. She chose to make sure that he'd be taken care of."

"I get that, James."

"Do you?"

"Yes."

"'Cause I don't think you do." He lights another cigarette.

"It's nice to live in that world inside your head that abides by your little idealist wishes, ya know, where everyone is straight up about their intentions and never uses people or lies about anything. But seriously, that ain't how this shit works, and the quicker you get that and stop throwing these rushed judgments onto people who are living a life that you have no fucking clue about what it feels to live, then you'll actually be ready for the shit that's gonna get tossed your way." He takes another drag. "Once you get that people are always gonna let you down and hurt you in some capacity, that's when you actually start to cultivate something real with them."

"That's fucked up."

"That's the way it works, man. This is the game that moves as you play." He takes another drag. "The time I spent with your mom was incredible, and she shouldn't be blamed for doing what was best for Kenny. After he was born, though, she got restless. That's what people like her and me do. We get restless and bored. We don't like to sit that still, and that's exactly what happened. She acted out on the same impulses that have been with her for a lifetime."

"Does Steven know about you two?"

"No."

"Jesus."

"And I don't think you should bring it up when you go home."

"So I'm not supposed to talk about this whole fucked-up situation at all?" I snort.

"I didn't say that, man. Whatever you need to say to your mom and dad about your real birth father . . . that's your business. All I'm asking is that you don't say shit about my affair with her."

"Can I ask you something?"

"Shoot."

"Why should I give a fuck about what you want?"

"'Cause you had sex with my girl, and you're still fucking walking."

"Good point."

James puts out his cigarette and hops to his feet. "What time is your flight?"

"Ten thirty."

James looks at his watch and says, "We got another hour at least. How about I buy you breakfast?"

"Food would be great," I say.

a. breakfast with james

We walk on Sutter Street to Leavenworth and this spot called Golden Coffee and sit in a booth next to a window. James orders pancakes and sausage, and I order scrambled eggs and bacon. And to be real, I'm still bitter with James. I get what he's saying and all, but that doesn't stop me from thinking how it's just a contrived way of being and a shitty way to justify things. I'm confused and angry. But I mask it now, because this trip has meant so many things to me on so many levels. I'm conflicted is what it is. I feel betrayed, used, and spent. But I also feel accomplished and proven, like I have carved myself out of stone. I'm older but still the same age, yet any innocence I was maintaining before the trip is gone, even though I feel like a child, still unwrapping life one sheet of paper at a time.

The range of emotions and the masks people wear. The meaning underneath the meaning underneath the meaning that can't truly explain anything.

The real human experience.

I ask James what's going to happen between him and Caralie.

"I honestly don't know," he answers. "But she is moving back with her parents at the end of the month."

"How do you feel about that?"

James stretches his arms to the sides and rests them on the top of the seat. "It was my idea." He looks out the window, his shades still on. His shades, almost always on.

"For real?"

"Yeah, Kaden. For real." He looks back at me. "And I think it's the best thing for her right now. With everything that's happened, I started thinking about how I was fucking her life up. How I've been sheltering her from having to endure the struggles that come from taking care of yourself. How I've been sucking up the days from maybe the most important time in her life."

"You really believe that?"

He leans forward, nodding. "I do, man. This life that I live, it's not for everyone. Most people can't hang with it. They want to at first, and then they just drop from your life one day, and it hurts. You usually never talk to them again. The kids I'm close to . . . Ryan, Reed, Ally, Gerry, and a lot of the other ones you didn't meet, I get something from them every day. I pull from those experiences and use them to create things." James leans in even closer, almost like he's talking into a camera, and he says, "I relish my debauchery. I don't regret it or shy away from it and pretend that I'm gonna stop it. This is who I am, and I'm not going to change for anyone. Anyone! And my real family is the kids I share these insane moments with, not those strangers in Springfield that I cut off the day I turned nineteen."

Pause.

James takes a sip of his water, then takes on the exact same pose.

He says, "And the big thing with Caralie is that she didn't grow up like I did. She came from a very close-knit family, and I've done everything I could to pry her away from them, and in the end I'm not sure that was the best for her. I mean, I fucking love that girl to death, but at the same time, looking back on the last three years really hard, I'm thinking now that I've been doing more harm than good."

Pause.

He rubs his mouth and clenches his jaw. "It's like this,

dude. I didn't get to where I am, all the success I've achieved, with anyone else's help. I started writing books one day, and I fucking pushed myself harder than anyone I know has ever pushed themselves, and I made it. I fucking made it. I'm more successful than any chick I've ever fucked or any dude who's ever fronted on me. I cut myself from stone and have done it the way I wanted to, and that's why I won't change. Because no matter how gnarly and cynical I can get, I'm still better than so many people here, because I take care of my shit no matter what and make things happen for myself. I might party hard and fuck up sometimes, but that hasn't stopped me from being great at what I do and being able to afford to live the way I want to live. But looking at Caralie, she's so smart and talented and beautiful but isn't doing shit, which makes me think that our relationship has taken away from her, and at this point I think we need to look at what we got and then she, not me, she needs to decide if it's really the life she wants to live anymore. Because as much as I want her by my side for fucking ever, I think an even more terrifying prospect than losing her is me standing in the way of her full potential. That's the deal, kid."

James sits back and looks out the window, and I think about what he's just said to me. It's intense, and I have a whole new respect for him. He's still a shithead, but he does love Caralie, which seals the deal for me.

"I care so much for her," he says, as this old Chinese man brings our food over.

James tells him thanks, and I say, "So be honest again with me. Do you think you two are gonna be able to make it work?"

James stabs a piece of sausage and shoves it in his mouth. "Nope," he says, chewing. "But the point is that we're gonna try to, man. I'm even going to go over to her parents' house for dinner next week. So yeah, we're gonna try. And who knows, maybe with her not being so domestically supported by me, with her being back so close to her family and friends, with some space between us, maybe we'll be able to get it back to the way it was when we first started seeing each other. That's the goal, man. That's all I can hope happens."

"Damn," I say. It's the first time the whole week that James slipped off his asshole mask. The first time I've seen any real passion from the guy, and I like this side. I say, "I hope it works for you, then."

James nods and looks down at his plate and then forks up another piece of sausage.

b. good-bye

After eating, I check out of the room, and the two of us stand on a corner and wait for a cab.

We both smoke cigarettes, one last social stick between two acquaintances.

"At least when you get back to Iowa, you won't be able to say you had a boring time here," James says.

"Shit, man. I don't wanna go back there."

"Well, you have to. Your mom would fucking lose it if you weren't on that plane home."

"So what?"

"Dude, she loves you so much, and if she knew what the fuck had gone down with you on this trip . . . the coke, the drinking, you fucking my girl—"

"By the way," I interrupt, "I don't regret that at all."

"You shouldn't, man. And I don't even care that much. Everything she's done to hurt me I've brought on myself."

"Can I ask you something, then?"

"What?"

"What the hell is wrong with you?"

James pauses and looks up at the sky, and a smile slices across his face. He lets out this strange laugh, then looks back at me and says, "Nothing, man. But it's completely out of control."

I start laughing, and I can't control it. The giggles overtake me, and I'm buckled over, my hands on my knees, face beet red as a cab pulls up next to us.

"Shit," I sigh. "Thanks for that."

"Sure thing, mang."

The driver gets out and puts my bags into the car, and I drop my smoke and smudge it out with my foot.

"I guess this is it," I say, sticking my hand out.

He shakes his head. "Nah. Fuck that. Come here," he says, pulling me in to him and hugging me. "It was good having you here, kid. This has definitely been one of the strangest weeks of my life."

"Really, James?"

Pause.

He lights another smoke. "No."

"You're fucking nuts, man."

"And you fucking loved it."

"I did."

The two of us bump fists one last time, and then the driver asks me if I'm ready to go.

"I guess so."

James hands the driver sixty dollars. "You're taking him to SFO."

The driver nods, and I step into the cab, and James goes, "Hey, you're forgetting something."

"What's that?"

"A grifter," he says. "What is it?"

"Motherfuckers living the way they want to."

He smiles. "Good man."

I shut the door and feel like crying. It all hits me at once. How I'm leaving San Francisco and going home. It's nuts for me to go back. To what? There's nothing for me there except a conversation I need to have with my mom and the need to see Jocelyn's face and tell her everything. But that's it. And there's water running from my eyes as the driver puts the car in drive, and then we move. We're off. I'm out of the city.

Just like that.

THIS IS NOT A LOVE STORY.

These are the words that have been scraped into the ceiling of my tiny, shit-hole room. My boxlike dungeon. My brand-new fucking home.
Below that,

There are no happy endings.

Sometimes I think about who the fuck carved this shit in here. A lot of times, actually. Because I have a lot of time on my hands to think about everything. Around here this is what passes as entertainment.
You wake up.
Think.
You eat.
Think.
You shower.
Think.
You write some shit down.
Think.
This is what my days and nights consist of.

This is my life.

My life.

I can't wake up and fuck some hot girl anymore and get fucked up on some shit, and it sucks, but I have nobody else to blame except myself. I made all of the decisions that led me to this point, so even if I tried to point a finger, I would only be pointing at myself, and there's no need for that. Not anymore. I'm well past that shit now.

But still, I sometimes catch my mind wandering around. Walking backward. I catch myself thinking about the things that have happened and how if I'd just done this or that differently, I might be in a different place right now. Who knows where. Maybe getting loaded in a room and going off to some wicked Lightning Bolt shit. Maybe booze cruising down some highway smoking cigarettes, jamming out to the Replacements. Maybe lying in some bed next to Laura, bodies covered in sweat, holding on to her, Greg Ashley flowing from some nearby stereo.

Laura.

I always catch my mind racing back to her, especially to this one night in particular, Christmas night two years ago, when I was home briefly from college.

This night jumps out because it was the night before I left for my trip to Hawaii, the trip where everything changed and flipped upside down for me. The night when Laura stood across from me and told me not to go. "Stay here the rest of your break and be with me."

No way, I told her. I've been stoked for this trip since like two months ago.

"Fine," she said. "Just go. Leave again. But get me something awesome."

What do you mean?
"Buy me some cool shit from Hawaii."

Pulling my shirt off, I crawl into bed and look at the ceiling.

This is not a love story.

I look below that.

There are no happy endings.

Travis Wayne

"YOU LOOK KINDA WEIRD, MAN."

How's that?

"You almost don't look like the same Travis," Chris tells me after picking up a small mirror with two lines of blow on it.

I take the mirror from his hands. Set it down on the coffee table in front of me, right next to an issue of *Vice* magazine—the drugs issue—and even though I actually think I know what Chris meant by that, I still ask him:

What's that supposed to mean, dude?

Chris swings his bloodshot, pitch-black-circled eyes over to his roommate and childhood friend of mine, Kyle, then quickly back to me, and says, "You've totally lost your edge, man." He sniffs. Swipes his nose. "Your face looks all worn out and sunken in. You look out of shape. You're pale. Pale, Trav. You've been in the fucking desert for a year and you look pale, man. Unbelievable. I mean, I remember when you came back to the city during Christmas break and you came over here one time in the middle of the night in a fucking limousine, wearing a pair of shades with like three scarves hanging off your neck, a bottle of champagne in your hands, totally name-dropping a couple of the dudes from the Brian Jonestown Massacre that you and Laura were hanging out with after a show. And now look at you, man. You walked off the airplane an hour ago with your shoulders bunched up, looking all timid and shit while you were waiting for your luggage at the bag claim. And no sunglasses. It's June and you weren't wearing any sunglasses. Your swagger's gone. That's what I mean, man," he finishes, before dipping two of his fingers in a glass of water and sliding them up his nose real fast.

"Come on, Chris," Kyle says. "Don't be a dick. You should be happy because our rad friend is back from Arizona. I am."

Thanks, man, I say.

Chris rolls his eyes.

Jamming a blue straw that's been cut in half up my right nostril, I snort—

Once.

Twice.

Breathe.

My eyes start watering.

I go, Do you guys ever feel like you're locked inside a car that's moving really fast?

"What kinda car?" Chris asks.

Like a fucking red Monte Carlo with a black racing

stripe cutting through the middle of it, and there's some superintense Fantômas shit jolting from the car speakers, like Mike Patton and Buzz Osbourne just completely losing it, but no steering wheel. The car doesn't have one. And the car is so out of control, right? It's swerving all over the road, and you're crying, pounding your fists against the window trying to jump out of it, trying to bail from it, and then all of these people start popping up on the road, like your parents and your sister and your friends, and the car is playing human dodgeball with them. It's trying not to run anyone over, but it's not slowing down, either, and then some junkie babe pops up in the middle of the road and the car destroys her, leaving her mangled body in its burnt rubber path, and then it keeps on going and going even though it can't maintain anything close to the same speed.

Pause.

You two ever feel anything like that?

"I'm a fucking coke dealer," Kyle says. "All I do is run over junkies. Night after night, again and again."

And Chris goes, "Nah. I never feel like that. But if I was in that car, instead of Fantômas blasting, I think I'd be listening to early Faith No More, the Chuck Mosley days. That shit would really blow your mind during a human dodgeball game."

"You think you'd have a choice?" Kyle snorts. "The car he's talking about doesn't even have a steering wheel, so no way that you'd be able to pick out the music. No way, man."

"I'm just saying," Chris snorts right back. "Early Faith No More would be the better choice to listen to in that particular situation. Don't you think, Trav?"

Maybe.

I lean forward. Wipe a thin line of coke residue off the mirror with my thumb and rub it back and forth against my gums a bunch of times until my mouth goes numb. Then I light a cigarette.

"You gonna be all right?" Chris asks me. "You look like your heart's just been ripped from your chest."

Plugging my nostrils with my other hand, I snap my head back and sniff superhard.

I think I'll be okay.

I look at the clock that hangs crooked on the dirty white wall in front of me, just above this black and white poster of PJ Harvey sitting on a bar stool, legs spread, panties showing. It's five o'clock.

Shit.

"What's up?" asks Kyle.

I gotta meet my parents for dinner soon. Like in an hour.

Chris starts laughing.

The three of us are watching this new Queens of the Stone Age DVD, and when I see Kyle get out of the blue reclining chair he stole from a nursing home recreation room last summer, I say, Yo, Kyle. Will you grab me something to drink?

"What do you want?" he asks.

Water.

And Kyle says, "No problem, dude."

Then he walks back into the living room a few moments later in his blue Dickie pants, his white Death from Above T-shirt, his left arm sleeved, his black hair butched with two thin lines shaved into each side of his head, and hands me a warm glass of water.

I take a drink and light another cigarette and look hard at Chris, who's wearing a pair of dark blue Levi's, a plain black T-shirt, and a pair of Vision Wear high-tops, and I ask him when the last time he slept was.

"This morning. What about you?"

On the plane ride here.

Kyle goes, "What happened to your car? What happened to all the shit you took with you to Arizona?"

I shrug.

Sold most of it. Fucked my car up like two nights after I got back to school from Hawaii.

Both of them smile and then I start asking them about what's been going on since I left. . . .

Not much.

What's new . . . ?

Not much.

I ask about everyone I can think of.

Cliff: *Livin' with his dad. Being a loser. Fuckin Natalie Taylor.*

Michael: *Gettin' wasted. Destroying meatpits. Lurking on Kennedy Street.*

Claire: *Being totally hot.*

I swallow a huge glob of spit.

Laura . . .

Silence.

Laura . . .

Silence.

Laura . . .

Nothing.

Chris starts blushing. He rubs his eyes. Shakes his head slowly from side to side.

Laura . . .

"I don't know," Kyle finally jumps in. "I don't see her that much anymore. She pretty much hangs out with different people now. But the last time I saw her at the Glass Castle, she was still looking good, man. She still had that whole Kate Bosworth thing going for her."

It's not a thing, I say. She really looks like that Bosworth chick. Maybe it's Kate Bosworth who has that whole Laura Kennedy thing going for her.

"Come on, Trav," Chris grunts. "Get real. Why do you even care what she's up to? She probably hates you."

I just wanted to know, Chris. What the fuck.

"What happened to you, anyway?" Kyle asks. "You came back for Christmas, flew to Hawaii, went back to Arizona, and cut everyone off."

Things got, ya know, complicated.

And Chris goes, "Things have always been *complicated* with you, Trav."

Did I do something to you, Chris? Cause you're being a total dick to me right now.

Chris shoots a look at Kyle, and Kyle goes, "You pretty much are, man."

Facing me again, Chris goes, "No, Trav. You didn't do anything. You just look different and talk different."

Pause.

He lights a cigarette. "It's making me a little nervous."

Well, your jaw's sliding around all crazy cause you're tweaking so hard and that's kinda freaking me out.

"I know it is," Chris says back. "It's been doing that every time I get high lately. I should probably chew gum when I do this shit."

Probably.

Kyle dumps some more coke onto the mirror.

Last night I called him and I asked him if he'd pick me up from the airport this afternoon but to not tell anyone that he was, which he didn't. Except for Chris.

And he went, "You're coming back? Do your parents know?"

Yeah. But they already have plans and can't pick me up. My dad sounded pretty pissed off.

"But I thought you wanted to stay out there for the summer," he said. "Maybe even do some traveling."

I need to come back, man.
"Why?" he wanted to know.
And I told him:
Kyle, just pick me up.
He cuts two more lines then he hands me the mirror.
One.
Two.
Goddamn this is some good shit.
Breathe.
And I'm really back.

About the Author

Jason Myers was born in 1980 and raised on a farm outside of Dysart, Iowa. After high school he studied film at the Academy of Art University in San Francisco. His first novel, *Exit Here.*, was published in 2007. This is his second novel. He lives and works in San Francisco.

GRITTY.
ELECTRIFYING.
REAL.

Find your edge
with these
startling and
striking books.